P9-BYU-405

The Righteous Revenge of Lucy Moon

The Righteous Revenge of Lucy Moon

Bill Brooks

FIVE STAR
A part of Gale, Cengage Learning

GALE
CENGAGE Learning

Farmington Hills, Mich • San Francisco • New York • Waterville, Maine
Meriden, Conn • Mason, Ohio • Chicago

Five Star™ Publishing, a part of Cengage Learning, Inc.

LIBRARY OF CONGRESS CATALOGING-IN-PUBLICATION DATA

Brooks, Bill, 1943–
The righteous revenge of Lucy Moon / Bill Brooks. — First edition.
pages ; cm
ISBN 978-1-4328-3009-0 (hardcover) — ISBN 1-4328-3009-0 (hardcover)
1. Murder—Investigation—Fiction. 2. United States—Social life and customs—19th century—Fiction. I. Title.
PS3552.R65863R54 2015
813'.54—dc23 2014041380

First Edition. First Printing: April 2015
Find us on Facebook– https://www.facebook.com/FiveStarCengage
Visit our website– http://www.gale.cengage.com/fivestar/
Contact Five Star™ Publishing at FiveStar@cengage.com

Printed in the United States of America
1 2 3 4 5 6 7 19 18 17 16 15

To the memory of my little sister Pat Brooks.
I will forever miss our laughter and tears together.

Chapter 1

Mama's dead. Somebody used a shotgun on her, Daddy Sam said. Daddy Sam is not a man of many words.

I was on my honeymoon in El Paso when I got the telegram. Jim and me.

Come on home, Lucy.

So Jim and me got the first KATY flyer out of El Paso eating boiled peanuts in a greasy paper sack while we waited, the Texas sun as hot as a fry pan on our faces.

Jim and me had only been married five days and still breaking each other in. Hardly ever got out of bed, took our meals in our room. Maybe I shouldn't talk out of school, considering the surrounding circumstances and all, but teaching Jim to be a tender and considerate lover was sort of like teaching a horse to ride a bicycle. But, God love him, he sure did try, often substituting rambunctiousness for tenderness.

I said, "Jim, why'd we come here if this is all you want to do with me, we could have done this grappling back home." Lord, wasn't no satisfying that man for long if you catch my drift. He may not have been well-schooled in the ways of a woman's true needs and wants, but he had a boundless appetite.

Jim's a tall handsome man-child what carries a bird's-head Colt butt-forward in a leather holster for all the world to gaze upon. Keeps another little two-shot skull popper in his inside jacket pocket. Jim says he doesn't believe in going about at a disadvantage in a world full of bloodthirsty types who would as soon shoot you as to look at you. Cut your throat too, he says, and that is why he also keeps a honed letter opener slid down the shaft of his boot. I'd tease him by saying I was surprised he didn't carry a rock tied around his neck as well, case he ran out of guns and knives. He'd give me one of his incredulous looks and say, "Lucy, I saw Eddie Foy one time in Dodge and he was funny. You ain't funny."

"Who is it shot her?" Jim asked when I read him the wire.

"Don't know," I told him. Daddy Sam left out all the details except for how. I wished he'd given more details.

So we packed our kit and got on down to the Union Station and waited for the midnight run munching on the peanuts a half-blind man with a spotted dog sold us and rode it two days and nights until it pulled into Danby which was as close as the train line could get us to where Mama was. We rented a hack and drove the rest of the way to Hadley's Jump getting in late afternoon, the sun ablaze across the land so gold and pretty it looked like what I imagined Heaven must look like and started crying thinking of Mama strolling those golden streets with no one to accompany her. Wasn't any in our family who preceded her in death I know of would have likely been waiting for her. Ours was a family of mostly gamblers, hell-raisers and whoremongers, but for Mama and me.

Daddy Sam was sitting out on the porch steps with a yard full of men hanging round, half of 'em with their fingers hooked into handles of crockery jugs of shine home brew. There were saddle horses and cabs parked all over the yard. Somebody had strung up black crepe along the porch rails and put a wreath of sorrow on the door.

Daddy Sam stood up to greet us and shook hands with Jim then hugged me.

"Lucy," he said. "Your mama, God rest her soul, is in the

house yonder, laid out in a nice way. I had her put in her favorite dress—the black velvet one."

I went on in while Jim stayed out in the yard with Daddy Sam and the men. Even in death, the sexes are separated by unwritten bonds, it seemed to me.

"I don't ever attend funerals or a wake," Jim told me one evening under a mortal moon. We'd been sitting on a blanket by a lake his hands cupping my bare breasts which he said reminded him of Chinese apples. I think he meant pomegranates.

We'd not yet married and were in the early stages of our sparking.

"That's a hell of a thing to bring up," I said when he blurted it out. "Why would you even think about such at a time like this and you pawing me like a school kid in a candy jar?"

Said Jim in his sheepish way, "Hell, Lucy, all a man like me thinks about is fornicating and death."

I probably should have bid him farewell then and there, but when a gal is taken with a man's handsomeness, she will overlook an awful lot. We women can be our own worst enemies sometimes.

"Why is it that you don't go to funerals?" I asked.

"Death will get on you if you get too close to it," he murmured in my ear. "I'm a fellow of many superstitions."

He was too. Wouldn't walk under a ladder or let a black cat cross his path. Would toss salt over his shoulder at meals and wouldn't shave after dark and only bathe on odd-numbered days. Said all the men in his family were that way.

He had those real smooth gambler's hands he treated with lanolin oil, said a man must take care of the tools of his trade, and smooth hands on a man is something a woman does appreciate, that much I'll give him.

And speaking of hands, Mama used to tell me, "Lucy, you

can tell a lot about a man by the shoes he wears, the company he keeps and the shape and size of his hands." She did not say why this was so.

I always trusted Mama's judgment when it came to men for she was well versed in them, having had a string of lovers Cleopatra would envy.

Mama said that too many young women don't know what real passion is because they'd marry the first galoot that came along pitching woo and promised them the moon when those pumpkin heads did not have a pot to leak in or a window to throw it out of.

"Lucy, honey, a woman doesn't know what she wants until she samples what all's available. Men can carouse and carry on all they choose and nothing is said, but a gal does it and she's called a strumpet, or worse. Don't matter what you're called as long as it ain't miserable. And miserable you will be if you marry the first fool who comes along and asks you."

Yes, Mama.

Mama always said she was a freeborn woman, and I knew her to have taken plenty of lovers before Daddy Sam come along. She never married any of them, preferring, she said, to just get along until she couldn't anymore.

"Why hitch your wagon to just one horse, Lucy Mae?"

Now, Daddy Sam, like her other men, was pretty as a Tennessee walking horse. And like most of Mama's lovers, Daddy Sam had a spotty past. He confessed things to her that she shared with me because that's what a mother and her daughter do: share personal things they wouldn't dare tell anyone else, not even their lover.

Mama told me that Daddy Sam told her he'd killed some men in New Mexico and maybe one or two in Missouri. Said he couldn't be sure exactly how many, because he didn't wait around to see if they were graveyard dead or just shot all to hell. Said he was pretty sure that some of 'em were graveyard dead. Claimed he never shot anyone that didn't deserve it. I thought when she told me, "Of course he'd say that."

But that wasn't all Daddy Sam told Mama, either.

He said he and some friends of his had robbed a couple of banks and maybe a train or two. Said he never robbed no individuals, but that banks and railroads had the money to cover their losses and after all they were the true criminals.

"Stealing from a thief ain't stealing at all," he told her.

Daddy Sam had been married before he met Mama, but his wife had passed. He said that she had been raped and murdered by a couple of heathen brothers he tracked down and took revenge upon—the two fellows in New Mexico—and that's how his bloodletting ways had begun. Said if it hadn't been for that tragedy he'd probably still be a deacon in the Holiness Church over in Lincoln, Nebraska, where he hailed from originally.

"Lucy, I think Sam is half a liar sometimes, and the rest of the time he prevaricates. But he could have pillaged the entire earth and I would have still fallen in love with him for he is a right pretty man and you know how it is with me and pretty men with a taste for adventure," Mama said. Mama also told me that she had been putting away money on the side without nobody but me knowing about it.

"I'm not getting any younger, Lucy," she said. "And I ain't getting no prettier either. Day might come when no man will want me and I'll be on my own. That's the other thing, child, as a woman you have to make sure not to rely on any man entirely. They'll all just disappoint you in the end. Our little secret, remember."

Yes, Mama.

Jim often mentioned how alike me and Mama are, saying, "The old cherry sure didn't fall far from the tree, did it, Lucy?"

I would tell him he had the mind of a guttersnipe, but he just got a laughing fit. I never could stay mad at him.

There were womenfolks inside the small house, including Vinita, who was Daddy Sam's brother's wife—Oren like the rest of the men out in the yard—gathered around Mama's coffin which was built of pine with some flocked wallpaper pasted over to make it look nice. The wallpaper must have been Daddy Sam's choice because it was a pattern of blue stripes and red roses, hardly befitting something so somber. Leave it to men to lack a sense of style. I hated it.

Most of the women were wearing widows' weeds, long black dresses, with faces as bloodless as death itself. Even Mama looked more lively than any of her sisterly clan, but for Auntie Lizzie and Auntie Myra who weren't really my aunties at all, but girlfriends of Mama's who, as she'd told me, had worked in the sporting houses before they married local galoots from in and around Hadley's Jump and improved their lot—though not by much. Mama laughed when she told me this.

"You ought to see the men those tarts hooked their wagon to, Lucy. But I guess when you're in the whoring business, you can't be choosy about your betrothed."

She was born with devilment in her bones. All three of her real sisters were merrymakers like Mama, but they had preceded her in death: Auntie Ida died of milk sickness, Auntie Mamie died along with her infant baby in childbirth, and Auntie Louisa died of rattlesnake bite when she was just ten years old.

"We were the devil's own spawn," she'd laugh whenever recalling their days as children then three of them as young women. "Lord! The trouble we got ourselves into and the boys we corrupted. If our daddy had a known he'd have beat us bloody with his razor strop. But we kept our own council and backed each other's play just so we could get away with the things we did." How often I begged her for the most intimate detail but she'd just shush me and say, "Lucy Mae, now there's just some things Mama can't speak about." Then titter like a schoolgirl.

Mama, lying there, eyes closed, lips pursed, hair all fixed the wrong way didn't even look like her, at least to me. Vinita slipped up beside me and whispered, "Lucy, she looks so peaceful, don't she?"

"No," I whispered back. "She looks dead."

Mama did not look like the lover of so many men and I thought about them briefly as I stood over her coffin.

Teddy Blue was the first one I recalled living with us, a Lone Star cowboy who never had enough change in his pockets to buy two beers at the same time. He had a way of wearing his Stetson pushed back with a lock of sandy hair hanging over his forehead and a winsome smile. Mama ended up carrying the full freight of their existence together, even working for a time as a sporting girl, or so I believed, though she never admitted to it. Still so young and me just a tot, Mama was as devoted to Teddy Blue as a coon pup to its master. To his credit, he always was nice to me and her as I recall, never raised his voice and I never knew them to have an argument. I asked her, little as I was, why he didn't have a steady job.

"Well, Lucy," she replied after a moment's thought, "I reckon some men just can't stand steady work," she said. So I asked her what it was attracted her to him.

"Honey," she said, "I'm just a sucker for a pretty man who keeps me guessing and wanting him all the time and Teddy is that in spades."

Teddy was killed in a dispute over a dice game. Stabbed to death by a Caddo Indian from Tahlequah one rainy night behind a billiard hall. I remember Mama's sobs when word came and the two of us went down to the undertaker's where they had

Teddy stretched out and how cold it was in that damn icehouse they had him in. His boots were off and his right big toe stuck through a hole in his sock.

"Oh, Lucy," Mama sobbed. "I should have darned his socks but I was never no good at being a domestic. Least I could have bought him a new pair."

I told her not to blame herself for Teddy Blue's misadventures and that it wasn't going to matter to him anymore whether he had darned socks or not.

After, there was a string of nameless men who'd come around, stay a night or two then ride off. But then came Johnny Waco, just as bad as Teddy ever was at everything and twice as handsome. God how that man did shine when he smiled. Mama said the first time she laid eyes on him, she wanted to rip her clothes off and tell him to go right to it.

Johnny moved in with us there on Homer Street in Dallas. I was just then on the verge of womanhood and my bosoms nearly as big as Mama's.

"Girl, you're going to bust out the top of your dress soon," Mama said teasingly. "I'll have to get out my shotgun to hold the boys off."

I never told Mama this but after Johnny had been around a while he had thoughts of deflowering me. To tell the God's own truth, I'm not sure if he'd tried I would have fought very hard not to let him. Many a night I lay up in my room listening to them going at it and it gave me the itchiest feelings. And as young girls blossoming do, I began to daydream about me and Johnny doing what he and Mama was doing and God, I knew it was so wrong to think such a thing.

When I confided to my best friend Eliza Atkins my feelings, she laughed and said, "Oh, Lucy, every girl wants to steal away her mama's lover, don't you know that?"

I said, "No, I did not know that."

She told me that her own stepdaddy had tried to mess with her and I asked how and she said, "He touched me down there once and kissed me on the mouth."

Mama claimed Johnny was the daddy of my half brother, J. R. But that might have been an unfortunate falsehood, since I recall her as telling me once when she'd been drinking that it was a man named Benbow who might have got her pregnant with J. R. Benbow, as little as I recall him, was a fellow who came by a few nights and had a slight limp, but still very handsome. Apparently she'd been seeing both of them at the same time if any of it was true. J. R. didn't seem to me to favor either of them.

J. R. is a big tall boy almost twenty with a dour outlook on life. He never was a happy child and now he was a unhappy man. He and I were always at odds with each other, mean as he was to me. I looked about but didn't see him anywhere when we arrived and was relieved I didn't. J. R. had, a few years ago, left for parts unknown and good riddance too, far as I was concerned. Hadn't seen him in the yard, but that didn't mean nothing. He could have been hiding in a tree for all I knew.

My two not-real aunties approached me and lifted their mourning veils and I saw that their cheeks were rouged and their lips painted red so as to distinguish them from the dead, I suppose. Or, perhaps they didn't have many opportunities out here on the high lonesome to gussie themselves up. Any occasion would do, even a funeral. The sweet fragrance of their perfume—I imagined it to be French—tempered momentarily my sorrow. They might have been whores, my two aunties—but they were good whores as well as Mama's closest friends.

Now you might wonder why Mama would let Daddy Sam move her into such a godforsaken place as the Pistol Barrel of Oklahoma when she thrived best in towns that had all the accoutrements a freeborn woman such as herself required.

Well, she told me that it was Daddy Sam's brother, Oren, who lured him there with speculation that there wasn't a lawman with a lick of sense who would scout up in there without he had a posse of a hundred men and even then it was unlikely. Daddy Sam reckoned such a place was just the spot for him to reside in without having to worry about being arrested or molested for any of his past deeds.

I'd never in my life seen such a faithless land where about the only real entertainment you could have would be to kill yourself. Hadley's Jump was a collection of shacks and hovels, saloons and whorehouses and little else but the basics to sustain the populace in and around it. Wind all the damn time, sweltering in the summer and freezing in the winter and nothing to recommend it except if you were a wanted man, for there certainly was plenty of that type about and according to what Daddy Sam told Mama and she told me, any lawman would be a damn fool or suicidal to come in there trying to arrest anybody.

Mama claimed at first that she didn't mind as long as she was sleeping in the same bed as Daddy Sam every night. But more and more in her letters to me, I could sense she was growing weary of it all—living so forlorn when what she craved was dance and beer halls, lively music, and most of all millinery shops. Mama purely did love hats, great big ones with feathered plumes. You hardly never seen Mama without her velvet dresses and her hats. But the last couple of years she never had too much occasion to wear her finery, such she told me in her letters and on occasion when I'd go and visit her.

In my last visit she pretty strongly stated that she might not stick that much longer if Daddy Sam didn't soon agree to come up with a better plan and move her to a city. Said she'd like to move to Tulsa or at the least Tahlequah.

"After all," she said, "a woman can only be distracted from the realities of her existence just so long no matter the love and passion she has for a man. And, to be honest, Lucy, even a handsome man can get to be old news after so long. You wouldn't want to eat cherry pie every night the rest of your life, would you? Wouldn't you need a slice of pumpkin once in a while?"

"Yes, Mama, you would," I said. I wanted to take her then and there away with me but knew she wasn't yet quite ready to abandon Daddy Sam. She still loved him probably more than she should have.

And now I had to look at my yet beautiful and youthful Mama lying there cold and still as stone in that peculiar decorated coffin. I know it was wrong to think it, but I thought Johnny Waco would never have let her lie in a casket decorated in wallpaper of blue stripes and red roses. Johnny had style and there were many days after Johnny's passing I'd wished I'd had availed myself to him. Such a terrible thought at a time like this, I know. Johnny had more style than even my Jim, though Jim, I have to say, is a lot more considerate and less vain than Johnny Waco was. That's the problem with a beautiful man—they can be vain as hell and not even know you're in the same room with them at times. I do believe that the only person Johnny ever fell in love with was himself.

Auntie Lizzie and Auntie Myra stood either side of me as I looked down onto Mama's peaceful countenance.

"Oh, Lucy, honey," Auntie Lizzie said putting her arm around my waist.

"What's wrong with her face, it looks odd?" I asked.

Neither of them wanted to say but coughed politely into their tatted hankies like they were truly genteel and highbred women.

"It's just . . . ," Auntie Myra tried to explain.

I looked closer.

"What's this?" I said pointing to one of Mama's cheeks that looked like the skin was sloughing off.

Auntie Lizzie leaned in close and whispered, "Lucy, honey, that's undertaker's putty. They had to use it because some of them shotgun pellets went a little high. It was either that or keep the lid down and nobody wanted to have the lid down."

I kissed Mama's powdered and cold forehead and stomped outside and got between Jim and Daddy Sam and yelled, "Who the hell did that to her?"

Daddy Sam looked grieved and no longer the handsome man I remembered him as the last time I saw him. He looked like he'd aged twenty years. Oren sat on the corner of the porch, his legs dangling and holding to a jug.

"Can't say for certain, Lucy. Could have been one of several people. Your mama had a tendency to anger certain people. You know how high-minded she could get. But, it could also have just been an accident, too."

"Accident! Who the hell would have shot Mama and then not confessed to it if it was a accident?"

Daddy Sam looked around at the yard full of men, some reclined on the grass with their jugs like they were on a picnic, some smoking and telling jokes to one another in low voices, but I could see them grinning. Oh, I was mad as hell at the lot of them.

"Hell, Lucy, I just couldn't say for sure," Daddy Sam said.

"Did you call the law in on this?" I said.

Daddy Sam ran his forefinger in under the paper collar of his Sunday shirt and said, "Law? Lucy, they ain't no damn law up in here. It's the reason your mama and me is living here in the first place. I thought you knew that already."

"Well, she ain't living here no more, now is she?"

He swallowed hard, shifted his weight from one foot to another like a man who has to pee real bad.

"Well then, are you going to do something about this?" I said.

"Course I am, right after the funeral, I'm going to look into it. An eye for an eye and a tooth for a tooth, like it says in the Bible. I ain't forgot my preaching days. Whoever did this to your mama will be made to answer to God's law not man's."

"Then I aim to go with you, me and Jim."

Jim coughed and said, "Lucy, maybe it's best you let Daddy Sam handle this and you not get involved directly. Case things go bad. I couldn't stand to be without you, honey."

Well that about slapdash floored me. Jim, my own husband, and us not even over with our honeymoon yet, not backing my play.

"I never figured you for no damn yellow coward, Jim."

"Ah, Lucy . . . ," he moaned. "Now don't be that way, darlin'."

I stormed off, my eyes blurred with hot tears from sorrow and disappointment. The onliest one I could trust and confide in completely was in a box and would never ever whisper another word to me nor I to her. Gone forever. And the yard full of men out there who you'd expect to take action and take revenge for her death, well, they were just lounging about as if awaiting the latest baseball scores.

I walked as far from that death house as I could go then fell down and lay in the grass and wept till my ribs hurt.

I told myself one thing: This will not stand.

Chapter 2

We buried Mama the next day out back of the house beneath a sheltering gum tree just where the land rises slightly, and of course it would rain cats and dogs. I mean rain like you never seen before. It come down so hard it knocked down the brims of men's hats and soaked the dresses of the women folk—neighbors, including Auntie Myra and Auntie Lizzie who said, "It's like the Lord is crying hisself over your mama, Lucy."

Daddy Sam did the preaching but you couldn't even hear his words because of the hiss of the rain. Some of that cheap wallpaper started to peel off Mama's coffin and I wanted to cuss Daddy Sam for his cheapness.

I had decided during the night I'd go on the scout for Mama's killer even if I had to go it alone. Jim was humping me and all I could think was what I was going to do to the rotten bastard who'd shot her. I don't think Jim even noticed I wasn't there; he just pumped away like he was digging a posthole or something, working up a sweat and me not even paying any attention to him.

Afterwards he sat up on the side up in the bed and smoked a hand-rolled, the tip of it glowing in the dark like a cat's eye.

"You know, Lucy, whoever shot your mama has probably fled the country. They probably read about who it was and skedaddled. Why, they could be anywhere in the world by now. I don't know how you and Daddy Sam expect to track 'em.

And then how you going to prove it was even them if you do track 'em?"

"Jim, you're a damn idiot."

"Ah, Lucy, now don't be that way, honey."

Jim could get awful whiny at times and it made me want to slap him.

"Well, I reckon as long as *you* get what you want," I said. "Everything is just fine, ain't it?"

"Now you know that ain't true," he said.

I got out of bed and looked out the window off in the direction of the little grave site where I knew Mama was resting beneath the earth all alone. Such a lively woman with so many high adventures and it made me as sad as I've ever been.

"Jesus, Lucy, you look beautiful standing there," Jim said. "Come on back to bed and let ol' Jim take your mind off things."

"If I had a gun right now, Jim, I'd shoot your lights out."

He was silent for a minute and all you could hear was the burn of his shuck as he smoked it.

"Well now that's a hell of a thing to say to your own husband," he said.

We got Mama buried in spite of the deluge and all gathered in Daddy Sam's and Mama's house and changed out of our wet duds into dry ones. The womenfolk had filled the table with all kinds of food: roasted duck, a ham, bowls of boiled potatoes and turnips, green beans cooked in bacon fat, meat gravy, pies and cakes.

The rain had quit by the time folks dug in and most of the men took their plates outside on the porch to eat and palaver including Daddy Sam and his brother Oren. Jim slunk out too and left me with those women.

My aunties and I found us a quiet corner and ate with our plates on our laps.

"Did you get you some rest last night, honey?" Auntie Lizzie asked.

I looked at her. Auntie Myra was eating like they were going to come and haul her off to jail any minute. I glanced across the room and Vinita was pecking at her food like a bird. I felt sorry for her without really knowing why. Sometimes I look at somebody and read heartache in them and feel bad.

I wanted to say to Lizzie's question that my husband found it more interesting to keep me awake half the night with his needs but instead chose to say, "Gee, ain't this bean salad good?"

Auntie Lizzie patted my knee as if she knew.

About that time in strode my long-lost brother J. R., lankier than I remembered him as being, but just as dour. He was dressed in a slicker that came down to the top of his tall boots he'd stuffed his trousers legs in. His Stetson hat was stained dark from the earlier rain and overall he was as gloomy as a storm cloud.

"Good of you to show up," I said sourly, for J. R. was one of those men that never failed to disappoint, of which I'd noticed in my life was just about all of them.

"Little sister," he said coming over and removing his hat to reveal the rest of his thick yellow hair. Damn if he wasn't the spitting image of Johnny Waco, even had Johnny's frost-blue eyes.

"I tried my best to get here before the burying," he said.

"What kept you?" I asked. "Mama would have wanted you here."

He shook his head and offered me a peevish glance

"I had some business in Tahlequah," he said. "Took longer than I thought."

"You mean business more important than burying your mother?" I asked. I always found it hard to know when J. R. was telling the truth. He was devious.

Jim come in just then carrying his empty plate and went to the table to refill it. The man could eat like a horse. All that nighttime activity had left him famished I reckon, damn his sorry soul.

He saw J. R. and come over and greeted him like a long-lost brother, even though I never heard either of them say a kind word about the other. Jim offered his hand for J. R. to shake but J. R. ignored it and, instead, concentrated on me.

"Don't you go to starting on me now," he said. "I did my best. It ain't like I could grow wings and fly here."

I wanted to bite his nose off.

"Go on and get you something to eat," I said instead.

I couldn't sit still and got up and went outside and wandered over to the horse corral and stroked the nose of a big friendly bay who came over to the rails. I always loved a horse. A horse has got something no other living creature has: a quiet and mysterious nobility. If only God made men like that.

It was then I noticed a fellow squatted down on his heels eating from the plate he was holding. A fellow all by himself set off from the others. He had his hat notched back and was watching me but not in that way most men will watch a woman, but in a way like he was studying me to pass a test. He nodded slightly when I looked at him, then went back to eating like I wasn't there. He was the color of a copper penny and longish red hair the color of dried blood, or maybe rust. I figured him for a half-breed cause of that red hair. I don't recollect ever seeing a redheaded Indian. Oklahoma was full of Indians of one sort or another, and then there was a awful lot of mixed breeds what with white men marrying Indian women and Indian men marrying white women. I reckon it was their land to start with and even though the government had them pretty much whipped, at least, they'd given them Oklahoma to carve up as they seen fit—at least for a while they did. But then ol' US Sam turned around and let the whites rush in back in '93, so it was a hell of a country no matter how you looked at it. Real interesting, too. And the wildest of it was still the Pistol Barrel which remained untamed and unfettered and a fearful place if you needed the law to help you.

He was a right handsome man in a dangerous sort of way, ol' starry eyes was.

Every man I looked at out in that yard to me was Mama's potential slayer, him notwithstanding. I made a note to ask Daddy Sam about him, who he was and what was he doing around here, the only red man among the white.

Chapter 3

By midnight everybody but me was drunk as coons from drinking hard cider and mash whiskey somebody had brought to the wake, Daddy Sam and Jim included. They'd built a big bonfire out in the yard stacked with cottonwood limbs thick around as a man's leg. They passed the jugs and howled like coyotes. I was disgusted with the lot of them. What did they have to celebrate but their own foolishness? Maybe Daddy Sam thought this was some way to honor Mama's passing, but I surely did not. Mama wasn't opposed to having a glass of firewater, as she called it, and, in fact, she could drink as good as any man when she wanted to. But I doubt she'd much care for having men howling like coyotes crazed on liquor as a way to note her passing.

I watched from an upstairs window.

But here's what I really noticed: that fellow earlier out in the yard—the redheaded Indian, how he stood off to the side and declined the jug whenever it was passed to him. I could tell it was him because of the crown of his hat, how high and round it was, like the Mexican vaqueros wore down along the border. I had a hard time peeling my eyes from him. There was something mysterious about him that drew you to watch him.

And as I stood watching how he stood apart, something told me he was the one who shot Mama. I couldn't tell you why, exactly, I felt that way, but believing in my heart he'd come to gloat, to prove he could kill a woman with a shotgun and get clean away with it. I admit I wasn't thinking straight, so filled with grief and anger as I was without a minute's peace about any of it.

I went through Jim's kit and found his revolver there beneath a silk shirt, one I'd bought him as a wedding present. The shirt was stained with gun oil. Just like a man to wrap a gun in a fine silk shirt then complain about the stain later when he tried wearing it.

I took the revolver out. It was heavy for its small size and its pearl grips were smooth and shaped like a bird's head, small enough to fit a woman's hand as well as a man's, the sort of gun a gambling man would carry. When he first acquired it, he had me practice shooting with it, said it was the same sort of gun Billy the Kid carried cause he had small hands. Said Jesse James also carried one like it and Jim had the gunsmith put on the pearl grips to imitate Jesse's.

Well, I knew that for a damn lie because Jesse and his brother Frank were shirttail relatives of Mama's and would come on occasion to visit and eat supper with Mama and her paramour at the time, Clell Miller. All this she told me later when she thought I was old enough to hear about it.

She told me Clell was a real quiet man and getting words out of him was like pulling teeth. She said Clell was later killed trying to rob the First National Bank up in Northfield, Minnesota, with Jesse and Frank and the Youngers. Said he was shot so many times he looked like a sieve. Mama said she wasn't overly broken up too bad about Clell since theirs had been a short-lived affair. She said it was Jesse who had asked her to put Clell up when he was suffering a gunshot wound from another earlier foray and she agreed to do it because she admired both Frank and Jesse and that her and Clell just sort of ended up sharing the same bed up until he rode off with Jesse and them on that fateful ride.

She confided Clell wasn't much in the lovemaking department and they never actually did what needed doing to make a baby. Said he was a bit of a mama's boy and a clumsy lover. Knowing what I knew of her and her later-on lovers, I asked her why she even allowed Clell into her bed.

"Desperation, I suppose it was, Lucy. I was on my own, run off from my family and hardly knew anything about men. Clell was my first, sort of."

She'd showed me a postcard of him, one taken in Northfield of him in death, an unsightly man if you ask me.

Mama went on to explain, "My daddy worked me like a government mule," she said. "My mama was sick in bed all the time and I was practically a substitute wife, field hand, chief cook and bottle washer. I couldn't wait to flee my home and ran off with twelve stolen dollars and a carpetbag of clothes. It was Frank James I met while working in a house in Saint Joe, Missouri, who was kindly to me and helped me find a place to live."

At this point she sank into a quiet reverie for a few moments, sat there looking out her bedroom window, the summer light filling the room and touching her lap.

What sort of house? I wanted to know.

She dropped her gaze to me.

"Just a house where women who are desperate work, Lucy." I was too young yet to understand what that meant.

She went on to say how nice a man Frank James was and how she discovered that him and Jesse and the rest of the Jameses were some sort of distant relatives which made it all the better.

"Anyway, Lucy, when Jesse and Frank came to me later on with Clell in hand suffering a bullet wound and asked me to care for him, I could not refuse. Things just sort of took their own course between Clell and me. But I never did love him but just as a friend."

I remembered a time when Jesse and Frank would come and sometimes stay at our place later when I was a girl still. How tall and domineering they seemed. And when they'd eat supper, how they took out their guns and laid them on the table while they ate. Biggest guns I'd ever seen till then, not the little ladies' sort of gun of Jim's I was now holding.

It wasn't the first gun I ever handled and Jim wasn't the only man who'd taken an interest in teaching me to shoot. There were lots of things Jim didn't know and I didn't see any reason to tell him some of those things. Fact is, the first man who showed me how to shoot was a neighbor boy lived down the road from us in Dallas when Mama and me was living with Johnny Waco.

The neighbor's boy was Davey Sawyer and he would have been pretty but for his bucked teeth. His daddy was a preacher and if Davey's any example, it's true what they say about preachers' kids: they're hell on wheels. Davey smoked and drank and diddled girls like a full-grown man, me unfortunately being one of them—right there in the back of his daddy's church. On a pew. That's all I'll say about that.

But Davey was a fool for guns and had two or three, including a great big ol' Walker Colt. He said it was powerful enough to knock over an ox. He insisted teaching me to shoot. I had to hold it with both hands and when I pulled the trigger it jumped clear out of my hands. Davey whooped and shouted, "Goddamn, Lucy!"

Davey was a first-class cusser. I won't even talk about the dirty things he said to me in the church that afternoon. Lord, my ears still ring every time I think about it.

What surprised me was how much I liked firing a pistol. And before you know it, I could hit seven cans out of ten. I liked shooting bottles best because of the way they'd shatter—like flung diamonds.

Well, that was my first experience with guns but not with boys. Funny thing was, Davey didn't last long in this world. He drank some sort of bad whiskey he bought from a drummer passing through and it poisoned him dead. When the sheriff caught up with the drummer he learned that the fellow made his whiskey out of charcoal, rubbing alcohol, snakeheads and sugar with some arsenic thrown in. Sheriff said there were at least two dozen rattler heads floating in the brew when he looked in. The sheriff arrested the fellow and had the marshals take him to Fort Smith where Judge Parker sentenced him to the House of Corrections in Detroit.

I hid Jim's pistol in the folds of my nightdress and went downstairs and out the front door. I aimed to kill that redheaded Indian boy, more sure than ever he was the one who shotgunned Mama.

I crossed the yard in my bare feet and the wet grasses felt like cold tears on them and I was reminded of the Biblical tale about the whore who washed the feet of our Lord Jesus. I think I must be going crazy to think such things at a time like this when I am about to kill my first man. I am crazy. The spirit of the Lord must have come over me, for I think, as I crossed to where ol' Copperhead is standing: I am washed in the blood of Jesus, but not nearly as much as you're about to be you murdering son of a bitch.

Ol' Copperhead is standing off from the others and hardly anybody notices me at first for they are pie-eyed drunk and singing Irish shanties. The flames of the fire are licking at the night like they're trying to eat up the blackness.

Copperhead sees me and just stands there, even when I bring the pistol out of the folds of my dress and aim it at him and cock back the hammer.

I guess it was then some of the others noticed what was happening and turned round for I heard Daddy Sam say, "Jesus H.

Christ, child, what in hell are you doing with that hog leg?"

"I aim to kill this murdering son of a bitch," I said.

Still Copperhead just stood there looking amused and I thought, Was he any other man, he'd be wetting himself by now. But not him. He was cool as an ice beer, hardly twitched an eyelid. The fear rose in me, clutched at my throat and caused my hands to tremble.

Then, Jim shouted, "Lucy, put that damn gun down before you shoot somebody."

"You shut the hell up!" I yelled.

Daddy Sam run over and got between me and Copperhead.

"Lucy, now, you go easy," he said. "Why is it you want to kill Red Dog here?"

"Well, he's about to become a dead dog," I said smartly.

Daddy Sam must of figured it and said, "Honey, Red Dog didn't shoot your mama; I seen him in Hadley's Jump the day she was killed."

"You're lying to me, Daddy Sam."

"No, I ain't, honey. If it was him what done it, I'd have shot him myself, don't you know that. Now, please, lower that pistol before you kill somebody innocent. Please?"

I lowered it then eased the hammer down.

"Well, goddamn it," I said to nobody and everybody. "This just stinks. You all are worse'n a bunch of hogs yourselves. Somebody ought to haul your worthless hides to Tahlequah and sell the lot of you for a penny a pound." Then I stomped back into the house and got in the bedroom and locked the door so Jim couldn't come in and disturb me. I wanted nothing more to do with any of them that night.

In my dreams, ol' Copperhead and me was sitting on a blanket under a large willow with a creek burbling nearby and we were talking sweet to one another and I knew before another minute, we'd be shucked out of our clothes and even sweeter things would happen.

Then, I was awoken by Jim pounding on the door.

"Let me in, Lucy."

"Go away."

"Ah, Lucy."

"I can't stand it when you start whining."

"Ah, Lucy."

"Go away."

He pounded once or twice more then left.

I went back to sleep hoping to pick up the dream where it left off, but all I dreamt about was Mama lying in her coffin staring up at me saying, "They shot me, Lucy. Oh, how it hurts." She was crying. I woke crying too.

CHAPTER 4

When I opened my eyes again the room was full of morning light and from beyond the open window I could hear birds singing. I slipped from the bed and went to the window and looked out. The sky was as clear and flawless as blue glass and I felt happy, until I realized Mama was gone.

The sun was on the other side of the house and the house's shadows lay out in the yard nearly to the pile of the bonfire ashes. Several crock jugs and bottles littered the grass and more than a few sleeping men. It looked like they'd fallen straight out of the sky and had smashed to earth and I thought good riddance. I did not recognize Jim among them. Oh, well.

I dressed in some riding clothes. I aimed to ride into Hadley's Jump and nose around and see if I could hear anyone speaking about Mama's murder and who might have done it.

Mama had once consorted for a short time with a Pinkerton detective when we lived in Fort Smith—in between Teddy Blue and Johnny Waco. He'd originally come to the house asking questions about the James-Younger gang. Somehow he'd heard Mama's name mentioned, probably through her brief entanglement with Clell, but this was several years after Clell ended up in a dirt bed.

The Pinkerton fellow's name was Finch Byrd, and I thought his mama must have foresaw her son was going to be a little fellow and that's why she named him Finch. That, or she had a good sense of humor. It was somewhat strange to name a boy

Finch who already owned the last name of Byrd. But then fo
is strange in naming their babies, like Clell Miller's mama.

Anyway, Finch came around one winter afternoon when th
land was covered in about two feet of snow making it look lik
one of those Currier & Ives postcards.

Finch stood there with snow on his hat brim and the shoulders of his black coat and asked Mama if he could come in and ask her a few questions.

She allowed it, for in spite of his pint size he was a good-looking man with heavy black mustaches and coal chunks for eyes. He had the whitest skin I ever saw on a man.

He saw me and said, "My what a cute little girl you have there, missus. She's the spitting image of you. What's your name little darling?"

"Lucy," I said.

"Lucy," he said as if testing the sound of it on his tongue.

"And who is this little tyke?" he asked, looking at my half brother, J. R., who was around two years old but already big for his size. Big and brooding.

J. R. offered him a sour look like he wanted to take a bite out of the Pinkerton's leg bone.

Mama offered the Pinkerton to take off his hat and coat and join us for dinner.

I watched and listened careful as Finch asked Mama about Jesse and Frank James and the Ford boys, Bob and Charley, who were at that point part of Jesse's new gang the way Finch told it. Mama said she didn't know anything about any of them, hadn't seen them in years.

"Well, I understand you are related to these boys is that correct, Missus Moon?"

"The bloodline is obscure," she replied coyly.

"Obscure," he repeated. "That's a fine word."

Mama had been without the company of a regular man for

several months by that time, doing her best to care for me and J. R. She would often leave us alone in the evenings after she'd tucked us into our beds. She'd say, "I'll be back soon. Mama's got to go work now, children. If you need something while I'm gone—and I do mean emergency wise, you go next door to Mrs. Choir and get her. I shouldn't be long."

I would lie awake and listen until she came in again, sometime late at night or very early in the morning. She'd come in and go quietly to her room.

I didn't know then what she confessed to me later—how it was she was able to afford to keep us together in this nice little house. And I sure don't blame her none, either, but instead, bless her for doing only what a woman could to keep herself and her babies together.

At first I was shocked at what she told me. But then she explained it as only Mama could.

"Lucy, I don't just do it for the money. I enjoy it, too. And long as I can pick and choose who I want to let pay me for my company then who am I to deny him? But it's me who does the picking and choosing and me who sets the price for what my time is worth and a woman has just as much right as a man in following her fortune."

Explaining it that way, it didn't sound so bad. Plus she said it was only temporary until the right man came along.

Well she sure enough was sizing up Mr. Byrd as he regaled her with stories about his job as a Pinkerton and how well it paid if you caught the ones with big rewards instead of the little fish as he put it.

"I don't mean to offend, Mr. Byrd," I overheard her say after they'd been sitting there several hours and her listening to one story after another about his exploits in the capture of violent men, "but considering your slight stature, isn't it terribly dangerous, the work you do?"

"Slight stature? Well now, Belle, may I call you Belle?"

She nodded.

"Well now, Belle," he said. "It ain't the dog in the fight, it's the fight in the dog that matters."

She gave him her best smile and Mama could smile the stars down from the sky when she wanted to.

Detective Finch ended up staying around for a week or so and in spite of his often expressed bravura, he was decent to us and even tried to get J. R. out of his gloom by letting him ride his horse, Stanley. But J. R. would have none of it. As for me, I listened careful enough to pick up several pointers of the Pinkertons' methods of finding and capturing miscreants, which I now aimed to employ over in Hadley's Jump the nearest thing to a town there was.

So I saddled Daddy Sam's big gelding and put Jim's bird's-head Colt into the saddlebags and headed for Hadley's Jump.

Jim woke from his stupor on the porch just as I swung aboard, and cried out, "Lucy, where the hell you going?"

"Go back to sleep, you loafer," I replied.

Then I rode off toward Hadley's Jump, a ramshackle of mostly saloons and cathouses, tobacco spit and mud. Wasn't for the few buildings standing some would call it a buffalo wallow.

I aimed to elicit (another word I learned from Mama) information about Mama's killer, or killers, whichever the case may be, and seek revenge.

A feeling come over me as I rode with the wind in my face and bloodlust in my heart—a feeling of something grand and worthy, as if I was doing God's work while He was off doing something else. The idea of finding Mama's slayer and killing him on the spot was like a kind of lust, for I got a tingling feeling that I only felt when Jim and me, or a few before Jim, consorted in intimate ways. I knew right then why some men get to liking it—killing, I mean—the same way they do bedding a woman.

I hadn't killed anybody yet, but there was a growing hot wetness flooding through me with every loping mile.

I let out a whoop and put the quirt to Old Joe Harper—what Daddy Sam had named his horse for reasons I know not—and Old Joe Harper flew like he had wings carrying me surely to my death or glory.

CHAPTER 5

I walked Old Joe Harper brazenly down the center of the main drag in Hadley's Jump. Sloe-eyed hatted men leaning against porch posts holding glasses of beer and stogies sticking from their ugly mouths gave me consideration as I passed them by.

"Hey, there, little sister," one of them called. "Climb on down off that big hoss and have a drink with me."

I cut a glance toward the voice but I don't know why. I figured all the manhood in the town were naught but blackguards, loafers and law dodgers. This one had a face full of gray-black beard. All I could see were the shine of two eyes peering out under the shade of his felt hat. He waved to me as if I'd just waltz over there and fall into his arms. I ignored him further. But he wasn't the only one called to me, there were others. Men in wrinkled baggy trousers looking like trash their mamas threw out. Hooting and hollering their lascivious invites, as if.

I looked about for any sort of jail or sign of the law, though I knew there wasn't one last time I'd been here a couple of years ago with Mama when I visited—this before I met Jim—and we came in to buy her a hat and have lunch. Like I said, Mama was hell for hats; any kind as long as they were big and plumed with feathers. Those and her velvet dresses and high buttoned shoes. She was the picture of fashion.

I hoped maybe since that previous visit some sort of law might have taken root. But no, it was still a dirty, filthy, enter-at-your-own-risk sort of town far as I could discern.

The air rang sharp with the sound of a blacksmith's hammer striking steel as I rode past a sooty shed where a big, thick hairy man paused his horseshoe shaping long enough to toss me a hungry look. I paused long enough to ask about some sort of law in town.

He showed me a mouthful of teeth looked like winter fencing blown crooked by a bad winter.

"Surely you are mistaken," he said. "Why there ain't never been no law in this town. Why would there be?"

"Good question," I said. "Maybe because it would keep down the killing and clear out the trash I see standing about."

He brayed like a mule.

"Jesus Christ, but you are a looker, gal. You come on back in my shed here and I'll show you something about what a smith can do besides shoe horses."

He had the same expectant look as a dog waiting for you to drop him a supper-table scrap.

"I'd as soon drown myself in the Niobrara River," I said and moved on, his braying following me. Never heard a man laugh like that.

Tell the truth, my bravado was beginning to wane. I felt as though I'd rode into a great den of inequity or like I was Daniel in the old lion's den about to be eaten alive, bones and all.

"Lucy," I thought, "what the hell were you thinking coming here without at least Jim backing your play."

I passed a dentist office squashed in between two saloons. There was a big wood tooth hanging over the doorway on which was painted:

DR. POPE, DENTIST WE PULL TEETH—CHEAP

Shudder the thought.

Two doors down was a barber's red-and-white-striped pole and a fellow sitting in a chair out front getting his hair cut by another fellow who looked like he needed his cut. I wondered if a righteous woman ever did ride the streets of Hadley's Jump or was I the first.

I recalled Detective Byrd saying how a saloon was a good place for a body to gain information if he was coy about it. I planned to be coy if I could summon the nerve to go into one of those bagnios with their eager-eyed souses standing out front.

Thus far, the only female I saw out on the town was me. I figured the other women were either chained to cookstoves or lounging on sofas in the altogether waiting on their next customer.

Either do it, Lucy Mae, I told myself, or turn tail and run back to the house.

So I reined in at the next saloon and dismounted and wrapped Old Joe Harper's reins around the hitch rail then reached inside my saddlebags and took out the bird's-head Colt and slipped it into the pocket of my trousers leaving just enough sticking out so it could be noticed if I were to attract unwanted company.

Soon as I stepped up on the walk, two bummers—one either side of the door who were leaned against the bar's wall tried to block my entrance.

"Now, little sister, why is a sweet lass such as yourself coming into a place such as this?" one of them said while the other grinned like a possum.

"I guess you ain't heard," I said. "But women get thirsty too. So please move out of my way."

He pushed off the wall to step in closer. His breath was worse than a hog's breath. "Well now—" he started to say.

I cut him off and said:

"Without you helping your friend hold up the wall, I reckon it is bound to fall over."

He snorted, said, "You hear that, Charley. She says the wall's bound to fall over without me helpin' to hold it up."

Charley made a sound like somebody snipped off his tail.

"Gar-dam!"

Hog Breath reached out and grabbed my forearm, saying, "How 'bout I show you a place much better'n this one here, where you and me can do the fandango? Why what I got, little sister, you ain't never seen."

"What would that be, a two-headed pecker?"

They both laughed hard again.

And while they were enjoying themselves, I reached with my free hand for the bird's-head Colt, but before I could pull it, Hog Breath unhanded me and stepped back. Had this peaked look on his pitted face like something sour he ate was about to come up.

"You children having fun?" a voice asked.

I turned around and about dropped the skull popper.

It was Red Dog.

"Why we was just funning, Red," Hog Breath said.

"Come on," Red Dog said with a jerk of his head to me.

I don't know why, but I followed him up the street to—lo and behold—an ice-cream parlor where we went in. He bought us each a dish of ice cream much to the dismay of the clerk's querulous face. Putting a pair of liberty dimes on the counter, we took our ice creams outside and ate them sitting on a wood bench.

"You best eat that before it melts," he said. I was still a bit dumbfounded. I suppose I had the damnedest look on my face. So we ate our ice cream and watched horse riders and teamster wagons go up and down the street as if we were interested.

"How's yours?" he said.

"Cold, and sweet," I replied.

He smiled. He had a good smile.

I noticed too the gun riding his hip, wore it like Jim and most men wore theirs: butt forward so they wouldn't snag the hammer on something and shoot themselves in the leg. Men weren't always as dumb as they seemed. But then, I supposed it only took once for word to get around, something like that.

He scraped out the last of his ice cream then licked the spoon and said, "That's mighty tasty."

"You want the rest of mine?" I asked.

"Well, if you're not going to eat it."

I had no real appetite thinking about Mama like I was, how I wished she was here to eat ice cream too, and all the other things she was bound to miss in the coming years.

Jim and I had talked a few times about having us some children. I knew Mama would have loved grandbabies. She would have played the piano and sang to them and we'd all go to town and eat ice cream. I could see us doing that.

"What's the matter?" Red Dog asked, a spot of strawberry in the corner of his mouth.

"Nothing," I said.

"She's okay, Lucy."

"Who is?"

"Your mama. She's in a good place."

"How would you know?"

He tapped the side of his head.

"Induns know things white folks don't."

"What sort of Indian are you, anyway, what with that red hair? You dress and talk like a white man. And is Red Dog your real name?"

He seemed to think about that a moment as if he wasn't sure.

"It's the only name I know to go by. Pap was Irish, he said. My ma's folks was some Cherokee and some Choctaw with a little bit of Creek thrown in. Might be more, the bloodline is often confused, depending on who you're talking to."

"And the red hair I reckon is from your Irish daddy?" I asked.

In the bright sunlight it looked redder, less the color of rust or dried blood.

He thoughtfully licked the spoon from my dish now that he'd finished that one too.

"My ma said my daddy was a sergeant in the Seventh Cavalry. Got cut to pieces at the Little Big Horn. Funny thing is my other daddy, the one my mother was married to, didn't know anything about it till I was born and he saw all this red hair. He threw her out and we went to live with my mother's people. And so it goes."

He looked into his empty ice-cream dish.

"What about you, Lucy?"

"What do you mean, what about me?"

"I mean what all blood you got in you?"

"I got some Cherokee in me as well on my mama's side. My daddy I ain't sure of."

"Why ain't you?"

"Don't know rightly who my daddy was."

"Your mama never told you?"

I shrugged knowing Mama had taken many lovers in her life and it could have been any one of them, though she claimed it was a fellow named Joseph and I thought when she told me the name, how very appropriate he'd be named that.

"She just never said," I told Red Dog.

"Well, ain't we about a pair of mixed bloods," he said. "You're a pert gal even if you are mostly white."

"Well thank you very damn much! You sure are a silver-tongue devil, ain't you?"

He laughed.

"Shit," he said. "First time I laid eyes on you I knew you was something special."

Oh lord, I thought. Now this fool is gonna to try and cause me to have second thoughts about my new husband because he was already tempting me with his carefree manner and that he had saved me from possible danger. Tempting me without even trying. Lucy, you best keep those heartstrings in check or there will be hell to pay and ain't you already got enough trouble as it stands? I told myself. You shoulda learned from Mama about a woman letting herself be vulnerable to men.

"You want some more ice cream?" he asked.

"No. I got to get on back."

"I'll ride with you. I ain't got nothing better to do."

"Free country," I said, when what I should have said was: You go on, Red Dog, and leave me to attend to my business and don't be messing around with my fragile heart and vulnerable feelings.

But instead I just nodded and got on Old Joe Harper and Red Dog got on his horse—don't know if it had a name or not, but it was a speckled gray—and on back to Daddy Sam's place we rode.

Chapter 6

Jim was fit to be tied when he saw us riding up together. He gave Red Dog a murderous look but didn't say anything. Red Dog dismounted and led his horse over to the water trough.

"What you doin' with that damn buck?" Jim growled.

"I ain't doing nothing with him."

"Well, how come you two are together, and where you two been?"

"I don't see no point to this conversation," I said.

"Well, I damn well do."

I never seen Jim so hot under the collar mad. I thought I best calm him down to avoid a shooting. Jim usually carried a calm demeanor but not this time.

"I rode into Hadley's Jump hoping I'd learn something about Mama's killer," I said. "Then some fools tried molesting me, and Red Dog stepped in and stopped them. Then he rode back with me to make sure I didn't end up like Mama. You ought to be thanking him for keeping me from being molested."

I put a few tears behind it just to make Jim feel ashamed and ease him down off his anger and not pull a gun on Red Dog who I glanced over to and saw was standing there holding the reins of his horse as coolly as if he hadn't heard a word exchanged between me and Jim. Fact was, I was more feared for Jim's life if he went up against Red Dog. Red Dog struck me as the more dangerous of the two.

Daddy Sam came from the house just then, screen door slapping behind him like a pistol shot, and Jim jerked and spun around.

"You're as jumpy as a frog in a frying pan," I said. "What's wrong with you?"

"Nothing," he said angrily.

You always know there is something wrong with a man when you ask him and he says nothing.

"Lucy, Jim and me and some of the others is going to ride over to Wilson's place—a fellow what raises hogs—and ask him some questions. You remember Wilson?" Daddy Sam asked. I shook my head.

"Up around the bend yonder, where the river crooks back on itself, on the way to Hadley's Jump. Used to be a old schoolhouse that burnt down."

"Oh, I kind of remember," I said. "But why are you going to see Wilson when it's Mama's killer you should be going after?"

Daddy Sam's hat rested atop his head at a jaunty angle. It was one of those little sugarloaf hats like bankers wore. He had on a waistcoat over a white shirt buttoned at the throat, black trousers and black tie shoes. He wasn't the same man he was when he met and married Mama. Back then he looked like every other Western man: big hat, big kerchief draped around his neck, rough riding clothes, boots with spurs and a pair of holstered pistols and a Winchester rifle slid down in his saddle sock. He looked like something you'd imagine in a lewd dream—some fellow any gal would desire to steal her away even if for a night. Now he just looked like a banker with a banker's little hat and little potbelly.

"It might have been Wilson who shot her," Daddy Sam said.

"Why would a hog farmer shoot Mama?" I asked.

Daddy Sam shrugged.

"They didn't get along, the two of them."

"Cause of what?"

"Hell, Lucy, honey. I don't know it was anything particular, they just never got along is all. Your mama just didn't have a kind word to say for him."

"Well, I'm going with you over there," I said.

"Ah, maybe it's best you wait here and let me and the other men go over and talk to him."

"To hell with that."

"Now, Lucy Mae, that's just what I'm talkin' about, that fiery temper of yours. You're liable to let your mouth run away, and next thing you know we're all killing each other over nothing."

"I'm going. Period."

Daddy Sam nodded and we all got mounted and turned our horses out to the road but for Red Dog who stayed behind and I wondered why. Hell, I didn't even think about J. R. not going, either. Figured he was somewhere in the house still sleeping from last night's drinking. I guessed it was just as well J. R. stayed behind—he'd become such a gloomy fellow and I no longer felt comfortable around my own half brother. It was like we weren't even kin no more, both of us having long since gone our separate ways—not that we were ever close to begin with.

Mama wrote me several times referring to how she missed J. R., that he hardly ever wrote or visited and that she'd heard rumor he'd been in trouble with the law and possibly jailed at one time. I wrote back and said, "Mama, why worry about that boy; he's grown now and will sooner or later have to find his way in this world, just as we all have to."

She was quick to defend him, though I know not why. You'd think a mother would worry about her girls more than her sons—that men were better equipped to handle life's trials and tribulations, but with Jim and me it was just the opposite.

It took us about twenty minutes to ride to this Wilson's place. It wasn't much of a place: surrounded by a split-rail fence within which a dozen or so hogs rooted free and squealed at our approach as if we'd upset their day.

We rode up the lane back in to where Wilson's cabin was. It appeared a hovel, truly, with the chinking fallen out and the front door leaning on its hinges and the stone chimney looking about to fall down. There were three or four outbuildings, including a privy, a shed, a chicken coop and a lean-to. There was a stone grinding wheel out front, a big galvanized washtub on what passed for a front porch and two ladder-back rocking chairs. There was several cats of various colorations slinking about and a big blood-red rooster perched on a gate post that flew off squawking as we rode up. I always wondered what made roosters think they could fly.

Daddy Sam was about to hallo the house but it proved unnecessary, for Wilson was suddenly there in the doorway holding a rifle with both hands down in front of him like a prize bar.

"What you fellers want?" Wilson asked. His gaze went from Daddy Sam and the others to me. I noticed the curtains shift in the only window.

"Want to talk to you about the murder of my wife, Belle," Daddy Sam said.

"I don't rightly know a thing about it," Wilson said.

"It happened not far from here is where we found her body," Daddy Sam said. "Thought maybe you might have heard or seen something."

"No," Wilson said, shaking his head. "I heard about it—afterwards—but I never heard no gunshots or nothing. I was down at the river running my trotlines about the time they say it happened."

"You and her never got along now, did you, Wilson?"

"I ain't never had no truck with her, that is true," Wilson said. "But I never had nothing again her neither."

Wilson was a slight, short fellow whose body looked sunk into his clothes. His face was grizzled with days-old growth of silvery beard, the skin of his neck loose like a turkey's wattle. He had features that reminded me of some old hawk sitting on a stump waiting for something it could kill. Sunk-in cheeks and sharp beak of a nose completed his visage. His voice was real gravelly too. He reminded me of Jim's daddy—that mean old son of a bitch who tried to kiss on me at the wedding when I'd gone into the house to see about helping with the food. Snuck up on me in the kitchen and found me in there alone, said, "Jim's got himself a right pert bride." Then grabbed hold of me and tried kissing me on the mouth.

I pushed him off.

"Don't you ever do that again."

"Oh, now, I was just foolin' with you, Lucy. Ain't it proper for a man to kiss his new daughter-in-law?"

"Just about as proper as it is for his new daughter-in-law to put a knife in his belly," I said.

That is what Wilson reminded me of: a fellow you'd not want to turn your back on.

"You kill my mama?" I called.

He looked at me fierce then.

"You'd be Lucy, ain't that right?" he said.

"If you did, I'm gonna cut your throat, you old fool."

"Calm down, Lucy," Daddy Sam said.

"I dint kill your ma," Wilson said. "I don't shoot women no matter how bad they run their mouth. If that was the case the whole country would be littered with dead women shot by me."

"You own a shotgun, Wilson?" Daddy Sam asked.

"Yes, I own one and what of it?"

"She was killed with a shotgun," Daddy Sam said, "but I suppose you already know that."

"I heard, yes."

Then Wilson's wife came out and stood next to him. I was surprised for she appeared a great deal younger than he. Had bunches of auburn hair pinned up on her head and large bosomed from what I could see budging the bodice of her faded gingham dress. My first thought was: How's an old goat like him get a young handsome gal like that?

"What do you want with my man?" she asked.

"We're investigating the murder of my wife, Mizzus Wilson," Daddy Sam said.

"Yes, sir. I'm sorry to hear of your loss, but Estes has nothin' to do with it. He was with me when it happened."

"I thought you said you was down at the river runnin' your trotlines," Daddy Sam said.

"Me and her," Wilson said without so much as an intake of breath. "We work it together."

"Well, this ain't finished," Daddy Sam said. "We'll find the ones who did it sooner or later and when we do, it ain't gone be no arrest and taken to Fort Smith to stand trial. Only trial will be held will be under one of these big hardwoods with a rope."

"Let me know," Wilson said, "and I'll hold one end for you."

"Let's go," Daddy Sam ordered and we turned our horses around and went up the lane and back to the road.

"That's all you're going to do?" I said. "Ask him a few questions?"

"I can't prove he did it yet, Lucy, but if he did then I'll find out. It could have been Wilson, but it could have been others too. Sure don't want to kill an innocent man. Wilson wasn't the only enemy your mama made since we moved here."

"Who else?"

"Well, probably one or two jealous wives, I imagine. Every married man within ten miles was in love with her and you can bet their wives didn't like it much."

"Wasn't you jealous?" I asked.

He laughed.

"Hell, Lucy, you knew your mama better than me. She was a

flirtatious woman who loved the attention of men even though she was faithful to the man she was with. I didn't let myself get riled up over it. Anything untoward was to happen she'd have told me. 'Sides, what if I was to get on her about it? She'd resent that and then there would have been trouble between us. No, I let her have her head and trusted her, but I'm not a hundred-percent certain that some of those jealous wives did."

"Anyone you suspect might actually have done it—waylaid her on the road?"

"Might be one or two I wouldn't put it past."

"Which ones?"

A sort of begrudged smile etched his mouth.

"The real ugly ones," he said. "And that could be the majority of them. Now let's go back home and eat some dinner and let me cogitate my next move."

"I want to keep searching for her killer," I insisted.

"You can, but where you aim to start? You already seen how far you got in Hadley's Jump. No, best let's think this through some more and come up with a plan of elimination till we find the right one."

So we rode back to Daddy Sam's and ate some dinner of ham hocks and beans and cornbread with apple butter. Then, it being so blazing hot, we laid down for a bit of noontime rest with all the windows open hoping to catch a breeze coming off the river.

Of course Jim wouldn't rest until he got what he wanted.

I refused at first.

"I'm sweating like a strumpet in church," I said. "Is that all you think about?"

He gave me that possum look the way a wanting man will do to get his way.

"Well, what else is a man newly married supposed to think about, Lucy? Prove to me you're not taken with that damn dirty

Indian, Red Dog."

"Oh, Jesus, will you leave off with your jealousy."

"How's a man supposed to know he is loved when his wife refuses to do her wifely duty?"

"My word no good with you?"

"Of course it's good. But damn it, Lucy, it's been almost forty-eight hours and I'm a man with great hungers."

"Can't it wait until at least sundown when it cools off?" I asked.

"I'll be quick, Lucy, honest, I will."

"Well, since you're being such a romantic about it, go ahead but don't get upset if I'm not exactly oohing and ahhing the whole while."

"No problem," he said.

It was over in about the time it takes to drink a glass of water and I was never so thankful for a man's fast release as I was just then. The best I can say for it was it wasn't as bad as getting a tooth pulled by a drunken dentist.

I closed my eyes in spite of the heat and rested thinking at least I wouldn't be bothered by Jim's needs for the rest of the day.

At least until night fell.

Chapter 7

In the hot fitful sleep I dreamt of Mama and Jesse and Frank James and the Younger brothers, one of whom Mama said in the dream she'd been secretly in love with. Cole.

Cole was a large handsome man going bald by the time he was in his twenties. They say light-haired men go bald early. His brothers Bob and Jim were the same way. But Jesse, who was also fair-haired, was not, though he did have a receding hairline which he was somewhat vain about.

We were all in the house Mama and Teddy Blue had lived in in Carthage not long after Teddy was murdered in the dice game.

The Jameses and Youngers just showed up in the dream and we were all sitting around in the kitchen drinking coffee and Jesse was dunking bread in his and eating it with his fingers. Frank quoted Shakespeare whenever he could get a word in edgewise around the boisterous Youngers.

"If you prick us, do we not bleed? If you tickle us, do we not laugh? If you poison us, do we not die? And if you wrong us, shall we not revenge?"

"Lissen to the professor," Cole piped up and said.

Jesse just kept dunking his coffee and eating it like wet pieces of newspaper clinging to his fingers.

Mama was leaned up against Cole standing in the entryway and telling Cole how much she admired a masculine man and he was that all over.

"Hell is empty and all the devils are here," Frank quoted another fine passage.

"Amen to that," Bob Younger hooted.

"I wish I had more bread to dunk," Jesse said. Jesse, when he got onto something, could not be distracted.

Cole had his hands on Mama's bottom.

"I sure could love a woman like you easy, Belle," he said.

Then there was a big explosion and everybody but me ran outside and when they came back in they were all crying.

"They killed Archie and blew off Mama's arm," Jesse wailed.

"Who did?" I asked.

"Those damn dirty Pinkertons," Frank said.

Then Cole was playing a guitar and his voice was as sweet as an angel's as he sang "In Thy Twilight's Keeping I Shall Rest and Await the Lord's Coming."

"What's done cannot be undone," Frank quoted again.

"They will all pay," Jesse bemoaned. "Sooner or later, everyone must pay."

Somehow I knew in the dream Jesse was already a goner, his brains blowed out by one of his own guns that his cousin Bob Ford had snatched when Jesse's back was turned.

Then something woke me and it took a moment or two for me to realize I'd only been dreaming, that I was still in bed in Daddy Sam's house. I felt a presence but when I looked around nobody was there. The light had mostly gone out of the day and I quickly dressed in a wrapper and went out and downstairs where Daddy Sam, Jim, and one or two of Daddy Sam's men friends were in the kitchen passing a bottle of liquor around and talking of revenge. They hardly noticed my entrance. Daddy Sam was planning ways of revenge in an overly loud voice; I thought it from the liquor.

It was still stifling in the house even though the sun had dropped beyond the trees and turned the sky brooding red. I wandered out of doors and stood for a moment on the porch hoping to catch a cool breeze blowing up from the river bottom. None was to be had.

I went down across the yard to where a path led to a small copse of trees that led into a thicker stand of hardwoods so deep and dark. I felt the need to just walk into the coolness of their trunks and remembered a little stream that eventually flowed into the river beyond and the idea of putting my feet in cool water was appealing.

I wasn't there very long, sitting on a stump at the stream's edge with both my feet dangled in the burbling brook when I suddenly felt the same presence as I had up in the bedroom.

I turned and there stood the shadowy figure of Red Dog.

"Evening, Lucy."

"Red Dog," I said with caution. For it had not escaped my vivid imagination that you should never fully trust a Indian no matter which kind. I still recall childhood stories told by some old Texas Rangers when Mama and me lived down in Dallas. How they told of the terrible things the Comanche did to white folks: rape and torture and burning folks alive and cutting off their noses. It raised the hair on my arms to hear them tell of it. Those old lawmen concluded that the only good Indian was a dead one and that they'd done their level best to make as many good Indians as they could. I remember asking Mama if the stories were true.

"I'm afraid they are, Lucy Mae. The land is washed by blood of both red and white." To ease my troubled spirit she would play lively tunes on the piano and sing until I was over my fear.

Washed by blood, I thought. Wasn't that the same thing preachers said about our Lord, that He was washed by blood? My child mind wondered if it was Comanche who killed him. "What you doing out here, Red Dog?"

"Looking for a scalp to take," he laughed. "Yours would make a real pretty one."

"That's not funny," I said angrily.

"Oh, Lucy, I was just fooling with you. I would never harm a single hair on your pretty head."

"Well, all right, then. You can sit down if you like. Just don't get no funny ideas and leave your scalping knife where I can see it." He clucked his tongue and shook and unsheathed his knife and plunged it into the dirt as he sat down next to me on the ground. The scent coming off him was that of wood smoke, a not entirely unpleasant smell.

"How'd things go over to Wilson's today?" he asked.

"I think that old man did it," I said.

"What makes you think it was him?"

"Daddy Sam said him and Mama didn't get along and I heard some of those other men say how Wilson was known to have killed some other fellows down in Texas and some in Florida too. Even Wilson admitted him and Mama didn't get on too well."

"You want, I could go over there and kill him," Red Dog said.

"Why would you when you got no dog in the fight?"

"I'd do it for you, Lucy."

There it was again, that fooling with my heartstrings.

"You do know I'm married to that big handsome Jim don't you?"

"Yes," he said. "I know it."

"Jim was awful upset to see me and you riding in together today."

"I figured. He do anything to you?"

"Like what?" I asked. I thought maybe he meant when Jim insisted I give in to him up in the bedroom.

"Did he hit you or anything because of it?"

"No, he didn't hit me. He knows better than to try it, too."

"What'd you do if he did hit you?"

"I'd take a board to him is what. I'd wait till he fell asleep and wrap him up in the sheets and wale on him."

He laughed like he didn't believe me. I know, I sounded tough because I wanted to feel tough, to not seem weak in light of seeking revenge for Mama.

Something was pinching my feet and I quick jerked them out of the water.

"Minnows," Red Dog said. "They like to eat the dead skin."

"Well, they'll not eat nothing off me," I said.

Red Dog grunted.

"Even the least of God's creatures got to eat, Lucy."

"You fooling me? I don't even understand why some creatures even exist, for what good are they?"

"Minnows, you mean?"

"Not just minnows. I'm talking about things like mosquitoes. What is a dang mosquito good for? I believe God is all knowing and such, but I don't think He thought everything quite through enough. Figures, Him being a man and all."

"You are a willful woman, ain't you, Lucy?"

"Willful enough, I reckon."

"Why is that?"

"Because it suits me to be so."

The last little bit of light was leaking out of the sky and it shone on his face so that it was pure copper and his hair looked aflame, and in that moment he was a right handsome man. I guess that's why I did it: leaned over suddenly and kissed him full on the mouth then leaped up and ran off back to the house pausing only once to see if he was following me. But no, he hadn't and I don't know if I was pleased or displeased that he hadn't.

Lucy, you damn fool girl, I warned myself as I went into the house: he could have just as easily raped you and cut your throat and tossed your body into the creek. Maybe he's meant to kill every damn Moon woman there is alive.

When I came into the kitchen, Jim looked up with stardust in his eyes and I knew what he was thinking so I grabbed him by the hand.

"Come with me," I said.

The others made suggestive remarks about him letting himself get hauled upstairs.

"There's hauling and then there's getting your ashes hauled," I heard one of them say followed by a lot of hooting and guffawing and stomping of feet. Let a man put his mouth to a bottle and he's liable to say anything.

Through the register vents we could hear them carrying on down in the kitchen, Jim and me as we made love, my own passion equal or surpassing Jim's for once. But the whole time I was thinking about Red Dog, the smokiness of his mouth, those soft lips mine were pressed against, the illicitness of it all. Me, a freshly married white woman and him a dirty red savage. Why there would be murder to spare if it was learned I'd consorted with him. Something about that thought however made it all the more exciting. I still wanted to keep going even after Jim fell out of the saddle.

"Ah, Lucy," he moaned. "I'm all shot to hell. I need to rest a while."

"You either will or you won't take me when I offer," I said. "But a wife whose needs are left unattended can't be held accountable for what she might do, husband of mine."

He rolled over and looked at me with one eye.

"What's that supposed to mean?"

"Just what it sounds like."

"Now Lucy, don't go threatening me with cheating. You know I've a jealous nature and I wouldn't brook becoming a cuckold."

"Mighty big word for a man so little educated," I said. "Must have learned that one firsthand in the whorehouses you used to frequent before I came along."

He growled like a cur dog under his breath.

"Then you take care of your business, Jim Creed, or somebody else just might." I wanted so bad to blurt out my indiscretion with Red Dog I nearly had to bite off my tongue.

He made a lame effort to satisfy me but it wasn't any good at all and I finally pushed him away.

"Just go on to sleep," I said.

And soon enough he was snoring and I was back to thinking about kissing Red Dog and warning myself of the dangers of such, telling myself I was only wanting to play with fire because it was there to be played with.

Gratefully, it rained like somebody had slit the belly of the beast open and doused all the fire and heat that was afoot that night. I imagined it as washing away sins born in the heat of the day, the cooling air upon my damp and warm skin.

Chapter 8

When I awoke next morning everybody was gone but Jim and brother J. R., who was squatted out in the yard twining a garter snake through his fingers. Jim sat on the porch looking on with hooded lids and bloodshot eyes, his hair like chicken feathers.

"You ready for round two?" I teased.

He looked awful glum.

"I ain't had no coffee or breakfast either one yet," he said.

"And I don't reckon you're going to get any setting there watching my half-wit brother fool with that snake, either."

"Shit, Lucy, why can't you be more like a dutiful wife? Why you have to be such a hard woman?"

"I wasn't hard last night," I said. "But then you wasn't either, were you dear husband?"

He hung his head and moaned. He wasn't wearing shoes and his feet were big and white like slabs of lard and his toenails needed trimming, and all in all he'd lost a lot of allure since the first time I laid eyes on him. Give a man enough time and his true self will bleed through. He'll look like gold at first but then he'll turn to rust. Once they have you, they think it don't matter how they present themselves.

J. R. now held the garter snake up close to his face, its black tongue flicking as if he was going to kiss it.

"Too bad it ain't poison," I called.

He gave me an evil dark look and I wondered how it was he and I came out so different, even considering we had different daddies, we still had the same cheerful Mama.

"Maybe I'll find one, sister, and toss it in your bed some night. Let it bite you in a proper place so that ol' Jim there can suck the poison out. Would you do that, Jim?"

Now some would laugh at such a perverse joke if they told it, but not J. R. He was serious and I did believe from then on I'd be checking my bedcovers before I got under them.

Over the years I'd heard some rumors about my brother that caused my skin to crawl—how he'd once forced himself on a daft girl down in the basement of her daddy's store. It was said she only had the mind of a ten-year-old. I don't know how much of the stories were true but he had a wickedness in him you couldn't wash out with lye soap.

"You just try it putting a snake in my bed," I said, "and I'll clean your ears with a pistol barrel."

"Will you two shut the hell up," Jim cawed. "My head's about to bust."

"That wouldn't be any great loss. Where's everybody?" I asked.

"They went off," Jim grumped.

"Went off where?"

"To try and find who killed your mama, I reckon. They was gone time I got up."

"Why the hell didn't somebody wake me!"

"I reckon if they wanted you tagging along they'd done just that. But plainly they did not want you tagging along. Now go on in and fix me something to eat, damn it."

I ignored such ignoramus talk. Having not spotted Red Dog, I asked if he'd gone with the others.

"What you care where that damned Indun is?" Jim said painfully as if somebody was jabbing a fork into his neck.

"I *don't* care," I said and went back into the house making sure I let the screen door slap shut loud as a pistol shot. I heard

Jim cuss, then say, "Will you quite playing with that goddamn viper, J. R.?"

"Go to hell you alky," my sweet brother replied.

Maybe I'd get lucky and the two of them would kill each other before noon, which it nearly was judging by the sun.

I got dressed in my riding clothes and belted Jim's bird's-head revolver, not even sure where I was going to go next. I thought maybe I'd ride over to Oren's house, Daddy Sam's brother. He was about the only person I knew who lived in the area besides Daddy Sam. Oren always struck me as a kindly man—one who was settled with his wife, Vinita, and their brood of children. Talk about wild Indians. The place always seemed run over with kids and cats as I recalled how Vinita, who was much younger than Oren, looked to be a hundred.

In spite of her heavy load, Vinita had always been real nice and would ask me all about my life, the places I'd been, the things I'd done, whenever I'd visit her. We'd talk for hours while the men demonstrated their skills at swapping lies and drinking from a jug and pitched horseshoes out in the yard.

"You're just like your mother, Lucy," Vinita said. "I envy the both of you for being freeborn women, doing what you want, going where you want. I never traveled much out of Oklahoma." She'd said all this out of earshot of Oren, and I understood why: men don't like their women dreaming too much of other lives. It's a threat. They're afraid their wives will run off and leave them to cook and clean and raise all those damn kids he put in her.

Yes, the more I thought about it the more I wanted to go visit Vinita.

When I came out of the house Jim was still sitting there holding his head in his hands. His long unwashed hair hung down over his eyes as he cussed and talked to himself under his breath. J. R. was no longer in the yard playing with the snake but over by the corral feeding carrots to a donkey they had. The thing brayed every time J. R. teased it with a carrot.

I went on past Jim and he looked up briefly.

"Now where the hell you off to?"

"Going to pay Oren and Vinita a visit."

"What the hell for?"

"Because I damn well want to. Me and Vinita have a lot in common."

"Like what?"

"None of your business, like what."

For some reason I felt mean toward Jim. It was as if something between us from last night just broke, like a favorite cup you dropped and broke off the handle and you knew you could glue it back on but it would never be the same. That's how it had always been with me and men anyway.

"A husband and a wife isn't supposed to keep any secrets from each other."

I stopped and turned and looked at him in the true light of who he was: a man unshaven, disheveled, forlorn and wallowing in his self-made misery. He held no appeal for me whatsoever in that moment, and maybe he never would again. He was like a stranger wandered up to the porch just to get in out of the sun, a bummer come to beg for a piece of bread and my cupboard was bare.

"Jim, if I was to tell you everything I know your head would explode."

"What's that supposed to mean?"

"There's little worse than a stupid man who don't know he's stupid. I'm leaving," I said and crossed the yard to the corral and picked out the remaining horse, a blood bay with a bald face. I saddled the mare and swung aboard and of course J. R. couldn't stand just leaving me be.

"You know it ain't womanly to ride a horse like that," he

said. "Mama always rode sidesaddle, but you ride like a man. But I bet in your case riding that way it feels right good to you."

"I don't reckon you'd know what it is for a woman to feel good no more than what it is to make you feel good, you damn fool," I said and thumped my heels into the bay's flanks.

I arrived about an hour later at Oren's place which was at the end of a long curving lane creased by twin wagon wheel tracks with weeds growing up in the center.

Before arriving at Oren's, I'd had to ride right past the place where they said they'd found Mama's body.

I was fearful I would see bloodstains in the dirt, but there weren't any and I was relieved.

Vinita was hanging wash in the yard—shirts and long drawers and faded denims, some white blouses, and her underthings discreetly put on the middle line. She looked up from the basket and waved.

"Lucy Mae," she shouted and left off the wash hanging and came running toward me as I dismounted the blood bay.

We hugged like old friends.

"I'm so glad you came," she said.

She smelled of sun and soap and rinse water, a not unpleasant smell. It struck me that Mama was never a domestic in the way that Vinita and other women were. I don't recall ever seeing her wash or hang clothes, or clean nor iron either. Seemed like she always had somebody to do those things for her—a colored woman she'd hire to do the domestic chores: cooking and cleaning and such.

"It's such common labor, Lucy," Mama said. "I've too many artistic endeavors to take up my time without having to be a servant to some man or other." She much preferred to play the piano or paint or teach me to dance. Mama was such a good dancer, so light on her feet.

Somehow that always struck me as the wise thing—to not give yourself to common labor if you could help it. It has nothing to do with work but everything to do with dreams. I had dreams in spades, same as Mama.

"Come and let's sit in the shade and have some cold tea," Vinita said. I noticed how red and raw her boney hands were.

She went indoors while I sat on one of several handsome rocking chairs made from wild vines there under the porch overhang. The house and other buildings looked cobbled together—like Oren had started out with just four walls and a roof and added on as he went so that nothing looked like it fit together. Oh well, to each his own. There was an old hay rake rusting in the weeds not far from the house and a pile of old boards near a trash dump piled high with tin cans. A milk cow grazed at the end of a long tethered rope over near a corncrib half full of yellow cobs, and chickens plucked a bare patch of ground near a wired coop.

I recalled hearing Daddy Sam say once that Oren was tight with a buck and that if he could fix something up rather than buy a new one that's how he'd go. Looking around, I could believe it.

Vinita came out with a pitcher of tea and two glasses and poured them and handed me one then eased herself down into the chair next to mine.

"Whew," she sighed. "Sure is hot for this time of year."

"Indian summer," I agreed. "It's my favorite time of year."

"Mine too, but for the work of getting ready for winter. Just finished putting up green beans and okra," she said. "Anyway, Lucy, how have you been? Besides I mean the loss of your mama."

"Been good. Me and Jim were down in El Paso on our honeymoon when we got the word."

"Oh, that's doubly bad, the timing and all."

"Yes," I said.

She patted my hand.

"This is good tea, Vinita."

She rocked and stared off out toward a large patch of garden that was pretty well picked over. She had the clearest light-blue eyes I've ever seen on a woman, or anyone for that matter but for Jesse James.

"How do you like being married, Lucy?"

"Oh, well, I guess I've not been married long enough to form an opinion," I said.

She looked at me.

"No, I suppose you haven't. The first few months, maybe even a year isn't too bad, though it takes some getting used to the other person. Everything is new and wonderful when you're first in love. But it can be a terrible adjustment too."

I nodded.

"Is Jim a good lover?"

That caused my jaw to drop a little. I thought Vinita was a fire-and-brimstone Baptist from what little I knew of her.

"Well, yes, he does all right in that department," I said feeling my ears burn.

She smiled and sipped her tea.

"They are—in the beginning," she said. "Too bad it don't stay that way the whole time."

"You and Oren still do it?"

"Oh, Lord yes. He won't hardly leave me alone. But . . ." She leaned in close as if there was others around to hear. "I don't care for it very much."

"That's surprising," I said, "with all the kids you two got."

She looked on the verge of either tears or laughter.

"Children will wear a body out," she said. "And you know who's the only one of two people who has the children, Lucy. I love my kids, but I don't want any more. We have to make sure when we're at it that doesn't happen."

I nodded as if I understood what she was about to say.

"See, the man just sticks it in and gets his pleasure without much concern for the woman. Least that is how it was with Oren and me until I set the ground rules about no more kids."

She paused then and looked around.

"There's something I'd like to ask you, Lucy."

"Go ahead, ask," I said.

Again she leaned in and spoke in a low voice.

"Why you whispering? I don't see anybody around."

"Never know," she said. "Them kids or Oren will sneak up on you like bandits."

My turn to nod and take another sip of tea.

"Only man I ever had is Oren," she said. "So I don't have a whole lot to go by in that particular department. But Lucy, I imagine a pert young sprite such as yourself probably has had several lovers."

"A few," I said.

This got us to giggling like a pair of schoolgirls.

"Well, I was wondering in your experiences, have you ever come across a man who's taken tender care with you and made sure you'd gotten pleasure from it same as him?"

I didn't even have to think about the question.

"Yes, Vinita, I can say that I have. Maybe not the first one or two I got up with, but I learned to demand my share since."

"What's it like?"

"What's what like?"

"You know, that thing I hear women are supposed to feel when it's real right?"

"Oh, that. You never have?"

She shook her head.

"Well, there just ain't nothing to compare to that feeling, Vinita. I can't even describe it to you except it feels like your whole body is exploding with the greatest sensation ripping through you."

I fumbled for the right words.

"It's about like what you'd think heaven is like, you know, how the preachers describe the gold and glory—everything you ever wanted."

"Oh my," she said.

I could tell she was holding something back.

"Oren's never made you feel that way even once?"

She sat silent for a moment, then scarlet bloomed along her neck and eased up into her cheeks.

"Yes, I felt that way once," she said.

"Well, what'd Oren do to you that time to make you feel that?" I asked. "Whatever it was, just insist he does it each time he lays with you."

She shook her head.

"It weren't Oren," she said.

"I thought you said . . ."

"It was me. I was here all alone, way before Jurvis and Roy were born, the twins."

"I'm listening." She had me truly interested, this plain woman wore out way before her time, boney and long in the face with ears stuck out from her straight stringy hair.

"I was up in my room and it was hot, real hot, no air moving whatsoever, not a whisper. Oren and the children had gone off to Hadley's Jump for some supplies so it was just me here alone. And in spite of the heat it was peaceful. I'd undressed and lay on the bed and got to dreaming about one thing and another . . ."

She leaned in even closer.

"You must promise never to tell this to anyone, Lucy."

"Cross my heart," I said, and crossed my heart.

"Well, back then we had a colored man hired on part-time,

helping Oren out around the place, posting holes and patching the roof and such. The children were too young for such work and I had my hands full just keeping the house up."

She paused and took a long sip of her tea then licked her lips.

"His name was Bogartus and he was young and light-skinned, like a Mexican. I'd often see him working in the hot sun when Oren wasn't around, working with his shirt off. And it come to my mind a picture of him like that. Lucy, the man was pure muscle and the way his skin gleamed with sweat. He was a real nice-looking man.

"Next thing I know my hand was down there and I was imagining it was me and Bogartus and he was inside me."

She swallowed hard and beads of sweat dotted her forehead as she told the story as if it was actually happening to her just then.

"I'd closed my eyes is the only way I could see it all, Lucy. I knew it was wrong what I was doing, but I couldn't help it. I just wanted to feel what it was like with another man and I figured the Lord would forgive me my sins if I didn't actually commit adultery on Oren."

"And?" I urged, sitting on the edge of my seat, because I could see it too, the two of them doing it, this colored man with his darker skin against Vinita's almost bloodless pale body and her giving herself to him with all abandon.

"Well," she continued, though her voice was slightly shaky. "I felt something like you described, Lucy, that going to heaven feeling, and I shook all over. It seemed I couldn't stop even if I'd wanted to, even if Oren and the children had walked in on me, I couldn't have stopped what was happening."

"I understand, Vinita. I think you reached a climax, which is what women are supposed to do if the man is right about it."

She rested back, the glass held loosely in her hand, her chest rising and falling like she'd just run down to the river and back, all out of breath.

"I know, Lucy. But Oren's never made me feel that. I'd just like once for Oren or some man to make me feel that."

"So now you know how to make it happen, maybe you could show Oren what to do, what you like," I said.

"Oh, I never could," she said.

"Why couldn't you?"

"He'd see it as criticism against him. He'd get mad as hell."

"Well, let him, then."

She shook her head.

"I'm not you, Lucy. I got to keep my family together and give Oren no reason to go off and find somebody else. I got to keep him thinking he's taking good care of me."

"Then I suggest you think of Bogartus more often," I said. "Take care of yourself."

Without looking at me she said: "I do, Lucy. I just told you it was that one time, but it has been plenty of other times too, and not just with Bogartus. With other men as well. One time it was a drummer came around trying to sell me a family Bible big enough you could use it for a doorstop."

Her eyes glistened.

"I allowed him to sit a spell on the porch while I took measure of him. He was a very nice man, handsomely dressed if not handsome himself. Sort of short, but I kept thinking: What if I had this man come into the house and follow me upstairs?"

"But you didn't?"

"Oh, Lord, no. If Oren would have come in he'd have killed us both. Besides, I couldn't do that to him."

"But afterward," I said.

"Yes, afterward I went up to my room alone and me and that fellow had a real good time of it."

She smiled broadly.

"Vinita, you are a complete surprise, but a wonderful one at that."

I told her I better get back and she said she hated to see me go and would I come around again before I left with Jim to wherever we were headed once Mama's murder got solved. I promised her I would. We hugged and I rode off back to Daddy Sam's.

Vinita had put me in a peaceful and happy mood and the sun came down through the trees and dappled the ground so that it looked like I was riding over black lace. But then I neared that same spot in the road where Mama's body had been discovered and something shivered up my backbone.

I felt like somebody was watching from the woods that bordered the fence line. Like maybe whoever it was had a rifle or shotgun and was aiming it at me and about to pull the trigger.

I thumped my heels into the blood bay and galloped away home again.

CHAPTER 9

It seemed that fate was strong that day for Red Dog met me along the road. He was sitting there astride his horse, one leg crossed over the horn, casual-like, as if he knew I'd come along.

"Wondered where you went," he said as I sawed back on the reins alongside him.

"Why'd you wonder, I'm not hardly your business," I said.

"Been thinking about that kiss you gave me, what made you do it, sudden like that then run off?"

I felt myself grow warm and not just from the sun.

"I don't know why I did it," I said. "Sometimes I just do things and don't know why. I think smart folks call it being impulsive."

"You mean like kiss a fellow and get him eager then run away?"

"Is that what I did, get you eager?"

He had pretty teeth, straight and white as ivory in that dusky face of his.

"I'd damn say you did," he said.

His horse stamped its hind feet and twitched about like it was half wild like its rider, like it had a rambunctiousness nobody could get out of it, same as Red Dog who uncrossed his leg and sat up straight.

"Well, I'm sorry if I did," I said. "I didn't even mean to kiss you much less get you eager. I ain't that sort of woman."

"What sort of woman are you?"

"Not the sort to work a man up then just leave him be. I work a man up I aim to stay around till the job is finished."

"Damn'd if I don't believe you're telling the truth of it," he said.

"Listen, I've already told you, I'm a married woman and that little kiss don't mean a thing. Folks kiss other folks all the time without it meaning nothing. Why I just now come from kissing a woman friend, you think that means anything?"

He grinned even more.

"Well now, that is an interesting piece of news."

He reached round and dug in his saddlebag and came out with a brown pint bottle that had liquor in it.

"How about me and you go over and sit in the shade of those trees and have a little drink and talk about all this? About what you mean and what you don't."

"There's nothing to talk about. I got to get on back. Jim will be wondering where I got off to."

"Jim's not there," he said.

"Where is he?"

"Last I seen he was riding toward Hadley's Jump. Said he needed to get something to eat. Said his wife wouldn't even cook him breakfast. Seemed real down in the dumps over something."

That damn fool husband of mine, I thought.

"That true, what he said?" Red Dog asked. "About you wouldn't even fix him breakfast?"

"I reckon if he said it, it's true."

"Why I understand the two of you only been married a couple of weeks. Seems to me you'd not have any disagreements so early on in. They say wedded life is bliss. But then I ain't no preacher or nothing."

"You seem to take a real keen interest in my life. Why is that?"

"I'm a curious fellow," he said. "Always have been."

"Curiosity killed the cat, don't you know."

"I heard that but I never yet seen a cat that's been killed from being curious. Have you?"

"Yes," I lied.

"No you ain't."

A hot dry wind rippled through the trees and spun through the grass which was already turning brown, it too dying as everything must.

"I need to get on," I said again.

"Okay."

But still I didn't go for a moment and he didn't ride away.

"What you want from me anyway?" I said.

"Nothing you don't want to give," he said.

"Well nothing is what I want to give."

"Okay, then."

"Okay."

"Go on," he said.

"I'm going."

"Well go on."

"All right, I will."

So I thumped heels to my horse and went.

He sat there watching as I rode on and my bad self was thinking I should turn back and go over into the shade and have a drink with him and see what would happen next, but my good self was telling me to keep going, that I'm a married woman and if I need that sort of thing and Jim doesn't give it to me, then I should do what Vinita does. And I kept riding, but slowly and I looked back once and Red Dog was still sitting there on his horse in the middle of the road watching me.

Keep going, Lucy, I said to myself

Just keep on riding and get home and fix Jim a real big dinner for when he returns from Hadley's Jump and show him what a loving and faithful wife you are.

And when I got beyond sight of Red Dog I felt like I'd lost something—an opportunity to change the entire course of my life. But I did not know what the current course of my life was or where it was leading me to, so why bother to try and change it?

Still in all, the onliest person I could think about the rest of the day was that mysterious man, his hunger for me even though I didn't need or want any other man than Jim.

My husband.

A woman isn't supposed to want any other man than her husband, is she?

I thought of Mama. She was never in want of a man. I wondered if she'd ever been unfaithful to any of her lovers. I didn't think she was the type, but then I've learned you never know about a body, truly, no matter how close you are to someone.

Oh, hell, Lucy, go on back and get yourself right again and stop thinking about that goddamn Indian.

But when Jim crawled in the bed with me that night, the room so dark I couldn't see his face, it wasn't hard to let myself imagine it was Red Dog on top of me taking his pleasure.

Imagination can be a mighty powerful thing and the power overtook me.

That night, it was the best I ever had with Jim. Even he commented on it as he lay there panting like a dog.

"Damn, Lucy, I rode unbroken horses didn't buck as hard as you just did. That was great, honey. Just great. It's just getting better and better, ain't it?"

"Yes," I said in silent bliss.

It was, wasn't it?

Chapter 10

I rose before dawn and drew on a wrapper and went downstairs, Jim snoring like a bulldog in the bed still.

The house was silent and I went on past the parlor where Mama had been laid out and glanced in thinking I'd see her sitting in there waiting for me, that maybe this was all just a bad, sad dream and I'd just woken up from it. But the parlor was empty and the curtains hung lank from the tall windows like the sheets ghosts had left behind. Worst of all was the upright piano with its lid closed, the empty bench and sheet music laid open. It seemed that music would never be heard again in this house no matter who lived in it.

I eased out through the screen door and onto the porch and there sat Daddy Sam alone, a quilt over his shoulders just staring out at the nothingness of a yet unlit land. There was a jug between his feet.

Ground fog hung low over the yard, eerie and silent.

"Lucy," Daddy Sam said.

"What is it, Daddy Sam?"

"I'm just so sad about Mama Belle," he said. "Couldn't sleep, been out here all night for thinking on it."

I could smell the liquor on his breath.

I took the chair next to his and we sat like that without speaking further for a long time. The sun, when it came up, would rise over the trees that followed the river's course unseen in the distance, but right now you couldn't even see the trees.

"I want to kill somebody for it, Lucy," Daddy Sam said softly. "But I don't know who to kill yet."

He sounded as sad as any man I ever heard. His voice caused me to well up inside and bite my lip to keep from crying. He reached for the jug and tilted it to his mouth.

"She was going to leave me if I didn't move her off this place and into a decent town," he said setting the jug down again. "Not a place like Hadley's Jump. She said any place that didn't have at least two hat shops didn't deserve to be called a town. She tell you that, Lucy?"

"Yes, she told me."

He looked at me then and gave a big sigh.

"I tried to tell her if we moved into a city, they would have law who might arrest me for the things I done and begged her to give this place a chance, to hang on a while, that she might get used to living out in the beyond. I should have gone ahead and done what she wanted. If I had, she would be alive and here with us now. It's as much my fault she's gone as anybody's."

His voice cracked then and I knew he was crying in the way men cry, fighting it all the way so as not to seem weak.

I reached out and patted his forearm.

"It wasn't your fault, Daddy Sam. It was whoever shot her's fault."

He continued to snuffle and fight his broken heart and I just kept quiet and let him because to try and do otherwise would only make it worse.

Beyond his stifled sobs you could almost hear the air stirring along the ground, a ghostly whisper. The moon looked like a milky eye like you see in somebody who's blind.

After a time Daddy Sam rubbed his eyes and nose with the edge of the quilt.

"Lord, I'm sorry, Lucy, for acting this way in front of you."

"It's okay. I cried two buckets of tears since I got the news."

"It couldn't have come at a worse time for you, could it? You and Jim off on your honeymoon." He slurred his words slightly when he said it about Jim and me.

"There's never a good time for such as this to come," I said.

"True," he said. "Sometimes my words don't come out the way I want them to."

The land slowly was beginning to lighten with a soft gray light and what was shapeless now begun to take shape, the outbuildings, corral with its horses, the tree line. And that's when we saw a rider come loping up from down the road, up Daddy Sam's lane, casual as if he was just out for a Sunday ride.

"Who's that, Daddy Sam?"

"Hell if I know," he said. "Maybe you ought to go in the house and get me my gun, Lucy."

His voice had suddenly changed from that of a maudlin, half-drunk man to one of stern warning.

I jumped up and ran inside and found Daddy Sam's Winchester rifle and carried it out on the porch where he now stood, the quilt still draped over his shoulders and wearing nothing more than his union suit.

"Here," he said and reached out for it.

"Now you get back inside in case this here is trouble riding up to the house."

But I didn't move, couldn't move.

And this fellow rode up to within twenty or thirty yards till Daddy Sam shouted, "Who you be, mister, and what you want?"

"Whoa," the man said raising his palm. "I come as a friend of Mother Mercy Moon's. I heard she got herself dead and I came to pay my respects."

Daddy Sam lowered the rifle.

"Well come on in, then."

The fellow rode up and dismounted and dropped the reins to

a fine-looking buckskin and stepped up onto the porch. He wore one of those bowler hats and a long linen duster that came down to the top of his boots. He looked slightly familiar to me but I couldn't place him. Older gentleman with salty gray mustache and long face.

He held out his hand to Daddy Sam.

"Name's Frank James," he said. Then he glanced at me. "Is that you, Lucy Mae?"

"Frank," I cried. "Oh, Frank."

Something about his presence caused my eyes to well with tears that spilled down my cheeks as he hugged me to him.

"I'm so sorry to have heard of her passing, Lucy," he said.

He smelled of tobacco and bay rum and new shirt. Now that I knew who he was I remembered him and Jesse always wearing those linen dusters. They were wearing them the day they came and got Clell Miller to go with them to rob the bank in Northfield, only we didn't know they were going for that. I think they knew that if Mama learned of it she wouldn't have let Clell go. Jesse and Frank were always tight-lipped about their plans. I hadn't seen either of them since, and Jesse was long in his grave, that handsome man with his light-brown hair and clear blue eyes. All the others were either dead or in prison, but for Frank. He removed his hat and I saw he was bald but for the fringe of sandy-gray hair that horseshoed his skull. He'd aged right proper.

Frank held me to him a long time like a father would then released me.

"Lord, child," he said. "I would have come sooner, but by time I heard the news it was way too late. But I knew I had to come on anyway just to pay my respects to your mama. She was a very good friend to me and Jesse, and in this old world the one thing I know to be true is you don't get many friends—not folks like her, anyhow."

"Are you hungry, Frank? I can fix us something to eat."

"I could use a good hot cup of coffee," he said. "Maybe something to eat if you got it and it ain't too much trouble to fix it."

"No trouble," I said.

I rushed in and got the stove going—a fine Queen Anne four-plate Portland with nickel trimming. I put a pot of coffee on one burner, a fry pan of sliced bacon on another and a skillet of eggs on another. I put the pan of biscuits from the day before in the warmer.

I had breakfast whipped up in no time while Daddy Sam and Frank James sat out on the porch talking about Mama. I could hear them through the screen door and something about Frank's presence brightened my spirits—to think he'd come all this way just to pay his respects. Last I heard of him was what I'd read in the *National Police Gazette* that he'd be standing trial for his and Jesse's past crimes. That not long after Jesse was assassinated, Frank turned in his guns. Was quoted as saying he was tired of running and living the outlaw life and didn't want to be hunted no more. That he was ready to face the music and take his punishment. When I read that I about come to tears.

Frank was always the steady quieter of the two. Mama told me him and Jesse had had a falling out after the foiled bank robbery in Northfield and had gone their separate ways and Frank had sent her many letters from where he was living in Virginia at the time of Jesse's death. That's why he wasn't there to watch Jesse's back when Bob Ford and his brother Charlie killed Jesse. Jesse had formed a new gang that included those dirty little cowards. Oh how I hated them for it from the way Mama had told me about it. She'd cried at the news.

I got everything onto plates and we all sat down to eat there in the kitchen and Frank insisted on a prayer of thanks and in memory of the recent past loved ones and we bowed our heads while he spoke from the heart then ate like savages.

"I told Frank how it happened," Daddy Sam said.

Frank looked solemn.

"Perchance to kill the innocent is a far, far greater sin than mere murder," he said.

"Is that from Shakespeare, Frank?" I asked.

He turned his gaze on me. "No Lucy, it just came out of my heart."

To me Frank was a mythical figure. So much had been written and spoken of the James boys. There were even illustrated dime novels and songs about them. And now here he sat at our table looking no more than an aging school teacher and such notions as robbery and even murder I could not assign to him. I noticed too that when he lifted his cup to drink he did so with both hands, for they trembled noticeably.

"How's life been treating you, Frank?" I wanted to know.

His eyes were more gray than blue like Jesse's.

"Well, it's not been easy, little sister. Can't seem to find any lasting peace. Folks always coming up to me asking me about Jesse and what all we done and what all we were accused of doing. Scribes and newspaper reporters wanting to collaborate with me on books about our exploits, souvenir seekers. They'll just come up and knock on the door without consideration of me or my family. The newspaper reporters are the worst."

He swallowed the last of what was in his cup and I hopped up and got the pot and refilled it and Daddy Sam's too then took my seat again.

"You want some whiskey in that, Frank?" Daddy Sam asked.

"No thank you, Mr. Harper. I give up drinking and am a deacon in the church."

It didn't prevent Daddy Sam from spilling some liquor into his own cup.

"Good news is, Lucy Mae," Frank said turning his attention

back to me. "Bob Ford got his lights doused by a fellow named Ed Kelly up in Colorado where Bob was running a saloon. Used a shotgun on him."

I flinched and Daddy Sam paused with his cup halfway to his mouth.

"Oh, Lord," Frank said. "I'm sorry. I shouldn't have said it about the shotgun. Forgive my indecency. I reckon I'm just tired and not thinking straight."

"It's okay, Frank," I said. "Bob got what was coming to him. It was a cowardly thing he done."

"Damn all the killing," Frank said. "That it should come to this. It's not just those who are killed but it is the murder of memories of those of us who yet live, the slaughter of dreams."

Frank had a way with words few men had. His cup rattled against the saucer when he set it down again.

"I'm sorry for what all Jess and I were involved in, the way our lives turned out," he said. "It ruined our entire family one way or another. And now here I am an old man with naught but my name and that too is a curse. Nobody much wants to hire the brother of Jesse James these days unless it is to be a buffoon, something folks can buy a ticket to stare at."

"You've always got friends here, Frank."

"I appreciate that, little sister."

He pushed back from the table.

"Well, if you all would be so kind as to take me to Belle's grave I'd like to pay my respects proper."

His spurs rang when he stood up. He might not have any longer been the notorious outlaw he once was, for time and age had tamed him, but standing there just then in that long duster and those spurs strapped to his boots, he cut a fine figure.

"I'll take you," I said.

"Lead on."

We went out and across the yard and up the rise to where

Mama was interred—she'd want me to use that word instead of buried, for she loved better words, as she called them—and Frank gazed down at the crude wood cross Daddy Sam had fashioned.

He removed his hat and bowed his head and I saw his lips moving as if he was nibbling the words coming from him, then he put his hat back on.

"That's hardly a proper marker for her," he said.

"I know it. Daddy Sam's going to have one made of marble soon as he gets over to Tahlequah. I'm going to go with him to pick it out."

"How long was she with Sam?" he asked.

"A few years now."

"Was he good to her?"

"Far as I know he was. I mean she never said he wasn't and I'm sure she would have told me if that was the case."

"That's good to know, Lucy."

"What about you, you still married?"

He nodded.

"Annie's stuck by me through thick and thin," he said. "She's a better woman than I deserve."

"I'm glad to hear that," I said. "I know Mama would have appreciated you taking the trouble to come all the way here. She always spoke highly of you."

"Did she?"

"Yes. Always."

He fell silent.

"I guess I best be getting on," he said after a moment or two.

"Wish you didn't have to go," I said.

"Annie and them are waiting on me to return or I'd stay around a bit and you and me could catch up on all these years. I've often wondered how you and your mama were making out. Lost track of you there for a time. Of course I reckon you didn't lose track of me and Jesse, the things we done, the things we were accused of doing. Seemed like you couldn't pick up a newspaper anywhere in the country wasn't our names in it for committing some crime or other. We'd done all the things they accused us of there'd have had to been a hundred of us."

I walked with him back to the house.

Jim was up, sitting at the kitchen table when Frank and me came in. Daddy Sam was absent, gone off somewhere.

Jim right away got that look on his face whenever he seen me close to another man.

"Frank, this is my husband, Jim," I said. "Jim, this is an old friend of the family's, Frank James. You probably heard of him."

Jim had a fork of cold eggs halfway to his mouth and stopped when I mentioned Frank's name.

"He come all the way from Missouri just to pay his respects," I said.

Jim didn't bother standing up to shake Frank's hand and I don't think either one was sorry for it.

"I guess Lucy told you me and her were on our honeymoon," Jim said. I knew why he said it. He wanted Frank to know whose property I was, mark his territory like some old tomcat. As if it mattered to Frank at all.

But Frank leveled his gray-eyed gaze at Jim and said, "You make sure you take good care of her, treat her right."

I know Jim wanted to retort but was afraid to engage Frank James and I don't blame him. I doubted Frank wanted to get back into the killing business, but a man like him don't ever put it that far out of his mind, I reckon.

Jim just nodded and went back to filling his mouth.

"Walk me to my horse, Lucy?"

"Glad to," I said and linked my arm through Frank's if for no other reason than to show Jim I wasn't his or anybody else's property.

Outside Frank pushed a knee into the buckskin and tightened the cinch then dropped the stirrup down from where he'd hooked it over the saddle horn.

"He good to you, that man in there?" Frank said suspiciously.

"Why, yes," I said.

He looked down at me with that no-nonsense gaze.

"He ever treats you badly you let me know," he said. "I won't tolerate anybody hurting you, child."

I wondered why he was acting so protective of me, then realized it was because he was Frank James and men like him took their friendships seriously, as valued as a poke full of gold.

"I will, Frank, but don't worry. I'm capable of handling myself."

He nodded.

"You do seem that, Lucy Mae. You got a lot of your mama's grit besides her beauty." I must have blushed.

He leaned and kissed me on the cheek then hefted himself up into the saddle.

"Don't stay a stranger now," he said. "You all get over Missouri way, come look me up. I'd like that."

"I will," I promised.

Then he touched the buckskin with those spurs and rode away like a man riding off into the history books. I knew I'd never see him again.

Chapter 11

Back inside the kitchen Jim looked like he'd just eaten a roach.

"What's he want with you, a old man like that?" he asked.

"He don't want nothing with me. I told you why he come."

"You two seem awful cozy together, the way he was looking at you."

"Are you crazy?"

"Shit, Lucy. You think I ain't got eyes to see with. You think I don't know how men look at you, what they're thinking?"

"He's old enough to be my father," I said. "What in the hell is wrong with your mind?"

"Nothing's wrong with it. But there would be if I didn't see how you are all the time availing yourself to other men."

"You best shut up or I'm going to get a knife and stab you in the heart, you damn fool!"

"You know if I thought you were messing with that old man, I don't care if he is Frank James, I'd run him down and put a bullet in him."

"The only one'd be getting a bullet in him would be you," I shouted. I was mad as hell at this husband of mine.

Daddy Sam walked in and looked at Jim and me.

"Everything all right? Sounded sort of loud in here."

Jim clamped his yap shut.

"Everything's just dandy," I said having to bite my tongue to keep from screaming again.

"Well, Red Dog's outside," Daddy Sam said. "He says he

might have a lead on who all was involved in Belle's slaying. I'm going to get ready and ride over with him and see what I can find out."

"I'm going with you," I said and scrambled up the stairs to change into my riding clothes.

I heard Jim saying he was going along, too. I suspected it wasn't so much with the interest of seeing justice done as it was to not let me out of his sight with Red Dog around. But I told myself I no longer cared what he thought of me, and if it came down to a fight with Red Dog, well, I guess it just would and I'd soon enough become a widow.

Turned out that Red Dog was taking us to see an overgrown boy he called Cottonmouth who lived in a shed out back of the One Door Down Saloon in Hadley's Jump. Red Dog said the boy was an orphan and urchin and subsisted on running errands, swamping out the saloon and entertaining customers by playing his harmonica and dancing jigs for tips. Said the boy jumped off the orphan train when he was ten or so and made his way to Hadley's Jump.

"That's how I come to know him. Every time he sees me around he attaches himself to me like a lost puppy. Says me and him got things in common, like both of us being men of color. I make sure he gets something to eat when he's running empty."

It was another checkmark in my mental ledger on Red Dog, under the heading: Kind.

"Anyway, when I was in town last night having supper," Red Dog said, "Cottonmouth came up to me and said, 'You think there might be some reward money for information on who killed that white woman?' "

"I told him I didn't know but there could be and what did he know. All he would say was he knew something. I did my best to get him to tell me what he knew but he said the only way he'd say anything more was if somebody paid him for his information."

Red Dog shook his head.

"He's wise for his years."

"We'll pay him if the information's good," Daddy Sam said.

Jim rode morose behind us, I suppose to keep an eye on Red Dog and me, make sure we didn't do it in the saddle right in front of him somehow.

I promised to tell Red Dog soon as we were alone that he ought to be careful of Jim's growing jealousy and watch out.

It took an hour to ride to Hadley's Jump. It was still early when we got there. We reined in at the saloon and tied off.

"You all wait here and I'll go round and get the kid," Red Dog said.

Most of the businesses in town had just opened up—the saloons never closed. Stray cats and a couple of dogs trotted up and down the street and a solo wagon rattled past.

"What you aiming to pay this kid?" Jim said, as if it was somehow going to come out of his pocket.

"Whatever it takes if the information is right," Daddy Sam said.

I was proud of Daddy Sam and could understand why Mama had stuck with him the longest, though the fact was too, he had lived longer than most of her lovers.

Red Dog reappeared with a Negro kid who was dressed in a faded calico shirt and bib coveralls so washed out they were almost white. His hair was nappy brush piled upon his head. To complete the picture of impoverishment, he wore a pair of busted-out brogans, the soles tied on with twine. He didn't seem scared or reluctant at all.

"This is Cottonmouth," Red Dog said. "Go on and tell 'em what you know."

His eyes were quick and darting in his dark face as they looked at the trio of us.

"How much it worf to you all?" he asked.

"Depends on what you know," Daddy Sam replied.

"What if I seen somethin'?"

"Then that would be worth quite a lot, that sort of information."

"What's quite a lot figger to?"

"What would you say is quite a lot?" I asked.

He ruminated on this, scratching his scalp through the brush pile of hair.

"Fity dollars, I'd say," he said with a hopeful expectant look.

"Fifty dollars it is," Daddy Sam said, "if it proves what you saw leads us to the person we're looking for. Can't say for certain till I hear what it is you saw, though. Might only be worth five dollars, maybe even less."

"Well I reckon it'd be closer to fity, what I saw be worf to you," he said.

"Let's hear it and we'll decide then."

Cottonmouth held out his hand.

"How about you give me sompin' in good-faith money, case you decide it ain't worth no fity dollars, sompin' for my time anyways?"

Daddy Sam took out his wallet and put a five-dollar bill in the boy's hand. He looked at it like it was a golden egg.

"Now tell it," Daddy Sam said gently.

"I seen that old fool they calls Harrison toss a good shotgun into de rivah three days back. I figger at first it cause it's busted and he was just thowin' it away. But then that dint make no sense when he could jus have got it fixed. Then I hurd about dis woman had gotten herself shot dead with a load of buckshot. It got me to thinkin' maybe old Harrison was thowin' that shotgun in de rivah cause he the one done it, shot that woman."

"Why didn't you say something sooner?" Daddy Sam asked.

The boy shrugged.

"Who was I gone say it to?"

"You sure it was a shotgun?" Red Dog asked.

"I know a shotgun from other kinda guns."

"You sure you're not just making this up to make some money?" Jim chimed in.

Cottonmouth gave Jim a tortured look.

"I ain't no damn liar."

"Can you show us where this fellow, Harrison, lives?" Daddy Sam asked.

"I might could."

"Well, would you?"

The kid looked at the money in his hand.

"I suppose to be swampin' out the saloon inside there. Bebow pays me fity cents a day to do it, and they's other work I could maybe pick up round town heah that I wouldn't if I was to go ridin' off wif you all."

"Fine," Daddy Sam said and took out another dollar and handed it to the boy.

"That's two days' pay right there for your trouble," Daddy Sam said.

"I ain't got no hoss an it's a piece out dere."

"Jim, would you mind lending him your horse?" Daddy Sam asked.

"What? Give this nigger kid my horse?" Jim protested. "You can't be serious."

"Jim!" I scolded like a wife who was used to it.

" 'Sides, I sort of planned on going along," Jim said. But I knew why he had. Again he didn't trust me and Red Dog out of his sight.

"Lend him your horse, Jim, or, you can just get the hell out of my sight," I warned.

"Aw Christ almighty," he swore and handed the reins of his horse to Cottonmouth. The boy looked bemused.

"You best return him the same way you got him," Jim said then went on in the saloon.

"Lead the way," Red Dog said as soon as Cottonmouth was in the saddle.

My hopes rose that we were about to find Mama's killer. As Red Dog and I rode behind Cottonmouth and Daddy Sam I had the urge to reach out and take Red Dog's hand and hold it, to let him know how much I appreciated what he was doing to help, and maybe for other reasons too.

I've been thinking about you, I wanted to whisper.

Red Dog rode along nonchalant with no indication he was still interested in me and I wanted him to at least look at me with that same look he had in his eyes the other day on the road.

"Thanks," I said, hoping to draw his attention, some expression on his poker face.

"You're welcome," is all he said.

We rode the rest of the way to the old man's house in silence but for the clopping of the horses' hooves on the hardpan road.

CHAPTER 12

After we'd gone about three or four miles, the boy turned off down a narrow, weed-choked lane.

"He lives back up in here," Cottonmouth said. "Dis here take us down close to the rivah, his place sits right on it almos."

The trees seemed to close in on us from both sides and the sun wasn't full up yet and I felt my heart begin to quicken. I wondered what Daddy Sam would do if this proved to be the fellow—kill him on the spot, or what? I reckoned he would, but would that satisfy my own grief. Would that wash away the hurt and loss? I didn't have Jim's gun with me. I thought maybe I'd ask Red Dog to borrow his if it came down to it.

Cottonmouth slowed his horse then brought it to a stop.

"Why we stopping?" Daddy Sam asked.

"Cause I ain't gone up to that white man's cabin, no way. That ol' fool's libel to shoot us all an' special me, he see a niggah come in his yard. He's a mean ol' son of a gun. Got him a niggah gal wife too. I knows her. Her name's Josie. Used to be his slave gurl. Some say he come here from Alabam where he had a whole lot of niggah slaves but that the war done ruint him and not only that, but he killed his white wife and put Josie in her place."

"How come you know so much about him?" Red Dog asked.

"Workin' round a whisky parlor like I do, I hears things."

"How much farther is it to his cabin from here?" Daddy Sam asked.

"Jus' up round that bend."

"You wait here, then."

"Don't you worry, I'll be right heah waitin'," Cottonmouth said. "Smokin' me a shuck unless I heah a bunch of shootin', then I be gone in the wind. Like a haint."

Daddy Sam kicked his mount forward and me and Red Dog followed.

There in a glen of chopped-out trees, like a garden of stumps, sat a chinked cabin with a shake roof and a stone chimney all in good repair. Nearby was a wired chicken coop and a milk cow tethered to a long rope pegged to the ground. The privy stood a dozen yards beyond.

We barely got within sight when a trio of baying and barking hounds came charging out raising ten kinds of hell. Daddy Sam and Red Dog drew their revolvers. The hounds circled the horses and caused them to stamp their feet and get nervous.

"You damn dogs git!" Daddy Sam ordered.

It didn't seem to do a bit of good.

Then a figure showed itself in the doorway.

"Who the hell ye be?"

"Call your dogs off," Daddy Sam said. "Or I'll kill them."

"Why you sumbitch, you shoot my dogs and we'll go to fighting."

"Then call them off."

The figure gave a whistle and the dogs ran back to the cabin, stood there growling, their tails in the air waving as if they didn't know what they should do, be mean or accepting.

"Why is it you're trespassing on my land any goddamn ways?"

"My name's Sam Harper," Daddy Sam said. "My woman was murdered several days ago by somebody with a shotgun."

"I still don't know what the hell that's got to do with me or why you're trespassing on my propty," the figure said. He remained part in shadow, but the barrel of his rifle was plain enough to see.

"Maybe I should just shoot him and get it over with," Red Dog whispered to Daddy Sam.

"No, I want to hear him say it, tell me why he did it if he did," Daddy Sam said.

There was something cold and calculating about the way Red Dog offered to shoot the man, as if it would be like no more than shooting a squirrel.

"Somebody told me they saw you tossing a shotgun into the river a few days ago," Daddy Sam said. "It got me wondering why a fellow would do something like that: toss his shotgun into a river."

"You best get the hell off here," the man said.

"Not leaving until you explain it to me, tossing a shotgun in the river," Daddy Sam said.

"Then there will damn well be blood this day," the man shouted.

You could see the rifle barrel come up, but I didn't see Red Dog's hand jerk his pistol free, cock and aim it and fire all within a short breath. The explosion from that big gun caused my horse to rear and buck me off. The fall stunned me and my head spun and then my world went all dark.

Something cold and wet fell over my face. I opened my eyes to see Red Dog's face above me, his hand holding a wet rag.

"Well now," he said. "It's good to see you come back to us, Lucy."

I sat up but nearly swooned doing so. My head felt like it wanted to fly off my shoulders.

"What happened?"

"I reckon that nag of yours is a bit gun-shy," Red Dog said. "He bucked you off and you hit your head. Wonder it didn't dash your brains out."

"Feels like it did," I said.

"No," he said, feeling around my scalp. "Don't find any. Hell maybe you didn't have any to begin with." Trying to make light at my expense, he was.

Then I remembered.

"You kill him?" I asked.

"No, just knocked a little meat off him is all."

I looked toward the cabin and saw the fellow sitting on the ground in front of the door, a young Negress in a sack dress kneeling beside him putting a bandage on his hand, Daddy Sam standing over him holding the rifle but not aiming it, just holding it there in both hands down by his waist.

"What's going on?" I asked.

"Daddy Sam is questioning him a little more now that he's less disagreeable."

"Help me up."

I didn't fail to notice the strength of Red Dog when he practically lifted me off the ground. Didn't fail to notice either how he held me there close to him for a moment longer than necessary; the two of us just inches apart, face to face, as he looked into my eyes.

I looked right back, too. I wasn't in any big hurry for him to let me go. I wondered if he could sense the heat coming off me. Women know things without it having to be said, but men mostly have to be drawn a picture. Mama always told me to keep a man guessing as much as I could.

"Keeping a man in the dark, Lucy Mae, is one way a woman maintains her advantage over his strength. Women know what men can only guess at, and most of them are too lazy to even do that." She was not being cruel to the other species, merely pointing out to her only daughter how to play the game with men—how to even things out between the sexes.

Red Dog's hands were holding me by the waist and I liked

them there, but . . .

"You best turn me loose before something happens," I said.

"That a threat or a promise?" he said, offering me that dusky smile.

"I don't know what it is," I said, which caused him to smile even broader.

"Then go on, then," he said and dropped his hands.

I stood there a second longer.

"Go on, then," he said again.

It was becoming a game with us. A game we both seemed to enjoy.

"I am," I said.

"Nothing keeping you," he said.

"I'm going."

For one more second we held each other's gaze but it was like holding a hot poker: you knew you had to let it drop or you'd get burned real bad.

I walked over to where Daddy Sam stood, Red Dog holding back away.

"I'm sorry my friend had to shoot you," Daddy Sam was saying. "We didn't come for blood work, mister. But when you pull a gun on a man you can't expect him to do less."

"That's a goddamn Indun from what I see of him," the man said angrily. "Shot by a goddamn Indun."

"You think it would make a difference if it was a white man shot you?" Daddy Sam asked.

The Negress kneeling and tending to the man was pretty with buckeye-brown skin and dark-brown eyes. She was slender and looked to be about half the man's age. Pure African, you could tell.

"I'm going to ask you once more: Why'd you pitch that shotgun?"

"Didn't pitch no damn gun in no damn river. Don't know

who told you I did, but even if I did, what of it? It's my property—whatever I want to toss away and it's none of your concern."

"It is when it comes to who killed my woman."

The man looked ashen.

Red Dog stepped forward then, and this time with all deliberation withdrew his pistol, thumbed back the hammer and pressed the muzzle to the man's boney forehead.

"You best tell this man what he wants to know or I'm going to blow a hole through your skull."

Daddy Sam tried to interfere, but Red Dog looked at him coldly.

"You either want this man to talk or you don't," he said. "And the only way I see to make him do it is to give him the choice of his life or the truth."

The man's eyes lifted upward to the gun barrel, as if seeking his Lord in heaven above, but seeing none, his lips began to tremble.

"I . . . I dint shoot her," he said, his voice quavering. "Why would I? I dint even know the woman."

"It makes no sense what he's saying," Red Dog said to Daddy Sam.

"He's right," Daddy Sam said to the man. "Your story don't hold water. Not with me it don't. Now you got one last chance or I'm going to walk off and let this big Indian do what he's wanting to do: kill himself a white man."

"Well, goddamn it, you're white!" the man yelped. "Why'd you let him kill me?"

"Go on, Red Dog, shoot this old fool, I'm tired of talking," Daddy Sam said. The two of them exchanged a quick look and I was sure Daddy Sam meant it.

The old man flung his hands up.

"Don't! I found it," he said. "Thought I'd come into

something, a good shotgun. I picked it up and brung it home here. Then the next day I heard about the woman shot down. Heard she was used a shotgun on, and I knew why it was just laying there in those ditch weeds. I figured somebody like you would come round sooner or later, so I tossed the damn thing in the river."

Red Dog pressed the barrel harder against the man's head so that it was moved backwards several inches.

"Even a water head could tell a better story," he said to Daddy Sam. "Let me finish him and be done with it and you and Lucy can have some justice."

"I'm not lying!" the man squawked. His Nubian clung to him as if somehow he was precious, and maybe in a way he was if he was all she had. Maybe he was better than nothing in her case.

"Please don' shoot him!" she cried. "He all I got in dis worl . . ."

Daddy Sam took a deep breath and let it out, contemplating whether he should let Red Dog pull the trigger.

"Anybody kills Belle's slayer, it will be me," he said and placed his hand atop Red Dog's, forcing it away from the man's head.

"Which ditch you find it in, mister?" Daddy Sam said.

"Over near Wilson's bend," he said. "Between the fence and the road. It still had the spent shells in it."

That seemed to satisfy Daddy Sam that the fellow was telling the truth.

"Let's go," he said.

"What about this?" the man said indicating his wounded hand, the blood already soaked through the bandages his black mistress had wrapped around it. The bandages looked like they were made of torn bedsheets, not white but a dingy gray. His old hounds sniffed about nervously as if riled by the scent of blood. He kicked at them.

"Git!"

"I guess you'll have to wait to see how it heals," Daddy Sam said dismissively.

"Why, goddamn, you all come onto a man's property and shoot his goddamn hand near off and that's the end of it? How'm I supposed to work?"

My turn to anger.

"We don't even know if you're lying or not. And if we find out it was you killed my mama, that hand wound will seem like a mosquito bite time we get through with you. Now shut your damn piehole."

I looked at the dark child.

" 'Sides," I added, "it don't look like you work much anyhow. That's why you're keeping this slave girl. I can't even imagine how bad it is for you," I said to her.

We mounted up and turned back.

Red Dog gave me a look accompanied by a sly smile.

"Remind me not to ever get on your bad side," he said.

"Don't ever get on my bad side," I said.

CHAPTER 13

Daddy Sam insisted we ride straightaway to Wilson's place. He sent the colored boy, Cottonmouth, back to Hadley's Jump in order to take Jim's horse to him. I knew if we found Wilson, there would be blood spilled. No doubt about it. But something troubled my mind about it all.

"Daddy Sam," I said riding up alongside him, Red Dog trailing along behind slightly as if it was his duty to watch our back trail. "I wonder why, if it was Wilson who shot Mama, why he'd just drop his shotgun and leave it where it could so easily be found. Why wouldn't he just have kept it and denied everything? I'd guess about every man in the county has a shotgun."

Daddy Sam stared straight ahead.

"I've been wondering the same thing, Lucy. But maybe Wilson shot her and right away someone come along and he dropped it and ran. When I was in the war it wasn't unusual at all for soldiers to drop their guns in a panic and run off. Maybe that's what happened with Wilson."

"Wilson didn't strike me as a panicky sort," I said.

"You never know about a man, Lucy, till you see him tested," Daddy Sam said.

"Ain't that the truth," I replied, thinking of men I'd known, loved and hated.

We made it to Wilson's in about half an hour's time. But when we got there nobody answered the call.

Daddy Sam dismounted, sliding out his Winchester lever-action rifle from the boot.

"You watch for any movement," he said to Red Dog. "Lucy Mae, you hang back away case he comes out shootin'."

Red Dog eased out his own rifle and held it with the butt resting on his thigh.

"I'll shoot anything comes out that door with a gun, Mister Harper," he said.

Daddy Sam eased up to the front door and pounded hard.

"Wilson, you come out here, I need to talk to you!" Daddy Sam shouted.

No answer. He pounded again.

No answer.

Daddy Sam looked back at Red Dog and me, shook his head.

"I'm going to try the door," he said.

"Go ahead," Red Dog said.

"Be careful, Daddy Sam," I said.

He nodded and lifted the latch and pushed the door open, ducked his head in then went on in, the rest of him. In a moment he come back out.

"Nobody's here," he said. "Looks like that bird up and flew the coop."

He came back and mounted his horse.

"Has to be Wilson done it," Daddy Sam said. "Otherwise why would he have abandoned the place except he knew I'd learn the truth sooner or later. Innocent men don't run, guilty ones do."

It was by now noon, sun almost straight up overhead, the air thick with the threat of rain. Dark clouds were gathering in from the northwest and the distant rumble of thunder could be heard.

"What now, Daddy Sam?" I asked.

"I'm thinking on it, Lucy," he said glumly.

"We could go after him, find him and then . . ."

"We could," Daddy Sam said. "If we knew which way he went off to."

"Somebody had to have seen something," I said.

"Not if he up and left in the middle of the night," Daddy Sam said. "Which is most likely what he would have done—what *I* would have done if it was me."

I felt my heart sink.

"Then Mama's killer is going to get away with it," I murmured.

"I think we have to consider it a possibility, Lucy. I won't lie to you. But I aim to go into Hadley's Jump and put out the word and see if anybody's heard or seen anything of him anyway."

Daddy Sam had the sad hound dog face of a man disappointed in himself and the world at large.

"You all go on back to the house, Lucy, get dinner going and I'll come along directly. Maybe with luck I'll have some good news. Cheer up now. It ain't the end of things—not by a long shot. We'll get justice for Belle, you'll see."

I asked to go along but he waved me off saying he needed to be alone with his thoughts for a spell and he wouldn't be gone long.

"You and Red Dog ride on back to the house."

I was half ashamed of myself for wanting to be with Red Dog more than with Daddy Sam, just then. But truth be told, there wasn't anything I could gain by riding with Daddy Sam anyway.

Red Dog and I turned back on the road to home, walking our horses so as to afford us more time to get there.

"Sorry about not finding Wilson," he said. "I was hoping we could put an end to things and you could finish your grieving, Lucy."

"Me too," I said.

He rode close to me, so that our legs often brushed against each other.

"Your mama was a handsome woman," he said. "But she don't even come close to how pretty you are."

I might have blushed, or it could have been the last of the sun on my cheeks before the clouded sky closed in and snuffed it out.

"You're not going to start all that again, are you?"

"I ain't starting nothing, Lucy. I'm just stating facts."

"Let me ask you how come a sweet-talking scoundrel such as yourself don't have a wife or two, so you have to pursue other men's wives? Is it by choice, or do women just see right through you?"

He laughed.

"Well, maybe it's cause I've not yet found one to my liking until now."

"Oh, and you think I am to your liking?"

"Damned if I don't," he said.

"What about to my liking?"

"Well I don't reckon you'd a kissed me the other night if I wasn't to your liking."

"I already explained that," I said.

"Well it's been my experience that women often say one thing and mean another."

"Even though I'm married, and I might add, freshly so, that don't trouble you?"

"No, it don't, really."

"Are you without morals at all?"

"I just believe in going after what I see suits me," he said. "You never know how long you got to live. You might as well be as happy as you can while you can. Why'd I want to marry some homely woman and be miserable the rest of my days?"

"Well, Red Dog," I said. "Not everything you see can you

have. That's also part of life."

"That might be your rules, but it ain't mine."

"I've no intention of leaving Jim and running off with you," I said.

"We don't have to run off," he said. "I got a fine little place between here and Eufaula. Three rooms, fixed up nice. Got horses and chickens and a couple of hogs. Got good water, too. It's set up just right for a woman like you, Lucy."

"A woman like me? Well, then you ought to find a woman like me," I said. "Cause me ain't available. How many times I got to say it?"

"Then how come you kissed me if I'm of no interest to you, if your blood don't run hot every time you think about me?"

He just wouldn't leave that damn kiss alone.

"How many more times do I have to explain it?" I said. "That kiss was like me kissing a cousin or my friend Vinita. That's all it was. You need to drop that from your thinking or it's going to drive us both crazy."

The sky darkened and the first few raindrops splattered against leaves and then splattered in the dusty road.

"That sure enough come on us quick," I said hoping to change the subject, to distract Red Dog from the present conversation.

"It's gone drench us," he said. "Best find a place to get in out of it quick."

"Home's just a few miles on," I said. "We just ought to get on back there."

But then just as Red Dog predicted, it began to pour buckets. He shouted for me to follow him, and like a damn fool I did, back in through the trees until we came to a shack with half the roof missing and dismounted quickly and ran in under the half still remaining. The rain came down in a fury and the wind rattled the remaining piece of metal roof and blew rain in through the open windows and doorway.

"Whew, I'm soaked through," Red Dog said as we stood there in the slight protection from above.

"Me too," I said, and I was, wet to the skin.

"Maybe we should shuck out of these clothes," he said.

"You think you're smart, don't you?"

He grinned wickedly.

"We could end up catching pneumonia and dying," he said. "I don't know about you, Lucy, but I'm too young and in my prime to die of the weather."

"Forget it," I said. "I'm not undressing for you."

He began to take off his clothes, shirt first, and I saw his chest was hatched by several scars, some long like hard worms, and some puckered and round.

"How'd you come to be so scarred?" I asked.

"Oh, just the usual sufferings of a fellow like me," he said.

"Are those round ones bullet wounds?"

He looked down at himself.

"Yep, sorry to say that they are. Still got a piece of lead in me somewhere from one."

"Who was it shot you?"

"Just some damn fools is all," he said. And that's all he'd say about it.

"What about those other marks?" I asked.

"Them who don't have guns to fight with generally have knives and broken bottles. They're nothing."

He sat down on a rusted pail and tugged off his boots and socks then started to tug off his trousers. I turned away.

"That's not something I want to see," I said.

"Why ain't it? You've seen a naked man before."

"My husband," I said. "Not you."

"Just your husband?"

"None of your stinko business," I said.

"Well, there's no harm in looking at me, then," he said. "Less it's beauty you detest looking upon."

"It starts with looking and goes on from there."

"Don't have to," he said.

"Will you please shut the hell up," I said with mock anger, for I wasn't angry at all, but quite the opposite and that was upsetting to me as much as anything.

"Okay," he said. "You don't have to look, but as long as it's raining and I'm naked, I might as well take advantage of it."

I peeked over my shoulder as he went out and dug around in his saddlebags and took out a bar of soap and stood out there washing himself and singing loudly as if a happy fool, which is exactly what I took him for.

A happy, beautiful and forbidden-to-me fool.

Chapter 14

The rain quit an hour later and Red Dog dressed back in his still-wet clothes and gave me one last longing look to which I shook my head again even though it took everything I had in me to resist the temptation.

"Who'd know but us, Lucy?" he asked like a sad little boy denied a cookie.

"I would," I said.

"Is it because I'm an Indian?"

"Are you crazy? Being an Indian has nothing to do with it. Hell, you talk better than half the white men I know and you've got decent manners from what I can see but for your rampant sexual urges you refuse to keep to yourself. No, it has nothing to do with that. I told you, I'm a married woman and I honor my vows. Wasn't for that, well . . ."

"Okay," he said and we mounted up and rode on back to Daddy Sam's.

Only one there was J. R. sitting on the porch, a pint bottle of hooch rested between his boots and him smoking a cigar like he was the King of England.

We dismounted and Red Dog said he'd put the horses up and led them off and I climbed the steps up onto the porch.

"You know," J. R. said. "One of these days that ragged-ass husband of yours is going to kill that red nigger over you diddling him."

"You shut your filthy mouth," I said. "You don't know a damn thing about it. And how come while the rest of us are running around trying to find Mama's killer, you see fit to sit on your haunches swallowing bug juice and not lift a finger to help?"

He reached for the bottle and put it to his mouth and swallowed then wiped his lips with the back of his wrist as he held it up to the light examining how much was left.

"She's dead and whoever did it is in the wind," he said coldly. "What's the use of chasing my tail over it? What's done is done. It's life, Lucy, get over it."

"You always were about as useless as tits on a boar hog," I said.

He offered me a hard look.

"You're just like her," he said.

"What's that supposed to mean?"

"Always got to be the center of attention, get men to do your bidding, get ever'body to do your bidding. Neither one of you ever knew what it was to have to work for your supper, to face the cold hard facts of life. There was always a man, wasn't there?"

"Be damn glad there was, J. R., or you wouldn't be sitting there downing the sauce instead of spilled seed upon the ground, a gleam in some old card dealer's hand, still."

"I should have fucked you and broke you in right. Maybe I will yet."

His words were like a slap to the face. I was stunned.

I rushed in the house, angry and upset and confused. I wanted to kill him just to shut his filthy mouth.

When I got to my room I slammed and locked the door. I was also scared of him, scared of the depth of his depravity and what he might do or try to do.

I peeled out of my wet duds and rubbed my skin with a towel, then I got under the covers and pulled them to my chin for I was shivering terribly. For once in my life I was at a loss. Why did he say that to me? Did he mean it? Was he just being his usual cruel self and wanted to torment me with his foul mind?

I was still cold from the rain and it had begun falling again, pecking at the windows and casting the room into shadows. I realized that it was just him and me and Red Dog at home. Neither Daddy Sam or Jim had yet returned. What if J. R. shot Red Dog and came for me? My mind ran wild with possibilities.

I scrambled out of bed and searched through our luggage hoping to find a spare pistol of Jim's but there wasn't one and I knew he carried the bird's-head Colt on his person.

I heard footsteps in the hall and I froze. They stopped outside the door. I could hardly breathe. I wanted to cry out for Red Dog but that wasn't possible if he was still in the barn. The doorknob turned but the lock held. Then the knob was released and the footsteps went on down the hall. I exhaled.

If I could get out of the house and find Red Dog . . .

But I knew if I told him to, one of them would end up dead and it would be the worst hard luck if it was Red Dog who was. And even though I was afraid of my half brother, I wasn't sure I wanted to have him murdered over words, even harsh and terrible as they had been.

The more I thought about it, the more I thought that J. R. merely wanted to be hateful and cruel in the way that he was cruel. And what could be crueler to me than saying what he said? He had to have known that those words were branded on my mind and I would never be able to forget them.

I went to the window and looked out through the rain-streaked glass. I saw J. R. mounted on a horse, waving his bottle about, then kicking the horse into a trot out toward the road: to where, I neither knew or cared. I was just relieved that he was leaving.

I dressed in dry clothes and went downstairs to the kitchen

and began preparing dinner thinking the whole while that if J. R. came back and tried anything I'd run him through with one of the big butcher knives.

But he didn't come back and gladly so Daddy Sam and Jim returned later on instead and came into the house along with Red Dog who must have stayed waiting outside, which I was grateful for, because if Jim had come in and found me and Red Dog together inside the house, who knew what might have happened?

"Something smells good," Daddy Sam said, going to the sink and pumping up handfuls of water to wash his face and hands with. Jim didn't bother to wash up, just took a seat at the table. Then Red Dog took his turn at washing up and joined Jim and Daddy Sam and I served them hot beef sandwiches with slices of fresh onion and brown gravy and glasses of buttermilk and sat down to join them.

I could barely concentrate on anything and the food was tasteless in my mouth. Daddy Sam asked where J. R. was.

"Saw him earlier," Red Dog said. "When Lucy and me rode in, but then he left again."

Jim cut Red Dog a vicious look.

"When was that? That you and Lucy rode in? And where'd you ride in from?"

"We come in from Wilson's," he said. "Thought Daddy Sam would have told you."

"I forgot to mention it," Daddy Sam said.

"You and my wife seem to be spending a goodly amount of time together lately," Jim said.

Red Dog simply stared at him and I thought, Oh no.

"I reckon you could be right," Red Dog said. "But it's not what you're thinking."

"What am I thinking?" Jim asked, his voice edged sharp as a straight razor.

"The wrong thing," Red Dog said.

"Am I?"

"What is it you want me to say?" Red Dog asked.

"The truth," Jim said, raising his voice even more.

"You two leave off," Daddy Sam said. "Jim, there ain't nothing going on here but that we are all grieving. Tensions are running high as it is. You don't need to be adding to them with accusations you cannot back up. I know Lucy and I know Red Dog and I don't think either one would cuckold you. You're one of those highly jealous and suspicious types. I've known men like you, and I've known some of them to be wrong and get themselves killed or kill somebody over nothing at all. So just calm down while you're in my house."

Then Daddy Sam went back to eating having said his piece. It seemed to have broken the tension and Jim went back to shoveling food in his mouth like if he didn't get it et in the next three seconds he'd turn into a horned frog, or something.

Red Dog stood away from the table and carried his plate to the sink and went out. Jim's gaze followed him. I kept wanting to say something about J. R., but with nobody to tell it to unless I wanted to stir things up even more and I knew Daddy Sam was on edge as it was. Besides, I was too embarrassed to tell it.

"I think I'll ride over to Oren's and visit with Vinita," I said, knowing I needed to tell somebody who'd listen without acting the fool and go kill J. R. over it.

"You was just over there the other day," Jim said.

"So what? I can come and go as I please can't I?"

"Maybe I'll ride with you."

"Be my guest," I said. I didn't see no way of stopping him and I know why he wanted to go along: fear I'd meet up with Red Dog.

"Okay, then."

★ ★ ★ ★ ★

After dinner we took the rented hack and rode in silence, Jim and me, till we were almost there.

"When we going back to El Paso?" Jim asked.

"You know when," I said. "As soon as we find Mama's killer and get revenge."

"Revenge? What about just getting justice?"

"To hell with that. We Moons take care of our own. Besides there ain't no damn law here in the Pistol Barrel. Have to ride clear on over to Fort Smith."

"Well when is that gone be?"

"You know as much as I do."

"Jesus, Lucy. Sam says that son of a bitch Wilson has flown the coop and he don't have a damn clue as to where. We can't stay around here forever. We got to get on and start earning some money. 'Sides we never finished our honeymoon. I think that's half what's wrong with us now. First year's the hardest, everybody says so."

I didn't say anything more. I'd speak with Vinita, share with her my fears about J. R. and seek her advice. At least I had her to talk to and not worry about it turning into violence.

She proved a comfort to me, told me J. R. was just being cruel, as I suspected, and that if anything did happen to me just to tell her and she'd have Oren kill him and say it was an accident.

"Jesus, Vinita, you keep surprising me," I said.

She offered me a sweet smile and said, "Ain't I, though."

We palavered while Oren and Jim seemed to sit around outside and talk about the weather and horses and what all.

"You have any more meetings with your dusky lover?" I asked her.

More smiles.

"Yes, you?"

"No, don't need them," I said. "Got that dern hound dog outside."

"He looks the sort," she said.

"And you'd know this how?" I teased.

"Cause they all look the sort."

"Let me ask you something, Vinita."

"Go on and ask it, Lucy."

"Just between us, cross your heart."

She crossed it.

"You know Red Dog?"

"I know him but only just by sight. What about him?"

So I told her.

She put her fingers to her lips as if to hold in whatever it was she was thinking to say.

"Well, are you going to?" she asked.

"Lord, no. I'm married and would never break my vows."

"Well, for a Indun, he is a very handsome man," she said. "I'm not sure I wouldn't break my vows was the opportunity to present itself."

We tittered like silly schoolgirls.

"Maybe I'll send him around some dark night and tell him to peck at your window, then," I said.

And we tittered more.

On the way home again Jim tried to get me to pull over so we could make love. I refused. He cussed a blue streak.

"I get the feeling you don't desire me no more, goddamn it, Lucy."

"You keep up acting the way you are," I said, "you just might make it such."

"It's that goddamn Indun, ain't it? You're foolin' round with him, ain't you?"

"Please, Jim. Just be quiet. For once be quiet and stop accusing me of things. Can you do that? Please."

After I chided Jim to shut up, he looked contrite for once and hushed up and drove us on back to the house and he did not trouble me that night as I thought he would, but lay silent and unmoving next to me in bed and we fell asleep like that: not touching or troubling each other's spirits, and for once, it was good with him and I felt married to him and it brought me hope that everything would soon get better.

Chapter 15

When I woke, Jim was gone from the bed and the room. I languished there in bed for a moment not wanting to get up, to face another day of uncertainty and sadness, or fear and anger, but just wanting to feel my spirit at peace, if only for a little while longer.

When I did rise, I looked at myself in the full-length mirror after I slipped off my nightgown. I had not done so in a long time and something about catching my image looking back at me caused me to stare at myself.

Men said I was beautiful, and no doubt believed it. Even Mama would go on at length about my beauty saying how much I looked like her mother, my grandmother.

But a woman will always see her own flaws when nobody else will.

My hips were a bit too wide, my breasts a bit too small and my feet a bit too large to suit me. I turned partway round and gazed at my bottom. Just right, I thought with satisfaction.

Yes, I could see how men would want me. "There is power in such knowledge," Mama admonished me.

"Pretty is as pretty does, Lucy," Mama said. "And a woman can get anything she wants if she knows how to play her cards. Don't you ever forget that men want what you have and they will fight and kill each other to get it if they have to. Use your beauty wisely."

"Yes, Mama."

I dressed taking my time about it then went out and down the hall. Before reaching the stairs, I stopped at Daddy Sam's and Mama's bedroom. The door was open and I could see the room was empty.

I was tempted to go in but went on downstairs to the kitchen and poured myself a cup of coffee from the pot Daddy Sam always kept going.

I went out onto the porch making sure to keep an eye out for J. R. lurking about and maybe pouncing on me like a cat on a mouse. But no one was there. The horses were gone, the place quiet with sunshine in the yard and clouds like sailing ships in the sky.

I wondered where everyone had got off to. Not even Red Dog's horse was about.

Then I realized it was Sunday, not that it had much meaning. I never knew really if Daddy Sam was a churchgoer or not. Mama used to play piano in church back when we lived in Dallas and a few other places, but not regular. Red Dog didn't strike me as a God-fearing man. Red Dog didn't strike me as a man who feared anything.

J. R.? Completely godless. I imagined there wasn't a church or house of worship in the land that wouldn't fall completely down were he to enter.

For me, God was something residing inside a body's heart and soul, not in some building somewhere. He was in the trees and creeks and rivers, in the sky and grass and horses and birds and every wild thing. No, I had no need to go and find Him in church.

I sat and sipped my coffee and felt calm and thought of Mama and the times we shared and all the memories I had of her and how hard it was to believe she was actually gone.

I wandered back inside and upstairs again and went into her and Daddy Sam's bedroom and opened the steamer trunk resting at the foot of her bed hoping I might find something of hers in it, something personal I could keep.

I lifted up some folded dresses and pressed them to my face and her scent was still faintly in them—the lilac perfume she liked to wear on special occasions. She favored black velvet. Her underthings were soft cotton decorated in lace. There was a pair of high button shoes, bone gray and brand-new with the tag still on them. I wondered what she could have been saving them for. There was a tintype of her and Teddy Blue, Teddy looking stern standing beside her sitting figure; neither of them looking happy or in love. I found a small gold locket and opened it and there was a picture of Johnny Waco staring out with cold-blooded eyes but a slight smile on his lips.

Mama and her men, I thought with amusement. Even in death she would not let them go.

I found a packet of letters tied with a red ribbon and a diary bound in leather. I never knew she kept a diary.

I put everything back but the letters and the diary. These I took to my room to read.

I read the letters first. They were mostly one-page affairs from various lovers of hers, some of which I didn't even know about: A Maynard Fox from Waco who apparently owned a drugstore. He professed a hundred times his love and desire of her.

> *Please, please, dearest Belle, marry me and make me the happiest fellow in the world. I'd give all I own to be with you this very moment. And you'll never lack for the laudanum you need, or any other medicinal care . . .*

Laudanum? When had Mama been taking laudanum?

The next one was from a fellow in Huntsville Prison named Lee Spoon.

They'll hang me tomorrow, Belle. But I want you to know my last thought will be of you and the night we danced down in that beer hall in Amarillo. We had us a hell of a time, didn't we Belle? I mean a hell of a time . . .

I tried to recall the name, Lee Spoon, but could not. I remember there was periods of time when Mama would leave me in the care of a neighboring couple when we were young, myself and J. R. I was too young to know the true reason of her farming us out, but sometimes she'd be gone for months at a time. The neighbors were a kindly couple, childless and treated us well. They never would reveal Mama's whereabouts whenever I'd ask. They'd just say something like, "Don't worry, little Lucy, your mama loves you children. She'd never abandon you."

I recalled their house was a big old musty place always too hot in the summer and too cold in the winter, those cold howling winds at night rattling the window glass. In the summer there'd be rattlesnakes and missus would kill them with a hoe—chop off their heads and bury them, warning that even a chopped off rattler's head could still bite. Well, one eventually did kill the poor old woman. (It was rumored she was in the outhouse at the time.) Thankfully I wasn't there to witness it.

I opened another letter.

Dear Sweetheart. Oh, how I miss you. I know that you're only 16 and I 38 but it don't matter in the ways of love. My hart longs to see you again someday. I aim to go to Deadwood soon and make my mark, perhaps next yar. I've heard it is teaming with gold and easy pickin's for a interprizin type. I still have that pitcher of you in my head—naked in the moons lite. O, what glory you give a man. Yr. admirer, J.B. Hickok.

I made a mental note of the years and it could truly have been that Mama and Wild Bill had somewhere met if the letter was to be believed, and surely it must for why else would she have kept it?

Wild Bill was killed in '76 up in Deadwood Gulch. I rifled through the rest of the letters to see if there was another from him but there was not.

"Mama," I said aloud, stunned at the men she'd known and consorted with.

But if that letter was shocking, there was one other even more so.

Dearest Belle. I've not much time to write. Dingus and me are on the dodge, as usual. I know I left you in a hurry with no time to say our proper goodbyes and for that I am sorry. I just want you to know after receiving your last that I did not mean for it to happen but I take all responsibility nonetheless. We allowed a moment's indiscretion to mark us forever. I only wish I could be free to do the right thing by you and take my place by your side in the coming days. But you know I never lied to you about my situation—that of a married man—and so I know that you'll understand and accept the reasons why I can't be what I should for the child's sake at least. You'll soon have in another man the husband and father oh that I would otherwise be.

I am not at all sure that I will survive these outlaw days the way Jesse is pushing matters. The law is ever closing in on us and there has been talk about leaving the country and going to Mexico or possibly South America to escape it if a bullet doesn't find us first.

On that account it would not matter if I were free to be a husband to you or not and you'll be wise to find yourself a loving man better suited for you than I.

I must sign off. Yrs. Frank

I sat there holding the letter and trembling. Was Frank James my father? Mama never said who my real father was, simply that he was a young lover of hers who had been killed in a mining accident. She would only say that his first name was Joseph and their affair had been brief and that when her father had found out, he moved the family away to Texas. I asked her where the name Moon came from since her daddy's last name was Cartwheel. She said she took it and gave it to us all because I was born under a blue moon, that she liked the idea of it and to have a whole new name made it easier to gain a fresh start once she struck out on her own.

My head was spinning. I heard horses outside.

I hid the letters and diary under my mattress.

I could hear Daddy Sam calling my name from downstairs.

"Lucy, honey. You home?"

I went down to where he stood. Oren was with him, but Jim and Red Dog were not.

"Are you all right, Lucy?" asked Daddy Sam. "You look peaked."

I had a mouthful of things I wanted to say, to ask: did Daddy Sam know who my real daddy was? Had Mama told him? What else did he know about us, Mama and me?

"I'm fine," I said instead.

Oren nodded and poured himself a cup of coffee.

"Where's the others—Jim and Red Dog?" Daddy Sam asked.

"I don't know. When I got up everybody was gone."

"Oh hell," Daddy Sam said, going back out onto the porch again.

"What is it?" I asked, following.

"If those two has got off alone I 'spect only one of 'em will be coming back," he said. "They're like a pair of fighting cocks can't wait to kill each other."

He glanced at me almost accusingly.

"Lucy, you know I love you as much as Jesus hisself," he said. "But my best advice would be to pack your things and you and Jim go on back to El Paso before blood is spilled here."

"I'm not leaving till I find out who killed Mama," I said.

Oren came out just then, quiet-like, and stood there without speaking.

Daddy Sam hitched his hands in his back pockets, his hat notched back so that a hank of his hair—black but streaked with silver threads—hung over his forehead. The sun shone upon his face and I could see the creases that weren't there the last time I'd visited.

"It might take years to find Belle's killer, if then," he said. "What you aim to do, move in here, you and Jim, and go out on forays searching for a man who might no longer even exist, or not knowing where in hell he could be hiding?"

I started to say yes I would do whatever it took but I knew Daddy Sam was telling the truth: it was unlikely that no matter what we done we might never find the man who killed my mama and that grieved me almost worse than the news of her murder.

"You should listen to him, Lucy," Oren said, then stepped down off the porch and wandered over to the corral.

"Lucy, I've put word out all over Hadley's Jump about Wilson. I've offered five hundred dollars reward money, every cent your mama and I have in savings. And if I have to I'll sell this place for more money if that's what it takes to find Wilson. Sooner or later somebody's bound to know or hear something."

I looked at him and he at me.

"Did you know about Mama and Frank?" I asked.

"What about them?"

"Nothing," I said.

He looked at me with questioning eyes and I knew he didn't know, that she never told him.

"If it's okay," I said. "Me and Jim will stay a couple of more days then head back down to El Paso."

"You're welcome to stay as long as you like, Lucy. You know that. I just didn't want you to have your hopes of finding Wilson anywhere around these parts and give up your young lives, freshly married and all, thinking we'd get justice served real quick now."

"Yes, Daddy Sam, I know."

"Good," he said and put his arm around my waist and held me like a real father would hold his daughter and it made me sadder still to think my real father was way off in Missouri with his real family.

After an hour or so Red Dog came riding in alone and my fear rose over what Daddy Sam had said about the two of them going off and only one coming back—that Red Dog had killed Jim.

Red Dog rode up and dismounted and dropped the reins of his horse.

"I bet I could find a cup of coffee in that house yonder," he said as he mounted the steps.

I didn't say anything for a moment and he stood looking at me, mystified at my silence.

"You kill him?" I asked.

"Kill who?"

"Jim."

That devil smile he was so good at giving creased his mouth.

"No, not today, anyway."

I let out a breath.

"Yes," I said. "There's coffee inside."

He nodded, held still for a moment then went on past me and inside.

Jim did not return that night and one time I looked out my bedroom window into the yard full of moonlight and there was

Red Dog squatted on his heels smoking a cigarette—a long and mysterious figure and I could not help but believe that he had killed my husband. And for some reason I was only sad at the thought but not angry.

It seemed to me a very poor way for a wife to feel.

Chapter 16

Daddy Sam was already out on the front porch having his morning coffee when I came out.

"Somebody's coming, Lucy," he said. Daddy Sam had keen eyes, better than mine. Mama had warned me about using too much belladonna in my eyes, a trick she taught me when I began blossoming into womanhood; said it made the eyes more seductive. I guess maybe I used the drops too much for I couldn't see half as well as most folks.

"Who is it?" I asked. "Is it Jim?"

"No," he said. "He don't ride a horse like Jim. Jim flops up and down like he's beating the dust out of his britches. This fellow rides like he was born to it."

"Where you think Jim's got off to, Daddy Sam? He didn't come home last night."

Daddy Sam shrugged.

"He's your husband, Lucy. He have a habit of laying out all night long?"

I felt wounded by the question, as if I wasn't a good enough wife to keep Jim at home in Daddy Sam's estimation.

The man came into my view then and I could see he was a fairly big man riding a fairly big paint horse of exceptional beauty, black and white with a bald face and light-colored eyes.

He halted in front of the porch.

"You Mr. Sam Harper?" the man asked.

"I am."

"Name's Leviticus Book," the man said. "I'm a US deputy marshal out here from Fort Smith on orders of Judge Parker."

I saw Daddy Sam stiffen at the news.

"How come him to send you?"

The deputy eyed me over carefully, like maybe I was something he was considering buying.

"Account of the killing of one Belle Moon," the deputy said. "He heard she got killed, shot down. Wanted me to come and check into it, report back to him what I learned of it."

"Good of you to come," Daddy Sam said. "But I didn't file no report in Fort Smith. Far as I'm concerned this is a family matter to be handled by family."

"That right?"

"It is."

"You mind if I climb down and water my horse over to your trough."

"No, go on," Daddy Sam said. "Help yourself. There's some grain in that bucket yonder too, you want to grain him."

"Appreciate it," the deputy said.

While the deputy was taking care of his animal, Red Dog came from out of wherever he'd been overnight, somewhere around back of the house and stood at the edge of the porch.

"Who's that fellow?" he asked.

"Deputy out of Fort Smith," Daddy Sam said.

Red Dog nodded.

"What's he want?"

"Says Judge Parker sent him to look into Belle's murder."

Red Dog watched the man for a moment longer, then said, "I got to go on into Hadley's Jump and get some breakfast. I'll see you all around." He barely even looked at me.

"You can sit to breakfast with us," Daddy Sam suggested.

"No, it's all right," Red Dog said and went and got his horse and mounted and rode off.

The deputy came back over to the porch but not without noticing Red Dog ride away, though he didn't mention it.

"You want a cup of this coffee?" Daddy Sam asked.

"Sure wouldn't hurt any."

"Well, come on up on the porch and I'll get you some."

"I'll get it," I said and went in and poured a cup and came back out and handed it to the deputy. He gave me another thorough going-over, but briefly so as not to seem like he was staring. Thing with men is, they don't have to look at you long for you to be able to read what they're thinking.

"First off," the deputy said. "Has anybody been arrested or otherwise been put under for the woman's murder?"

"Nobody," Daddy Sam simply said without mention of Wilson yet.

"I reckon the way the judge explained it, he'd had some dealings with your wife," Deputy Book said. It was something between a question and a statement.

"We weren't legal hitched," Daddy Sam said, "if that makes any difference to the law in the matter."

"It does not."

Daddy Sam proceeded with his side of it.

"I know they knew each other at one time or other. Didn't think they were all that close he'd send a man over to look into her death."

The big man sipped his coffee, looked at it, sipped some more.

"Well, I ain't privy to how well they did or did not know each other," he said. "I just do what I'm told by the old man. So maybe you could lay it out for me exactly what happened to your woman."

Daddy Sam explained it, about some men finding Mama's body and the location, about it being a shotgun used on her. Then he mentioned his suspicions, saying the man Wilson was number one on his list. Daddy Sam also explained why.

"Wilson," the deputy said now staring into his cup. "Seems I heard the name, but can't say for certain, Wilson being a common name as it is. When'd he disappear from the area?"

"Yesterday. We run down a fellow who picked up a shotgun near Wilson's place. Thought he'd found himself a prize till he heard Belle had been shotgunned. Tossed it in the river for fear folks would think it was him."

"Hell, I imagine most folks have a shotgun or two for hunting," Deputy Book said.

"I'm sure of it," Daddy Sam said.

"I bet even you got a shotgun," the deputy replied with a steely-eyed stare.

"I reckon I do."

"Where were you, Mr. Harper, when your wife went off by herself and got herself killed?"

I could see the look that came over Daddy Sam. He didn't brook suspicion of his personal character none at all. But it struck a moment's doubt in my mind, I have to admit. I always figured Mama and Daddy Sam got along swell, like she did with most of her men.

"I was here, right here on my porch," Daddy Sam replied.

"Who was it come and told you the news?" Book asked.

"It was J. R., Belle's boy—this one here's half brother."

Now there was a bit of news I hadn't known. I kept quiet. If you're going to learn anything, better to listen than to be a flannel mouth, Mama always said.

"And what is your name, miss?" Book asked.

"Lucy," I said. "And it's missus, not miss."

"That a fact," he said. "Pretty name for a pretty gal."

He sure wasn't shy about what he was thinking.

"He around, this J. R. half brother of yours?" Book asked.

Daddy Sam looked at me.

"Lucy, you seen J. R. this morning?"

I shook my head.

"No, but I can check his room if you want."

"Why don't you do that, and get the deputy another cup of coffee on your way back if you don't mind."

The deputy handed me his cup.

J. R. took up residence in the back part of the house just off a summer kitchen. It seemed a good place for him to be, like his own private doghouse. Just a small room with a cot in it, the walls papered over with pages from a Sears Roebuck catalog. I noticed J. R. had several pages near the head of his bed featuring women's corsets and undergarments, renderings of them wearing them, and it made me wonder even more about his perversity of mind. I reckon it wasn't an accident he picked that room, either.

I came back out, stopping on the way in the kitchen and pouring the deputy another coffee and went back out again.

"Thank you, miss," he said when I handed it to him.

"He's not in the house," I said.

"I reckon he's not to home," Daddy Sam said looking over to the corral and not seeing J. R.'s horse.

"Know where he might be?"

"Hell, that boy could be anywhere, but most likely he's in Hadley's Jump drinking his breakfast or consorting."

"Consorting?" Deputy Book asked.

"Whores," Daddy Sam said. "Wished he wouldn't. Told him more than once those type women won't do nothing for a man but bring him to ruin. The Bible's full of such tales. But you can't tell that boy nothing. He's willful and mule headed."

"Willful, eh," the deputy said, sucking his teeth. "Anybody else here besides you two?"

"My husband, Jim Creed, came with me when we got word about Mama," I said.

"Was that him who rode off a bit ago?"

"No. My husband didn't come home last night."

Book rubbed his chin.

"That a regular habit of his, is it, miss?"

"I don't see how that's concerning you," I said.

"No, I reckon you're right. Where'd you all come from? You said when you got word. You all living around here?"

"We were on our honeymoon down in El Paso at the time," I said.

"I see. Well, where do you think your husband might be—seeing's how you two are newly married and all. Seems like he'd want to be with his bride."

"I don't know," I said.

He drank some more of his coffee then set it down on the floor by his boots and reached in his pocket and took out his makings—a pouch of Bull Durham and cigarette papers—and built a cigarette, taking his time, doing it, careful, with large blunted fingers. And when he finished and twisted off the ends he reached in another pocket and took out a kitchen match and swiped it against the porch post and held the flame to his shuck and drew in deeply before exhaling it.

"Hard for me to drink coffee without a smoke to go with it," he said, offering me yet another hungry look.

"Well if that fellow what rode off just a bit ago wasn't your man, who was that?"

I hesitated saying anything.

"His name's Red Dog," Daddy Sam said.

"Red Dog, huh. Now there's a name for you. What relationship is he to you all?"

"He ain't any," Daddy Sam said.

"That mean he works for you?"

"Sometimes he helps out. He's more a friend than anything."

"Looked Indian to me. He a Indian?"

"Yes, Cherokee mostly, his family was."

"He carry a shotgun?"

"Not that I know of," Daddy Sam said. "I never seen him with none."

"Don't mean he wouldn't know how to use one though, would it?"

"He didn't do it," Daddy Sam protested.

"You know this how?"

"I just know it is all."

"He headed off to this Hadley's Jump as well?"

"Said he was going in to get breakfast."

The deputy smoked a bit longer, swallowed the rest of his coffee and handed me the empty cup—saying, "Thank you, miss"—and looked off toward the road.

"I'll be getting on," he said. "For now. Need to see if I can track any of these men whose names you mentioned: this J. R. and your husband, Jim, was it?"

"Don't forget Wilson," I said.

"Wilson," he said. "And that fellow Red Dog. Ask 'em some questions."

"It's none of them what done it," Daddy Sam said defensively.

The deputy paused in his leaving, had one foot on the lower step, but turned halfway round.

"Like I said before, you know this how, Mr. Harper?"

Daddy Sam hesitated just a moment.

"And like I said, I just know it." Daddy Sam's voice was retrained, holding back his anger at being questioned.

"Well, then I'm sure they'll have no reasons not to answer my questions. The more names I can cross off the list of possible assassins the easier and quicker this will go. The old man likes for me to be thorough. Hell, he even docked me for some missing mileage I claimed in going over into the Nations one time to round up miscreants. Brought back a whole wagon full—

whiskey peddlers mostly. But that didn't cut no ice with him when it came to my paperwork. So you can see I don't want to have to report back to him that I didn't question every possible suspect when I had the opportunity."

He gave a tight smile then turned and descended the last two steps and mounted his horse, threw me one last look then rode off.

"Real talkative son of a bitch, ain't he?" Daddy Sam said.

"You don't think either J. R. or Red Dog could have been involved, do you, Daddy Sam?"

He looked up at me and shrugged.

"No," he said.

But I could see the hint of doubt in his eyes.

"Just supposing one of them had a hand in it," I said. "Which would be the most likely?"

"Lucy," he said. "Don't go suspecting our friends and kin now."

"I'm not. Just that I know J. R. can be awfully cruel and mean and I don't half know Red Dog as you do."

"I don't see it," he said rising from his chair. "Neither one of them. My money's on Wilson and it's going to stay on Wilson and when that deputy comes back I'm going to tell him to stop sniffing around and see if he and that bunch over in Fort Smith can get a line on Wilson and go and arrest him. Or, if they want to tell me where he is, I'll take care of old Wilson. The laws got powers I ain't even close to having. Goddamn them any old way."

Daddy Sam went inside and let the screen slap shut with a bang. I knew he was skittish about the law because of his own history. Figured he was anxious to get rid of the deputy as soon as possible.

I hadn't meant to irritate Daddy Sam or show my disloyalty, but the more I thought on it, the more I realized that of everyone concerned, I was the one closest to Mama, the one who loved and cherished her more than any of the others—Daddy Sam included. They hadn't been together long enough for him to love and ache for her the way I did—her own flesh-and-blood daughter. I had first dibs on sorrow far as I was concerned.

Yes, she'd given birth to J. R. with equal as much pain and effort as she had me, but J. R. was the devil's spawn, the unknown seed put in her by a man who wasn't *my* daddy. And if my daddy *was* Frank James, then I knew with certainty that J. R. had none of Frank's honor and kindness in him. J. R. seemed to hate everybody and everything, but for whores and liquor and poker and running wild and causing untold mischief.

I had to wonder if J. R. himself wasn't on the dodge from the law over in Kansas where Mama had told me she'd last heard from him, this being some time ago. Writing her and telling her he was in some trouble and could she wire him some money to get home on. She said she was going to do it even though I advised her to cut him off. But she wouldn't.

She'd said, He's my own flesh, Lucy, same as you. You just don't understand a mother's love for her kids till you have some of your own, which I hope is soon now that you're about to marry Jim Creed. Mama seemed to like Jim when I introduced them. I think it was because Jim was a lot like some of her past men, bodacious, handsome, and a sweet talker. He complimented her on her looks and the way she dressed and flattered her with all manner of talk.

Red Dog?

Well, Red Dog was and remained a mystery to me. I'd no doubt he'd done some very bad acts in his life—murder maybe one of them. I couldn't figure out why he'd want to kill Mama, unless it was to rob her. Or she'd done something to him to make him harbor a hatred nobody knew about but himself.

But it *did* seem that Wilson, what with his packing up and taking off like he did, was the main culprit. Like Daddy Sam said, innocent men don't run, and Daddy Sam was an expert on such matters, himself a runner from the law and justice.

I felt more disheartened than ever.

Chapter 17

But the bird of bad luck wasn't yet finished singing.

About noon they brought Jim home—in the back of a wagon, covered with a tarpaulin, his boots sticking out.

A colored man in a busted-out straw hat drove the wagon and Deputy Leviticus Book rode alongside, large and looming as a figure could be.

Course I didn't know they had Jim in the wagon when it came up. I was inside the house washing dishes from our breakfast earlier. Daddy Sam was out in the yard splitting wood when I heard him call to me.

"Lucy, you best come out here."

I came out to the urgent sound of his voice, thought maybe he'd chopped off some toes; it'd be just like Daddy Sam to do something terrible and not yelp and scream but just call for help.

I heard him say to the colored man, "Olney, what's you got in the wagon?"

Then Deputy Book seeing me nodded his head once.

"Sorry to be the bearer of bad news, miss, but would you come and have a look?"

I still didn't know what it was and I came down off the porch the same time Deputy Book dismounted his horse and handed the reins up to the colored driver.

I went around to the back of the wagon and I saw Jim's boots. I knew they were his because he favored them fancy stitched, with roses in the shafts. I'd bought them for him as a wedding gift and he'd given me a gold locket with our wedding photograph in it.

Deputy Book lifted away the top part of the tarp to show Jim's slack face as if he was just sleeping, but for the dark round wound in the center of his forehead, a trickle of dried blood slanted down toward one eye. His skin was the color of cigar ash.

I must have gasped or uttered something, for before I knew it Deputy Book had his arm around me holding me up.

"Is that your husband, miss?"

I didn't need to answer. Daddy Sam answered for me.

"That's Jim Creed, my daughter's husband," he said, a touch of anguish in his voice.

"I had to be sure," Deputy Book said. "Figured it was easier to bring him here rather than to send someone to fetch you. Hired this fellow and his wagon for the task. Sorry for your loss, Miss Moon."

It wasn't that I was all that much in love with Jim. We'd barely gotten to know each other well enough for it to be true love yet. Ours was more to do with desire and lust I guess some would call it. Jim was a right pretty man and when he wanted to be tender he was a good lover. When he proposed to marry me I knew I didn't love him yet, but figured I could learn to love him like I should—like a wife ought to love her husband, but I hadn't yet reached that point. And the fact that Red Dog had raised desire in me had proven it. Now, gazing upon Jim's stony face I felt terrible.

I looked toward Daddy Sam for some help.

"We'll see he's buried. If you want, Lucy, we'll bury him next to Mama." I guess I nodded.

"Olney, will you help me carry this man to the icehouse then assist me in digging a grave? I'll pay you for your time," Daddy Sam said.

"Yes, suh," the colored man said. "I'm sorry to have to bring him home like this to you, missus." I glanced up into what I thought was the face of God if God had been a colored man—so tender and sorrowful were his eyes and it made me cry just looking at him, for it seemed he had more sorrow bringing my husband home than I had receiving him.

"It's okay, Olney, appreciate the use of your time and wagon," Daddy Sam said.

I watched as they lifted Jim from the wagon and carried him over into the icehouse. Deputy Book still held me around the waist.

"I'm okay," I said trying to wriggle free from his grasp.

"You sure?"

There was something nearly lecherous in his asking.

"Yes, I'm sure."

"Let me help you up to the porch, sit you in one of those rockers."

I allowed it.

Once seated he squatted on his boot heels before me.

"I know it's a shock to you," he said. "But, you know anybody who'd want to shoot your husband dead, miss?"

I shook my head.

"He didn't even know anybody around here. Jim's from over near Ardmore, originally. He just came home with me to attend to my mama's care and burying."

I don't know why I said it, but I added, "Mama and them came to Ardmore for our wedding."

I dabbed my eyes with the heels of my hands.

"I asked around in Hadley's Jump there what happened, if anybody had witnessed anything," he said. "But those folks are pretty tight-lipped. His body was found this morning in an alley next to the saloon. You sure he didn't make an enemy while you two were around here?"

I thought about it a moment, wondered if maybe Jim had fallen in with one of the town's demimondes and perhaps she or her pimp might have taken advantage of Jim and he fought back and they killed him. Or somebody tried to rob him. Jim was the sort to put up a fight if accosted, but not one to openly seek trouble out if he could avoid it. His was not of the trouble-making nature.

I shook my head.

"Jim didn't mess around on me," I said, but unconvinced in my heart that he might not have considering our most recent troubles in the bedroom and out.

The deputy looked at me strangely, as if I was a book written in Greek he was trying to decipher.

"Didn't mean to cast unnecessary aspersions," he said. "Just trying to figure out who killed him and why."

"Well, he didn't have need of any other woman," I reiterated.

"Yes'm, I can see that he wouldn't have, a woman looks like you."

His gaze was falsely sincere.

"A real tragedy losing your ma and now your husband so close together," he said as he worked at building a cigarette, casual-like, unhurried.

I could only think of Red Dog as Jim's killer. I knew if I said what I was thinking that the deputy would most likely arrest him and probably take him back to Fort Smith to stand trial, and if found guilty, most likely he'd be hanged. What I didn't know was whether or not I wanted to be responsible for blaming him when I did not know for sure if he shot Jim. But if it was him, I felt directly responsible. I shouldn't have fooled around with Red Dog, even as little as I did. Men get damn strange notions when it comes to being toyed with by a woman.

Sometimes one little kiss and they think they own you.

Daddy Sam walked back to the house with the colored man, Olney, who was walking slightly behind like he had no right to walk alongside a white man.

"I'm going to take Olney inside and feed him something before we get started on digging a grave," he said to no one in particular. "Some of those hoecakes and bacon from earlier."

"There's plenty," I muttered.

Olney was carrying his busted straw hat in his hands and he looked as ancient as a sea turtle, his worn-down-at-the-heel brogans shuffling over the porch planks as he entered into the house with Daddy Sam.

"How long were the two of you married, you don't mind my asking?" Deputy Book asked, exhaling a stream of blue smoke, the smoke from his shuck curling up around his face causing his one eye to squint.

"Not long," I said. "Just under a month."

He squatted there, his arms crossed at the wrists, the cigarette smoldering between his fingers, chewing over my words, no doubt weighing and measuring everything said and unsaid. I never did trust a thoughtful man. I always wanted to hear what they were thinking, not guess at it.

"You think it could be the same one killed your maw killed your husband?" he asked.

"I don't know. I think that Wilson killed my mama and Wilson's fled as far as anybody knows. So I reckon if he killed Mama, then Wilson wouldn't have been the one to shoot Jim."

"No, I reckon not," he said. "If Wilson's gone and flown the coop it surely wasn't him. Funny thing is," he added, "I went out to Wilson's and he sure must have fled in a hurry. Every stick of furniture was still there, even a fry pan with charred bacon strips left in it. Don't you think that is odd?"

I shrugged.

"I reckon if he was fearful that he'd been found out, he might well have run off in a quick hurry," I said.

He took another draw on his smoke and exhaled it skyward and laid those mud-brown eyes on me again, waiting I reckon for me to add more to the conversation.

I didn't honestly know what to think, my mind was in such turmoil. I knew that the weight of Jim's killing hadn't settled on me as much as it would later on, tonight when I was alone and it was silent but for the house settling and that's all I had to do was think about it.

"What about you?" he said.

"What about me what?"

"I mean, what you gone do now?"

"I don't know," I said. "Is it something I should do now?"

He looked off toward the wagon then the icehouse.

"No I reckon it ain't," he said. "Just curious is all."

"Curious about what, exactly?"

"Well, I ain't a married man, myself," he said. "Never have been. Single my whole life. But it don't mean I'm opposed to marrying. Just means to say I ain't never found a woman I'd want to give up my freedom *to* marry."

Spoke real casual as if it were any other day, any other circumstance and we were old companions whiling away the time.

Lord, what was this man even talking about, I asked myself.

"I imagine your line of work wouldn't make you a real good candidate for some woman, being gone off to arrest miscreants and such all the time," I said, feeling rather mean-spirited toward him for being so casual about the circumstances in the midst of my sorrow. I wanted him to know what I thought of him.

He looked up at me through the veil of smoke, that one eye still squinting.

"That's true enough, miss. I was just thinking aloud, is all."

"Thinking about what, exactly, Deputy?"

If someone was to later on ask me was he a handsome enough man—say someone like Vinita when I told her, I'd have to say yes, he was a fair-looking man in a desperate sort of way. Then what was it about him that put you off so much, Lucy, she'd probably say. And I couldn't give her an answer that would exactly describe what it was. It was just a feeling I had that he was cold-blooded in unspeakable ways.

He looked down between his hands when I asked him what it was he was thinking, as if now too embarrassed to look at me.

"Oh, sometimes my mind just rambles," he said. "A lot of foolishness, is all. Some might call me a dreaming sort."

"Go on and say it," I insisted. I wanted him to spit it out and get it said.

"Oh, nothing . . ." He hemmed and hawed and I waited staring directly at his hard figure kneeling there practically at my feet.

"Just that you seem like a real fine woman to me. And I know you ain't had time to grieve over your man or nothing . . ."

He paused long enough to draw on his nearly burnt down shuck then flicked it out into the yard in an arc of sparks.

"But I kindly was wondering if you'd consider letting me keep in touch with you after . . ."

Then he let the rest of it just hang there, like a rotten pear waiting for me to pick it and tell him what a wonderful and thoughtful offer it was. I wanted to say, Why yes, Mr. Deputy, I surely could use me a new man, and in a hurry too. For I'm nothing more than some poor simple girl who has to rely on a man for my subsistence. And you being so available and willing, why I think you'd make me a fine new husband. But is it possible you could wait just long enough for them in yonder eating hoecakes and bacon to dig a hole to bury my old husband in and cover him up before I jump on the back of your horse and ride off with you? Please? Pretty please? I'd sure enough appreciate it.

Instead, I said, "I'm in mourning, Deputy. I hope you can help find my husband's killer."

He nodded and pushed on his knees until he stood straight up.

"Yes'm, I understand completely. I'll leave you all to your work here and I'll go and try and do mine."

I could not wait for him to leave.

He stepped down off the porch and swung into the saddle.

"That fellow, Red Dog," he said before turning his horse about. "He might have been the one what killed your husband. How's your thinking on that, miss?"

My shame and sorrow had turned to anger.

"I guess I got no opinion on it," I said.

"It just makes sense he might. Him hanging around here in the vicinity of a good-looking young woman such as yourself. Maybe he got a notion if he got rid of your husband he could get set up with you."

It was all I could do to keep from cussing the man.

"Believe me, miss. I've seen lots of bad things happen when men get to fighting over a woman. Lots."

"I bet you have," I said and went inside before I spit fire.

Daddy Sam and Olney were sitting at the table, Olney sopping up the last drop of syrup with a piece of biscuit. Daddy Sam drank coffee.

"How you holding up, Lucy?" Daddy Sam asked.

"Not too goddamn well!" I said.

Olney's eyes grew into hardboiled eggs. I bet he never in his life heard a white woman cuss like that.

Daddy Sam didn't say a thing.

Olney plopped the bit of biscuit into his mouth.

"I'm ready if'n you are, Mistuh Sam. I need to git on back to the Jump purt soon."

Daddy Sam nodded and the two of them went outside and then I wept.

Chapter 18

Two hours later Daddy Sam and Olney had a fair grave dug near Mama's, the earthen mound of hers already starting to settle in. I watched as Daddy Sam paid Olney for helping him, both of them sweated through their shirts, then they shook hands and Olney drove off.

"I'll need to go into town and buy a coffin," Daddy Sam said. "You want to come along?"

"Yes," I said.

He hitched a team to his own spring wagon and I climbed up next to him on the wagon seat and he snapped the reins and we jolted off down the lane to the road and then over it all the way to Hadley's Jump.

We rode in silence for most of the way, each dealing with our own thoughts until Daddy Sam said it.

"You reckon Red Dog had a hand in this, Lucy?"

"Why would he?" I said.

"Honey," Daddy Sam said. "I've seen how he watches you. And I've noticed how you are around him. I got eyes and I know plain as anything when men and women have an interest in each other. I'm not saying I think anything went on between the two of you. I know you're decent like your mama was. Not saying that at all. But Indians can get funny thoughts in their heads, especially when it comes to white women and pretty ones at that."

"Red Dog never said an off word to me or tried nothing," I protested.

But in fact I knew that wasn't true. And I also knew that if Red Dog had shot Jim, then I was as responsible as he was. It was me who kissed him and led him on. I hated having to lie about it. The lie felt like I'd swallowed a rock that lay heavy and cold in the pit of my stomach. Lying to Daddy Sam made it even worse.

"Well," Daddy Sam said. "I like and trust Red Dog well enough, about as much as you can like and trust any Indian. And I surely wouldn't want to think of him as having any part of this. I reckon most likely Jim got mixed up with the wrong person is what it is. There are some bad actors in Hadley's Jump. The Pistol Barrel has always been a refuge for such types."

Then he fell silent a minute.

"It's why I came here," he said. "I don't know how much your mother told you the reasons for us moving here."

"She told me. Enough anyway," I said.

"I gave up my wild ways when I got together with Belle," he said. "I didn't want no more of that life. You can just run so long and then they'll either kill you, put you in prison, or you'll kill yourself. I quit the game when I met her. I was lucky. But that don't mean that somebody like that deputy won't come around someday with a warrant for my arrest."

"What would you do if that happened?" I asked.

"I been to jail, Lucy. I ain't going back. There's some things worse than death."

"I'd hate to think of that day ever coming," I said.

"As would I."

We rode on, the wagon rattling to and fro, its wheels riding in and out of ruts.

We came into town and it seemed every eye was staring at us, as if they knew our reason for coming. We could have been circus elephants the way they watched.

"Somebody sure enough knows something about this," Daddy Sam said. "But there is this false honor among the miscreants where they won't talk on one another because they're all in the same boat. You might as well cut out their tongues."

Daddy Sam reined us in front of a carpenter's shop which also doubled as the blacksmith. He wrapped the reins around the brake handle and got down and helped me down.

We went inside.

A muscular fellow with a chin beard like tangled black wire hanging down to the middle button of his shirt dozed in a chair. He opened his eyes at the sound of the door opening and closing. Slapped a troublesome fly away from his face.

They greeted each other and Daddy Sam told the man he needed a coffin made. The fellow looked at me from his begrimed face, his hands fat and rough as potatoes just dug out of the ground.

"I'm sorry for your troubles, miss," he said. "I heard about the shooting." The stink of his breath was highly noticeable.

"You hear who it was shot him?" I asked. I noticed sawdust flakes clinging to his beard.

He shook his head.

"Sorry, I couldn't help you on that account. You want to see what I got in stock, I got some made in the back," he said. "You all want to come look, pick you out one?"

We followed him to a back room that had four coffins made of pine planks rested on end and leaned up against the wall.

"I can paint or decorate any of 'em," he said looking at Daddy Sam.

I thought, You sure did enough of a poor job on Mama's coffin.

"What you think, Lucy?"

"Black," I said. "Just paint one of them simple black will do."

"You sure?" Daddy Sam asked.

I nodded.

"You want me to get Doc Ellis to do an embalming?" the smitty asked.

"Not necessary," Daddy Sam said. Then again, he looked at me. "Unless you want him shipped on to his people over in Ardmore, Lucy?"

I shook my head.

"He's got no close kin I know of. Mother, pa, brothers and sisters all dead already. Jim's was a family with real poor luck of the long living variety. He surely didn't have any better."

Daddy Sam settled accounts with the man. The smitty said he'd have it ready in an hour or so, paint it right away and set it in the sun to dry.

We went out again.

"Who's Doc Ellis?" I asked.

"Dentist," he said. "Doubles as a town doctor and embalmer, and not very damn good at either of 'em."

Red Dog was standing across the street leaned against a porch post watching us. The man had an uncanny habit of popping up places you didn't expect him.

"Maybe you should wait here while I go have a word with him, Lucy," Daddy Sam said.

"No," I said. "I'm going too."

"All right, then."

We crossed over. Red Dog did not move away from his vigil and I hadn't expected him to. He never struck me as the running kind.

"I guess you heard about Jim getting murdered," Daddy Sam said. I watched Red Dog's face, his eyes for any sign of guilt. But Daddy Sam might just as well asked him if he heard it was going to rain anytime soon for all the emotion he showed.

"I heard about it, yes," Red Dog said. His gaze never left me, as if Daddy Sam wasn't standing there at all. It was as if Red Dog was testing me instead of the other way around.

"You see or hear anything about who's responsible for it?" Daddy Sam asked.

"No. Just heard a man had been killed, his body found in the alley by the saloon. I went over and a bunch of gawkers was standing around. Then I saw who it was."

"You could have come and told us," Daddy Sam said.

"Didn't figure it was my place. 'Sides, that deputy showed up and took charge of things. Figured he'd get it told to you all. I waited on up the street. Seen him and that nigger, Olney, putting Jim in the wagon, cover him with a tarpaulin. Figured they was going to carry him onto the house. Reckon they did."

"You could have come along with them," Daddy Sam said.

"No," Red Dog said.

"Why not?"

Red Dog shifted his gaze to Daddy Sam.

"You know why not," he said. "Same reason you'd have for avoiding those badges. No need to mix up with 'em any more than I have to. They're like dogs, get to sniffing around and before you know it they latch onto you, lock you up in a cage, even if they got no reason to."

"Well, Book's wondering if you had a hand in it," Daddy Sam said. "He asked me direct."

"I didn't and you can tell him that direct next time he asks. He can wonder all the damn hell he wants to, it don't prove nothing."

"Tell you the truth," Daddy Sam said. "I was wondering myself."

Red Dog shifted his gaze back to me.

"You wondering too, Lucy? Maybe I killed your husband?"

"I don't rightly know what to think anymore," I said. "Seems like around here a body can get murdered and nobody knows or sees anything. But somebody surely knows, but it don't seem like nobody wants to say. Maybe the whole damn place is guilty of one thing or another."

"Probably so," he said. "But for me, that cuts it. I reckon I'll see you all around sometime."

He stalked off without so much as a glance back.

"Goddamn," Daddy Sam muttered.

"I feel twisted up," I said.

"Me too, Lucy. Me too."

We hauled the black coffin back to the house. Daddy Sam said he'd get J. R. to help us with the burying.

"If he's returned," I said. "Even then you might have to threaten him with a pistol to get him to do anything."

"He does skulk around like some old tomcat," Daddy Sam said. "Tell the truth, Lucy, and just between us, that boy sometimes gives me the spooks and I'm not one to spook easily. Sometimes I hear him talking to himself, holding a regular conversation. He fools around with snakes. I've seen him standing naked out in the yard sometimes when the moon is full, like it's affected his mind. He'll disappear for days only to show up again unexpected. Sometimes looks at you with pure hatred in his eyes and you not done a thing to him."

Daddy Sam leaned and spat over the side of the wagon.

"Tell the truth, wasn't for your mama wanting to care for him like some water head what didn't know any better, I'd have run him off a long time ago. I wished he'd never come back after he was gone the last time for nearly a year. The things I heard about him . . ."

I was surprised to hear Daddy Sam speak of the very things I'd thought about concerning my half brother.

"I know it," I said.

Daddy Sam glanced at me.

"You sure the two of you are even related, that your mama didn't find him along the side of the road somewhere and take him in out of pity? The two of you are like night and day, him being the night and you the day."

"I've wondered that myself several times, Daddy Sam." I didn't tell Daddy Sam that there was a real outside chance in my mind that it wasn't even Johnny Waco who was J. R.'s daddy, that it could have been someone else. There were some things Mama was very closed about when it came to her very person, even to me.

We'd barely finished talking about my devil brother when an explosion of quail burst from the brush and spooked the horses. They took off like a pistol shot. It was all I could do to keep my seat and Daddy Sam to rein in the team again. I was sure we were both going to meet our own deaths.

But Daddy Sam got them halted, cussing under his breath, sweat running down his face. We looked back and there was Jim's new black coffin busted all to hell having been pitched from the wagon bed.

We collected the boards and lid and put them back into the wagon, Daddy Sam saying how he could cobble it back together, though it might not be as nice a job as it had been.

"I reckon Jim won't know the difference, Lucy," he said contritely.

I touched his arm, tears streaming down my face.

"Are we cursed, Daddy Sam? It sure feels like we're cursed."

He held me close, one hand gently atop my head.

"No, honey, we ain't cursed. We've just hit a patch of bad luck is all. Seems like when things start to go to hell they just keep on going for a while. We'll work through this."

I calmed down and we continued on to the house.

"I'll fix us some supper," I said while Daddy Sam halted the wagon near the corral and set to work reconstructing the coffin.

I went inside and there sat J. R. at the piano fooling with the keys. He looked up.

"I hear old Jimmy grew a third eye," he said smiling.

"Yes, and you're going to help bury him," I said angrily.

"Shit, be glad to," he said and went back to plinking the keys. I detested him for lots of reasons, the least of which at the very moment was to see and hear him messing with Mama's piano. It was sacrilege in my book.

I called Daddy Sam to the house to eat and he came in with dark stains of sweat bled through his shirt, his hair plastered to his head. He washed his face and hands then wiped them on the dry towel.

"Was that you playing the piano, Lucy?" he asked. "Thought I heard it."

Before I could tell it, J. R. came in from his room in the back. He had the scent of cheap toilet water that the crib whores wear—that and sweat stink. He sat down at the table.

"That was me playing it," he said. "Thought I might take it up and start playing in saloons for my keep."

"Oh," Daddy Sam said as I filled his cup with coffee, choosing to ignore J. R.'s cup. Did the same thing when it came to dishing up supper. J. R. just sat there a minute looking at me, aggrieved I had not served him his supper. When I sat down, he got up and dished up his own supper and sat down again.

"Well, ain't this nice, folks?" he said. "Family, sitting down to supper together."

"We ought to say a blessing for Mama and Jim," Daddy Sam said.

J. R. commenced eating while Daddy Sam said a prayer asking for the Lord's care over the souls of Mama and Jim, imploring Him to take them into His heavenly kingdom.

"My mansion has many rooms," he quoted.

J. R. smiled around his food.

"You think God's got a big ol' house where every one of us goes when we die?" he asked. "Well, I hope I get me one with a big ol' pitcher winder."

Daddy Sam offered him a stony look.

"You be careful about speaking blasphemy," Daddy Sam said.

"Well, now that's sorta like listening to the pot callin' the kettle black, a man of your reputation preachin' to me," J. R. said.

I thought Daddy Sam was going to come out of his chair and flatten J. R. but he didn't.

"Why don't you shut your vile mouth, J. R., and leave a body be," I said angrily.

"Why don't you, Lucy?" he said. "Why don't all you all shut up with this ghost and holiness talking? People die all the time, shit, it ain't nothing but what it is."

He pushed away from the table taking his plate with him and stormed outside letting that damn screen slap shut causing me to near jump out of my chair.

"Next one we bury is going to be him I have my way," I said.

"Now, Lucy. Don't let him get to you. He's just a mean fully miserable human being. He's like those damn vipers he fools with, mean and low down."

I wanted so badly to tell Daddy Sam what J. R. had said to me the other day, but I held my tongue. I just wanted a bit of peace for once. I felt like I was barely able to breathe.

"Excuse me, Daddy Sam," I said and left the table, my meal sitting half eaten, and went out and off the porch where J. R. sat eating, and on past him out to the icehouse. I needed to look at my late husband, to say something kindly to him even though he could not hear me. But maybe his spirit could. Maybe it was lingering about yet and hadn't gone off to the heavenly home Daddy Sam spoke of and he would know that I wanted to love him even if I hadn't got the chance to fully do so.

I opened the icehouse door and stepped in. It was cool and dim inside. There were several large blocks of ice covered in sawdust that Daddy Sam must have had delivered every few days from Hadley's Jump.

A few sprites of light came in through some of the board cracks, just enough to see my late husband lying there half covered by the tarp. I shivered from the coolness or maybe it was being alone with death.

"Jim, honey. It's me, Lucy. I'm so very sorry for what happened to you. I never would have believed this would happen. Not this, not now. I know you loved me and you tried your best to make me happy and I should have been more loving to you. I hate it that we argued the last time. Just hate it, and I'm so sorry. If it was Red Dog who did this or any other and I find out, I will take vengeance on him myself."

I touched his face, his cheek. It was cold like stone is cold. I could not bring myself to kiss his dead lips. I wanted to as a gesture of my love and grief, but I just couldn't. So instead I touched my own lips with my fingers and then touched them to his.

I took off the locket he had given me for a wedding gift and placed it between his folded hands, strung the chain through his stiffened fingers.

"You take this with you, Jim."

I don't know why I thought it. It was such a bizarre thing to think. But I thought of Jim showing the locket to our Lord Jesus, the two of them smiling over it. Jim saying, "This is Lucy, my sweetheart."

"I have to go now, honey," I said and stepped out into the warmth of a low slanted sun whose light now spread over the ground like golden water and cast long shadows, mine included.

I went back to the house and J. R. was still there on the porch watching me.

He just couldn't leave it alone.

He said, "You two have one last time of it, Lucy?"

"If I had a knife, I'd cut your heart out and feed it to hogs," I said.

He just laughed.

I was trembling.

"What's wrong now, Lucy?" Daddy Sam asked when I came in. Tears were streaming down my cheeks from anger and pain.

"Nothing. I just went to the icehouse and paid my final respects to Jim is all."

Daddy Sam nodded.

"Well, might as well get over with the burial before night catches us."

He put on his hat and went out and I heard him say to J. R., grab some ropes from the toolshed and let's get this done.

I watched from the porch as they carried the coffin inside the icehouse and then out again, each at one end straining at the weight now that Jim was in it.

They carried it over to the dug grave and used a pair of ropes to put under the coffin so that they could lower it down. I was thinking I wouldn't put it past J. R. to simply drop his end and make a mess of it. But he didn't.

The sun was now near set beyond the trees bordering the westward side of the property, the light glinting through the leaves and branches.

By the time J. R. and Daddy Sam got the grave filled in, the air was dusky, almost a purple haze.

I carried Mama's old Bible out to the grave site and handed it to Daddy Sam.

"Maybe you should read from it, Lucy?" he said.

J. R. watched with eyes cold and empty as death itself.

"I can't," I said. "I'd choke up too much for it to sound proper."

"Okay, then," he said and opened it.

"This is from Corinthians," he said.

"When the perishable puts on the imperishable, and the mortal puts on immortality, then shall come to pass the saying that is written: Death is swallowed up in victory. O death, where is your victory? O death, where is your sting? The sting of death is sin, and the power of sin is the law. But thanks be to God, who gives us the victory through our Lord Jesus Christ. Amen."

Then he looked up and across at me.

"Anything you'd like to add, Lucy?"

"Ashes to ashes and dust to dust," I said. Daddy Sam nodded.

And it was finished. Night came on and up in my room I lay abed alone and feeling lonely, longing for once the touch of Jim's hand upon me, craving his kiss or hearing his silly laughter at something I'd said. And I wondered if I was meant for loneliness, meant for a life of constant sorrow.

"Mama," I said aloud, in a whisper. "Can you come and be with me tonight, just this once more?"

Maybe it was a trick of the wind, for I'd left the window open and night brought with it a cooling breeze that fluttered the curtains, for as I said it, the rocker in the room creaked once.

And I knew she was there and it brought me comfort.

"Thank you, Mama."

Chapter 19

Morning brought a pounding rain. Lightning shattered the bruised sky and the crack of thunder rattled the entire house. It woke me from a fitful sleep and I felt exhausted and unwilling to rise out my bed. I felt blue and empty, as if my body had no bones.

I lay for a time listening to the rain hammering down on the roof and pelting against the glass, then realized I'd left the window open and jumped quickly to shut it and nearly slipped on the wet floor.

Oh hell, I thought. What else can possibly go wrong?

I remembered then as I went back to the bed Mama's diary and pulled it out and propped myself up with pillows to read some of it.

The first entry was dated June 30, 1876.

Sick again this morning.

Today I read where General Custer and all his men were killed at someplace called the Little Bighorn in Montana territory. They were slaughtered by 5000 savage Indians and the Nation is in mourning. I feel sorry for their wives and families. Not the Indians, but those of the soldiers, I mean.

I also read about the Centennial Exhibition in Philadelphia and the many wonderful displays and would so like to go. They say it is like seeing the whole world all in one place.

Frank stopped by today and asked me how I was doing. I

had not seen him for almost a month—his last visit was when we went for a picnic down by the riverside. He said Jesse was eager to pull another job, but Frank stated he was less interested. He said because he was a married man now, he was less inclined to take risks like when he was young and single. I'd privately hoped that he would divorce and he and I would marry someday, even though no such declaration on his part had ever been expressed. Still, we had been intimate on several occasions, and I thought that he loved me.

To say I gave my virginity to him would not be wholly truthful, but still a girl likes to believe that the man she gives herself to is the one she loves and who loves her. It should be a lesson to me from here on. A girl can wish all she wants but it don't make it so. To Frank's credit, he never lied to me that I know of.

Overall, he seemed happy, but for the plans of Jesse to do as he put it, A job in Minnesota soon.

I warned Frank not to do it and he said he could use the money. Again I begged him not to even though he was married to another.

I reckon considering everything, I won't be able to see you anymore after this, Belle, he told me. I think we were both saddened by this revelation.

At least I was. He could have not told me anything, but he was decent about it in that respect.

Frank was nearly always serious, what with his books he kept in his saddlebags and his lost dreams of being a school teacher. But sometimes his droll humor came through as it did today. He said, Belle, you will never lack for male admirers, even when you're 90 years old they'll be lined up at your door. You're a regular mantrap.

I told him that was probably true, but what did it matter if the ones doing the admiring weren't the ones you wanted, to which he answered with a shy cough.

He stayed for supper but we did not become intimate this time since Mama and Papa were about and shared in our repast. I kissed him good-bye and wished him all happiness and once more begged him to give up his outlaw ways. He promised me he would and told me not to worry.

Nothing's going to happen to old Frank, he said as he waved his hat in the air and bid so long.

I had not told him my suspicions with regards my situation, for I did not want to ruin a good time, and besides, what good would it have done me?

I was capable of raising a child by myself if that is what it would come to. I am not certain I am pregnant, but the signs are all there.

And now off to bed . . .

So maybe it was true, I thought to the accompaniment of rain and blowing wind and early shadows.

Maybe Frank James was my father.

This I thought until I read a later entry, and then I wasn't so sure.

Daddy Sam called from down below.

"Lucy, you up yet?"

I went to the head of the stairs and saw his face looking up.

"I'm not feeling especially well this morning," I said.

"It's okay, I've already fixed myself something to eat. Warmed up some of those biscuits from yesterday with some butter and honey on 'em and coffee. You want something to eat?"

"No thank you."

"Well, I was thinking on going into Hadley's Jump. I know a fellow who might for the right amount tell me something if he knows it. He's a skulking fellow with good eyes and ears when he's not drunk or pretending to be. It's raining like Hades, but I thought I should see if you'd want to come along. I have an extra rubber you could wear."

"No," I said. "I don't feel up to riding in the rain."

"Okay honey, why don't you stay and rest up. This fellow might not even be there and it'd be a cold wet ride to town and back for just a hunch he might be there."

I eased down the stairs on bare feet trying to be as quiet as possible until I got within whispering distance of Daddy Sam.

"Where's J. R.?"

Daddy Sam shook his head.

"Don't know," he said. "I've not seen him around this morning."

I dreaded the thought of him skulking about.

Just then there was a knock at the door. Daddy Sam had closed it to keep the rain from coming in through the screen.

"Maybe that's him," Daddy Sam said.

I stood waiting to see if it was.

"Oh, it's you," I heard Daddy Sam say. Then I heard the flat nasal voice of Deputy Leviticus Book. Daddy Sam invited him in, for to do otherwise, I reckoned, might raise more suspicion as far as Daddy Sam himself was concerned.

I was in my nightdress still.

I heard them talking, Deputy Book saying he'd just come round to follow up on some things. Was J. R. about? He'd like to ask him some questions. Said he'd been asking around about him but nobody knew anything. Also wanted to talk to Red Dog.

This fellow Red Dog, is how he said it.

Daddy Sam tried putting him off, saying he hadn't heard from any of them, nor seen them.

"I was just leaving myself to go into Hadley's Jump," Daddy Sam said. "Maybe you want to ride in with me and if I see J. R., I'll point him out." I knew Daddy Sam was trying to draw him away from the house.

"No, that's okay," Deputy Book said. Then he asked if I was there.

"She's sleeping still," Daddy Sam said.

I don't know what made me do it but I stepped down off the stairs and went to where the two of them stood by the front door. There was a puddle of water that had dripped from the lawman's rubber slicker and formed around his boots.

Daddy Sam tossed me a warning look.

"What is it you need?" I asked.

"Oh, just wondered how you were doing is all, since I'd come out this way to question your brother," he said.

"I'm doing okay," I said. "Thank you very much for asking. Have you figured out yet who killed my mother or my husband?" I said it cold, accusing him of a lack of competence even though he'd only been around a couple of days.

He'd taken off his wet rain-crushed hat and held it in both hands upside down like a bowl.

"Well, no," he said. "Kind of hard to find out much of anything since some of the folks I aim to question are more scarce then hen's teeth and the rest of 'em wouldn't say squat if you pinched their noses."

Silence befell us all. Sometimes you just run out of things worth saying and this was one of them.

"Well, I best get on looking for these fellows," he said. "Thank you all for your time."

He left with only the puddle of rainwater to remind us he'd even been there.

"I'll check and make sure J. R.'s not around before I go off, honey. You keep the door locked if you're afraid of him," Daddy Sam said.

"Daddy Sam?"

"What is it, Lucy?"

"J. R. said something to me that scared hell out of me."

"Well, what'd he say, Lucy?"

I told him. His mouth dropped open.

"Son of a bitch," he said. "Why'd you not tell me before now and I would have run him off right then?"

"I didn't want to stir up more trouble. You had enough troubling you already."

"Well, as soon as I see him I'm going to run him off. You wait right here."

Daddy Sam left the entryway and went off and came back shortly with a small pistol.

"Lucy, you ever learn to shoot a gun?"

"Yes. But this one seems too little to do much," I said. "What about Jim's bird's-head Colt? Did he have it on him when they brought him home?"

Daddy Sam shook his head.

"Seems like whoever killed him must have taken it, Lucy. Leastways he didn't have it on him."

Then he held the gun out again.

"It's what they call a bulldog or belly gun," he said. "Easy to hide. But it will do the trick you hit a fellow right. Might be best if you put the first one where J. R. makes water to teach him a damn lesson."

It was small with rubberized grips but heavier than it looked.

"Careful, it's fully loaded," he said.

"Thanks," I said.

"You want, I'll not go into Hadley's Jump," he said.

I shook my head.

"No, if there's a chance this fellow you're going to see knows something you go and find out. With this, I'll be all right until you get back."

"Well, don't kill him less you have to," he said. "Nothing like blood on your hands to haunt your dreams. I won't be gone any longer than I have to."

He kissed me on the forehead then went on out. He'd already had a horse saddled and I watched him mount and ride off slapping the ends of his reins over the animal's haunches as he put it into a gallop, its hooves throwing clots of mud into the air.

I stood for a second holding the bulldog.

Then I prayed.

Come on, J. R., just you come on and try something with me and I will put an end to you and every damn vile thing in your head.

But it wasn't J. R. I should have been worried about.

CHAPTER 20

I'd locked the door and gone into the kitchen still holding the bulldog revolver and wearing my nightgown. I didn't even feel like getting dressed. I set the pistol on the table and fixed myself a cup of coffee and slathered a biscuit with butter and honey and sat at the table feeling listless and as unhappy as I'd ever been. The coffee was bitter and I added sugar and some canned milk to lighten it. The biscuit was dry and crumbly, a result of Daddy Sam's baking efforts. God love him.

I'd been but a few minutes eating and drinking and feeling maudlin when there was a knocking at the door again. My heart quickened. Then I figured it to be Daddy Sam come back because he'd forgotten something. He'd only been gone but a minute.

I went to answer it not even thinking.

There stood Deputy Book, big as life, his hat brim flopped down over his eyes so that he'd had to tilt his head back to peer upon me. I was momentarily too paralyzed to move, even to slam the door shut.

"What is it you want?" I asked, bravely even though the sudden reappearance of him standing there had my insides trembling.

Mama always warned me about showing any man fear.

"They will leap upon you, daughter, like a cat upon a mouse if they think you're afraid of them."

"Could you let me in?"

"No," I said. "Just tell me what it is you got to tell me."

"What are you afraid of?"

"Nothing. Either tell me what you got to say or leave."

"You sure are a fright. I never figured you to be afraid of someone like me, an officer of the law. Why is that? You got something to hide? That old man you call Daddy Sam? He hiding something he don't want the law to know about and you protecting him. Is that it?"

"Get off the porch," I said and went to close the door but he stuck the toe of his boot in then pushed it wide and me with it.

I ran toward the kitchen where I'd left the bulldog but he was right behind me and grabbed hold of me just as I got a hand on the pistol and got it cocked and ready before he twisted it from my fingers.

"Goddamn, you was going to shoot me, a federal marshal? Are you crazy, child?"

"You best leave out of here before Daddy Sam gets back," I said as calmly and coolly as I could muster, but truth was I was now most certainly scared for my life.

He looked at the bulldog in his hand as if it were something to behold and shook his head.

"Why this little pop skull wouldn't hardly do more than piss a man off if you was to shoot him with it," he laughed, but not in a humorous way.

"Well, then give it over to me if that's all you're thinking," I said.

He broke it open and knocked out the hulls that clattered to the floor then tossed it aside.

"Now listen here," he said.

"If Daddy Sam comes and finds you here like this, he will kill you," I said.

"Well, I hardly don't think such will come to pass," he said.

"Whyn't you fix me a cup of that Arbuckle and let's sit us a spell."

"Fine," I said.

I poured it with a plan in mind to throw it in his face and run, but when I brought it over he motioned and said, "Just set it on the table and don't get no ugly thoughts about flingin' it in my face."

I set it down.

Then he motioned me to sit down across from him and I did and he removed his flop hat and rested it upon the knob of the back of a chair and I couldn't hardly stand to look at him.

He sipped casual and built himself a smoke, taking his sweet time. I knew I was being toyed with and I didn't care for it one damn bit, but I didn't know what to do about it, big as he was.

"Now then," he said when he got his shuck lit and took a draw from it and exhaled a cloud of smoke into the room.

"I imagine you've had plenty of relations with men, haven't you?"

"What's that got to do with the price of tea in China?" I said.

He offered a crooked smile, the cigarette held between his fingers, the smoke from it drifting up.

"You what? Sixteen, seventeen years old?"

"I'm old enough," I said.

The crookedness of his grin grew more crooked.

"I just bet you are. I bet that husband of yours taught you a great deal of what a man likes. Hell, I bet he wasn't your first neither, was he?"

"What is it you want, mister?" I said getting some of my brave back. I figured if he was going to molest me, he was going to and no point making it easy for him.

"Well, now," he said. "I reckon the heart wants what the heart wants," he said. "Like the flesh wants what it wants."

"Meaning?"

"I think you get my meaning. I think you perfectly damn well know what a man wants from a young sweet thing such as yourself. You don't fool me none with all that effort of innocence. Hell, I bet your dear dead husband surely had to keep you on a short leash now, didn't he, gal like you? I can see trash written all over you. Pert is as pert does, is that it?"

"You leave Jim out of this," I said. "Don't speak ill of the dead, damn you."

"I wasn't speaking ill of the dead. I was speaking ill of you, sugar plum."

His eyes were wet and glistening and he ran his fat tongue over his lips like a dog slavering over a ham bone.

"You know if you molest me, I will track you down and kill you," I said. "I won't go to the law in Fort Smith and tell my tale to Judge Parker—ain't that who you said sent you cause he was a friend of my mama's?"

He nodded ever so slightly more amused I suppose than anything since he was at least twice my size, carried a big damn pistol on his hip and held all the winning hand.

"Well," I said. "I won't even bother going to Parker. I'll just hunt you down and kill you in the worst way a man can be killed. I'll cut off your peaches first and force you to eat them then I'll gut you like a fish."

"Stop, sugar plum, you're making me tremble so bad I'll probably make water in my pants."

His laughter filled the room and it wasn't even a good laughter, just loud and lewd.

He stubbed out his cigarette on the tabletop and drained his coffee then stood away from the table.

"Let's me and you go find us a bed so we can get this done proper. I'd not want you to think of me as some ol' border ruffian what just lifts a woman's skirts above her head and ruts her right on top of the kitchen table. No, ma'am. I'm the loving kind."

He came around the table and grabbed my wrist and jerked me to my feet and I tried to kick him but he got a good strong hold on me and brought his face down close to mine. His breath was rank as a swamp.

"Now, we can do this hard or we can do it easy like. You gone like it much better if we do it easy than hard. You unnerstand me?"

His grip on me was like being squeezed by a vice.

"I mean I'll slice up your face so no man will ever want you and I'll cut off your teats you fight me and I'll still take what I come after. So how we do this is up to you, sugar plum."

I didn't mind dying. I just didn't want to be cut up.

He waited for my answer.

I nodded.

"Good, now which way to your bed."

We trudged up the stairs. For me it was like walking the gallows steps.

In the bedroom he turned loose of me.

"Go ahead and shuck out of that nightdress and let me get a look at my prize," he ordered.

I bit my lower lip but did as he ordered, lifting the gown as slowly as I could hoping Daddy Sam would come back but knowing he probably would not and that I was going to have to go through with what the man with the gun and the advantage over me wanted.

He sat down in the rocking chair in my room and pulled off his boots one at a time then his dirty socks all the while holding the gun in one hand and all the while watching me closely.

"Go on, drop it," he said.

I let the gown fall to my feet.

He whistled.

"I just knew them would be some real fine bubbies," he said. "They are too, ain't they, Lucy?"

I didn't say anything.

"I said, ain't they fine bubbies, Lucy?"

"Yes," I muttered.

He tugged his shirt off over his head with a yank. His flesh was near white as lard. A few sprigs of black hair grew in the center of his chest. He was as thick across the middle as a bear and had large rounded and sloping shoulders.

"I can tell you're likin' what you're seein, Lucy, ain't you? I ain't built like that dead husband of yours. I'm built like a man, top to bottom. You'll see."

Again I did not respond and again he asked me the same question about liking what I was seeing.

"Yes," I said.

"Go on and say it," he said.

"Say what?"

"That you're likin' what you're seein'."

"I'm liking what I'm seeing," I said.

"That's better." He rested back, his lustful eyes taking every inch of me in.

"You know somethin'," he said.

I shamefully shook my head.

"Some gals I've known, some of them Fort Smith whores color their hair down there, figures it makes 'em more exotic. I'm glad to see you are natural, Lucy."

I wished worse than anything he would not say my name, it just made it seem more obscene to me when he called me Lucy.

"You ain't no whore, are you, Lucy?"

I shook my head.

"Say it."

"I am not a whore," I said as softly as I could.

"No, you sure ain't. But you want to know somethin'?"

I waited.

"I'm gone make you my little whore. I'm gone keep you as my own personal little whore. How'd you like that?"

I was ready to explode, ready to die if I had to.

"Either kill me or get it over with," I said.

He stood up then and unbuckled his belt with one hand as he stepped up to me. He took the cold hard muzzle of his revolver and touched first one of my breasts and then the other with it. It felt like a serpent's bite and I flinched when he did it. Then he did the unthinkable and lowered it to between my legs and touched me there with it. Not hard or rough, just a touch but it was worse than anything I could imagine.

"I knew a man over in Ingalls once used a skull popper on a woman in that way. Then you know what he did when she fought him?"

I kept quiet.

"He pulled the trigger. Yeah, shot right up inside her."

His face was inches from mine, his rotgut breath sickening.

"It was a damn mess," he said low and harshly. "They strung him up over it from a chinaberry tree. But I gotta tell you, Lucy. They was somethin' about him doin' that, you know, foolin' with her that away that worked on my mind. It touched real dark places in my mind."

I tried my best not to, but I began to tremble.

"You see there is a lot worse than most women think can happen than some things that *do* happen to 'em. Now what I aim to do with you ain't nothing even close to what that boy in Ingalls did to that woman. No, fact is, this will be real pleasurable. All depends on how you approach it, sugar plum."

He touched the side of his skull with the revolver's barrel then.

"Get your mind right and hell you might even want to take up with me once you seen what a real man can do for you. Now finish unbuttonin' me so I can step on out of these drawers."

My fingers fumbled with his buttons while he stroked my hair with his free hand and kept saying, "That's nice, real nice."

Finally his trousers fell and he stepped out of them.

"Now lay back on that bed, honey," he ordered.

"Be a man and put a bullet in me," I said.

He grunted.

"I'll put somethin' in you but it ain't gone be no bullet. Least not yet."

He got above me on hands and knees and I wished that the gun would go off accidental and kill me.

"Go on, put it in. I like it that way," he said.

I could not bear to touch him.

Please God, I prayed.

Then:

"Get off her," a familiar voice ordered.

The lout of a lawman twisted away and then there was a double explosion that felt like it rocked the room and momentarily deafened me. The big man tumbled off the side of the bed and I heard a gasp. But the gasp hadn't come from him.

I sat bolt upright and there, slumped in the doorway was Red Dog holding his chest and bleeding through his fingers. His gun lay on the floor next to his right hand.

I might have screamed. I might not have screamed.

I came off the bed in a rush, forgetting even that I was naked, not caring. He'd saved me from rape, possibly worse. I knelt next to him and he raised his eyes to mine.

"He got me, Lucy. Got me good."

"Let me see," I said taking his hand temporarily away to expose his rapidly staining shirt. I reached to unbutton it and Red Dog jerked and I thought it was because of the pain but I saw his gaze go from mine to something behind me.

I turned and saw Leviticus Book getting to his knees, a stream of blood trailing down his lower ribs and smearing his hip. He was alive and probably in a lot better shape than Red Dog. He reached for his gun which had landed a few feet away just under the rocking chair.

"My gun," Red Dog muttered.

I grabbed for it just as the lawman's fingers reached his.

"Shoot him," Red Dog said in a frightful voice.

Deputy Book grabbed hold of his pistol and was turning toward us.

"Why you damn Indian sumbitch," he cursed.

"Shoot," Red Dog managed as his eyes rolled up in his head.

I fired and saw the top of the deputy's head explode into a bright red spray like flung paint that splattered the wall behind him and he dropped as though struck by a sledge.

My hands were trembling so badly I could barely hold the big revolver and then I lowered it when the lawman didn't move again.

Jesus Christ, I thought.

Jesus Christ.

CHAPTER 21

Blood, and there was plenty of it, has the smell of copper when you get up close to it. I wasn't sure if Red Dog was dead or just fainted away. I looked over at Deputy Book and he sure enough was dead with half his head blown off. It looked just like a jar of pickled eggs dropped from a shelf.

My arms and legs and belly were covered in Red Dog's blood from holding him as I knelt there on the floor beside him. The air in the room was filled with gunpowder smoke that hovered like a fog. The violence was so sudden and over so quickly it seemed like a dream rather than a thing that happened.

Red Dog moaned and his eyes fluttered open and he looked at me.

"Am I dead?"

"If you were, do you think you'd be asking that question?" I said with relief.

"No, I reckon not," he said. "But goddamn it hurts like hell, getting shot does."

"I imagine so," I said. "Don't move and I'll run and fix some bandages."

"Don't worry, I ain't going nowhere."

He seemed pretty damn smart-alecky for a man shot through the brisket.

I rested him back against the wall then ran downstairs to the kitchen looking for something to plug up the hole in Red Dog, then ran back up thinking Mama might have kept something in one of the drawers of her old bureau with the oval mirror framed by what looked like a maple horse collar.

The best I could find was a pair of Mama's linen bloomers, they would have to suffice.

I ran back in the room where Red Dog sat slumped and pressed the pretty bloomers against his chest wound.

"Hold these till I get back."

He looked down.

"Yours?" he said with a weak smile. "I always hoped I'd get to see them, but not like this."

"Shut up you heathen and wait here."

"Not planning on going nowhere," he said.

I ran back down again and tried to think where I might find some medical remedy and it came to me there might be something out in the barn Daddy Sam would have used on his horses, liniment or the like, so I ran outside forgetting I didn't have a stitch on.

The barn smelled sweetly of horse and hay, a good smell if ever there was one, and I searched thorough the boxes till I found a small can of what looked like axle grease, pried off the lid and smelled of it. It had a nice fragrance so I figured it wasn't axle grease but maybe some blood-stopping remedy and ran back to the house with it and up the stairs.

I removed the blood-soaked bloomers and scooped out a dollop of the salve and smeared it over the bullet hole.

"What's that?" he asked.

"Something I found in the barn. Horse something."

I tore the top sheet off the bed and ripped it into strips and then took a silk hankie I'd bought for my wedding and used it as a patch and tied it in place with a strip of torn sheet wrapped around Red Dog's body. All the while he sat staring across the room at the dead deputy and the blood streaks on the wall above the body.

"How do you feel?" I asked when I finished.

"Like third prize at the county fair," he said.

"Now what do we do?"

"We need to get rid of the body and get me to a woman I know. An old witchy woman who maybe can save my life."

"Wouldn't it be better if I just rode and got Daddy Sam and brought him back, maybe with that crazy old tooth puller what passes for a doctor in Hadley's Jump, the one you was telling me about?"

"I'd just as soon we get on out of here," he said. "You don't mind."

"Why do we have to get rid of Book? Hell with him. He's dead, just leave him and let me get you to this woman you know."

"You think for once you could just do as I ask?"

He was ashen and I figured he was about to die on me anytime and it wasn't right of me to argue with a soon-to-be-dead man and have him go out of this world with ill feelings toward me.

"I'll go hitch the team to the wagon," I said.

"You might want to put some clothes on first," he said.

He might have been gunshot and near to dying but it didn't stop him from noticing I was naked as one of those women you see in a painting above a whiskey bar.

"If I wasn't so bunged up," he stammered, a stupid half grin on his face.

"Shut up and be still," I said, "or the devil's liable to just snatch you away." Then I quickly dressed in my riding clothes and went out and hitched the team to the wagon. It was something I'd learned as a girl to do, taught to me by Johnny Waco or Teddy Blue or one of them. Mama always said it was important to learn to do everything a man could do and not have to rely on them. "But," she added, "you let them do it if they're able, Lucy. It makes them feel potent to think they are capable. Men like to feel potent."

I got the team hitched and brought it up as close to the porch as I could get it and went up and got a hold of Red Dog under his arms and with his assistance got him to his feet. We went down the stairs like a couple of hundred-year-old decrepits, slowly and steady, him gripping a bloody hand on the railing. Then outside and down the porch and up and in the wagon bed.

"Now you got to go and get Book and haul him out," he said.

"Get him? How in hell am I going to get him? The man is bigger than you are and dead as hell and can't walk a step."

He shook his head.

"I don't know, but it has to be done. He's found shot dead ol' Parker will send out a dozen more deputies looking for his killer, which is you and me, Lucy."

"It was self-defense," I protested.

"It was, but he's still a federal man and who you think the law will believe, us'ns or the sight of one of their own, his head blown off? They won't know if we hide the body. Won't be able to prove anything."

I was confused, good Glory.

"I'll try," I said and went back in the house and back up the stairs hoping maybe I was mistaken about Book being dead and that he regained consciousness and was only hurt, the way you'll do when desperate and the mind starts playing tricks on you. But no, he was dead as hell.

I grabbed hold of him under the arms and dragged him to the head of the stairs, it taking every ounce of strength I had. It was like lugging around a steer. I got him to the edge of the landing and shoved and he slid and tumbled the rest of the way down leaving a smear of blood and offal I didn't want to even think about. I repeated the process out to the porch then rolled him off the edge into the wagon's bed.

"His clothes," Red Dog said.

I was winded and bloody but I went back and got Book's clothing and boots and gun and hat and carried all down and tossed it in the wagon bed.

"Now what?" I said huffing, short of breath and worried sick.

"Go on in and clean yourself up, wash the blood off. Get some blankets and pillows for me to rest upon and some of your daddy's clothes for me to wear, money too if you got any."

"Well, hell, why don't I just dance a jig and sing 'The Star Spangled Banner' while I'm at it?"

"Don't be foolish, Lucy. This ain't the time."

"You think not?"

He looked at me with the cold stare of impatience.

So I went in, washed the blood off my hands and face and grabbed some of Daddy Sam's clothes, blankets, pillows and all the money I had, which was the leftover wedding money given us by well-wishers for our honeymoon, and hurried back outside.

"The tarp," Red Dog said as I started to climb up onto the wagon seat.

"Huh?"

"To cover him up with in case we get stopped along the road."

I about cussed a blue streak but ran to the icehouse and got the same tarp that had covered Jim and brought it out and covered the deputy instead. We tied Book's horse to the back of the wagon with a lead rope.

"Which way?" I said.

"Take the west road," Red Dog said.

I started off, then suddenly remembered something and turned the wagon around and drove back to the house.

"Now what?" he asked.

I just imagined what Daddy Sam would think when he came

back and saw the place a damn bloody mess. I turned the team around and headed back to the house.

"Got to leave Daddy Sam a note lest he thinks it's my blood in there and I've been murdered and kidnapped. Otherwise he'll get some men and come after you and kill you without asking any questions nor giving me time to answer any."

"Well sumbitch," is all he said.

I ran in and found pencil and paper and wrote a hasty note.

Daddy Sam, don't worry, I'm fine. Just a little trouble while you were gone. Will contact you soon as I know where I'm going, which I don't know yet. Love, Lucy.

P.S. Anybody comes asking questions, you don't know nothing.

Then it was back in the wagon and hauling tail to this witchy woman's place Red Dog said could save his life. Said she was practiced in the arts of healing and anyone could save him it would be her.

"What about him?" I said nodding toward the dead lawman whose steer-sized frame jounced beneath the tarp as we rode the rutted road.

"I don't think she could help him none," Red Dog said.

"No, stupid, I mean what we going to do with him?"

"I know a place we can get rid of him," Red Dog said in a coughing sort of way. Frothy blood bubbled from the corner of his mouth. I knew then he'd been lung shot. And I knew too there wasn't much chance he was going to live.

I hurried the horses hawing and snapping the reins but the jostling became too much and Red Dog asked me to slow down.

"Damn it, Lucy, you might as well get you a limb and beat me with it," he moaned.

We rode what seemed like forever, clear till the sun dipped low and threw out a bright spray of its last glory into our eyes.

When we reached a place that had a stand of old cottonwoods that followed along a dry wash, Red Dog told me to turn up in there and I did and we went along about three or four hundred yards and he said for me to stop just where there were some weathered gray planks lying on the ground. Nearby were the remnants of an old stone chimney but no sign of where a house might have stood.

"Stop here," he said. "Drag them boards off that hole they're covering."

I got down and went and dragged the boards away and there was a black hole there wide as a man's shoulders.

I didn't need to be told further what to do.

I tugged and pulled until I had Deputy Book out of the wagon, then dragged him to the edge and pushed him in it. His bulk scraped the walls on the way down that ended in a dull thud and splash then nothing.

"Toss in his clothes too," Red Dog said, half sitting and looking over the side of the wagon.

I grabbed everything of Book's but for his pistol, a right handsome thing with ivory handles, and tossed it all down the well too, then covered the opening over with the planks again.

From there Red Dog directed me to the witchy woman's place and we arrived just as darkness was closing in around us.

"Go up and knock on the door and tell her I'm in the wagon," Red Dog instructed.

So I halted the wagon and got out and went and knocked on the door. It opened and there stood this old hag could have been any breed of human being—Indian, Mexican or Cajun or all three. She had a face like a shrunken old apple and black button eyes. Her hair stood out from her head like a brush pile waiting for the match to be struck. She leaned on a crooked stick for a cane.

"What you want?" she said in a shrew's voice.

"I got Red Dog in the wagon. He's about half dead. Been shot. Needs your help. Said you're the one could resurrect him," I said in short bursts of breath.

She looked at me like she wanted to cook and eat me for supper but then came along and looked in the wagon and poked him with her stick.

"He dead," she said. "Take him away. I can't do no good for a dead man."

He lay there unmoving, eyes closed. My heart sank. Don't ask me why. I couldn't have told you.

"Take him away," she said again with the wave of her hand and started back to her cabin door.

Then he coughed.

"He ain't dead," I shouted. "Come look again."

She turned back and looked in and poked him again, harder this time and he slapped a hand at the stick and said, "Stop doing that, goddamn it. It hurts."

"I guess he ain't so dead, eh?" she said.

"I guess not."

"Okay then. Bring him in, I look."

As I helped Red Dog out of the wagon, I couldn't help myself from saying, "I might just as well consider myself a mule for all the human hauling I've been doing."

He grunted, said, "Maybe you ought to, Lucy. You'd be the best-damn-looking mule I ever rode."

Chapter 22

I never thought it possible but Red Dog was still alive come the dawn, his breathing ragged, and all night long he moaned and talked crazy things and begged for water, which I brought him in a pail with a metal dipper, and fed it to him till the water leaked down the sides of his mouth. I wet a cloth and place it on his forehead until it grew warm and then dipped it and cooled it again and put it back. The old wretch came in and out of the room jabbering nonsense while applying poultices to Red Dog's wound. Each time, he would cry out in delirium.

"He gonna make it?" I'd ask. She'd simply look at me with her crazy eyes and go out again.

I took the liberty to look beneath the sheet at one of the things she used as a poultice and it sure as hell looked like a chicken's heart to me.

I am not by nature a praying person, don't know what to think about all that in spite of Mama's exhortations to me to believe in the Lord Jesus Christ as the one true Savior and that God was a good and kindly God. But I didn't see it that way, especially now that both my mother and husband had died so violently. Why would a good and kindly God let killers murder my family and then run loose? But suddenly I remembered, I was now a killer too.

So I prayed. A little, not hoping for great results.

"Lord, I am a sinner, it is true. But it has never been in my heart to do wrong, and the wrong I have done has been more accidental then intended. I imagine you might overlook a thing like that if you're up there listening.

"Now I don't know if Red Dog here killed my husband, or even my mama, but he saved me from some awful bad situation with that mean ugly ol' Deputy Book, and for that I'm grateful. He took a bullet on account of me, one that might kill him. I'd ask you to look at the big picture here and not just its parts, if you would. Thank you."

I drifted in and out of sleep as I sat by Red Dog's bedside. I'd hear the old crone snoring from time to time in the other room where she lay upon a narrow cot by the woodstove. I wondered what witchy women dreamed about if they dreamed at all.

A claw of a hand shook me awake.

She was there holding a cup of something that smelled downright awful.

"You drink," she said handing the cup out for me.

"It's him that's sick," I said.

"You drink."

So I took it expecting not to get more'n a swallow down as badly as it smelt, but upon tasting it, I was surprised at its unusual taste.

"This ain't half bad," I said.

She'd already gone to the bed and pulled back the covers and removed the old poultice, chewed up a new one and spat it onto the wound then bandaged him up again. She lit some sage and waved the smoke over him. Definitely an Indian thing, I thought.

Then she pointed at him and the cup and said, "Give him when he open eyes."

I nodded and she went out.

Two more days and nights came and went and Red Dog hadn't died, though he hadn't gotten much better, either.

Then on the fourth day, he woke and looked around and said, "Well, am I dead or is that you sitting there, Lucy, and not some angel come to collect me."

"Do you really believe in that stuff?" I asked.

"Maybe so, maybe not. There's things humans don't know about," he said.

"Well, you are alive, but I sure as hell don't see how you are."

He raised his hands and felt delicately with his fingers at the bandaged wound.

"Don't feel too bad," he said.

"Miracle upon miracles."

"Where's my clothes?"

"In a heap I reckon," I said. "Pardon me if I did not find time to wash and mend them."

He offered me a sly grin.

"Well, what you been doing all this time? Every time I opened my eyes, you had yours closed. Never saw a woman sleep as much as you do."

"Don't try and be funny," I said.

"We got to get going soon as possible," he said.

"Why? Nobody knows we're here."

"They will soon enough," he said. "I don't think it will take the law too long to figure out we killed that deputy and send a bunch of fellows to come looking for us. No, we got to clear out."

"I can convince them of the truth," I said, "that it was me who shot him and not you, that you were only trying to save my life."

"We already went over that. They'll want their pound of flesh," he said.

"You must have done something real bad to be so jumpy about the law," I said.

"Jesus God, you sure ask a damn lot of questions."

"I like to know who I'm dealing with."

"Me," he said.

"Well, gee whiz now I feel a whole lot better," I said sarcastically.

"What's in that cup?"

I looked at the smelly brew the witchy woman had concocted, reached for it and handed it to him.

"Hell if I know what it is, but don't let the smell put you off. Sort of invigorating whatever it is."

He smelled it, flinched then took a gulp.

"Does have a bit of a bite to it, don't it?"

"Getting back to this bad business you're involved in," I said.

"I killed a man," he said.

"Over what?"

"Some might call it love," he said. "Not sure that I would."

"A woman?" I clarified.

"No, a damn mule," he said. "Of course it was a woman."

"Let me guess," I said. "She was married and her husband walked in."

He shook his head as if I was the dumbest creature in the world.

"No, it wasn't nothing like that. This fellow way back thought I was messing around with his wife. I wasn't, though I did sort of like her. He came after me raged with jealousy, claiming that I'd molested her. I never. Found out later she was fooling around with a friend of mine and rather than tell the truth, she said it was me. I did my best to talk him out of fighting me, but he was a damn fool and paid for it with his life."

"You kill her too, seeing as how she lied on you?"

"No, but maybe I should have."

"So that's it then, the whole of it?"

"Yep."

"Seems to me the court might have taken into account your

side of it," I said.

"They might have, but this fellow was Indian Police over in the Going Snake territory. The deck was already stacked against me."

"So you killed a lawman?"

"Makes us even, don't it?" he said.

"Sort of does, I reckon."

"It's plain and simple: I get caught, I'll hang."

"I believe you're a decent and goodly man, Red," I said. "And I won't abandon you in your time of need."

He looked relieved.

"Thing is," I said. "That slug is still in you. The witchy woman poked around a little but she didn't dig that bullet out of you. Probably not at all safe to move you more than necessary."

"I'd just as soon die by that bullet than to get strangulated by a rope," he said.

"Yeah, I reckon I would as well," I said.

"You sure look good, Lucy. If I wasn't so bunged up . . ." He didn't finish the thought but I knew what he was thinking.

"Men ever think about anything else?" I asked.

"Not too much," he said with a pained grin.

The witchy woman came in just then. Looked at Red Dog then at me.

"Talk too much," she said, then turned and left.

Chapter 23

Three days more and we got Red Dog loaded in the back of the wagon and lit out for the borderland. Red Dog said he knew a fellow down in the Texas panhandle could put us up for a time. Said we'd be safe at least until he got all his parts working again.

I didn't say it but I was planning as soon as I got him down there to his friend's place, on heading for Daddy Sam's again. Figured I'd clear Red's name and my own and tell what happened. I believed the truth was the only way to clear my conscience.

The trip overland was long and arduous and we'd not make more than twenty miles in a day, if that. Some days it rained and turned the roads to mush and we'd make even less progress.

We camped near creeks when we could find them and in out of the wind, choosing to ride down into arroyos when we could. Otherwise we suffered on that open country, wind and rain and even a hailstorm once that left bruises on our arms and back.

The night wind was generally cold and had us shivering even wrapped in blankets. Red Dog suffered more so because of his wound which still leaked blood through his bandages and caused him to tremble something fierce so that I had to wrap up with him like we were a pair of cocoons, or more like raccoons, he said trying to make light of the situation.

Even huddled up together didn't seem to do much good. I tried building us a fire but the wind wouldn't allow for it.

Our first night after leaving the witchy woman's was terrible. We'd ridden through an ice storm and were soaked through in wet clothes and I'd not been so miserable in all my days.

"Seems like the entire world is against us," I said through chattering teeth.

"I've felt that way most of my life," he said. "You ought to try being a mostly Indian in a white man's world."

"You ought to try being a woman in any sort of man's world, period," I said.

"Shoot, if I was, I wouldn't lack for nothing," he said. Trying to be funny, I guess.

"Us women are treated no better than cattle. Just some man's property. Oh sure, they'll fight and die over us, but only because they want to own us same as they would a horse somebody tried stealing from them."

"I don't know how you can judge it if you've not been a man," he grumped.

"Well, men are born damn fools, I'll give you that. Mama always said God scooped out their brains and filled their heads with mush. So, no, I wouldn't wish to be a man not even for a day. You ever wished you were born a woman?" I asked. "Seriously?"

"Hell no," he grunted.

We tried everything and anything to distract ourselves from our misery but nothing seemed to work.

"The hell I ever ended up being in this situation?" I said.

"Don't be sour, Lucy, it doesn't suit you."

"You don't know a thing about me," I angrily reminded him once again.

"No, but it ain't for lack of trying to get to know you," he said. To which I did not respond.

"Why you're about to shake clear out of your skin, Lucy," he said. "Maybe we was to get naked under these blankets so we can press together and share our body heat."

"That some old Indian trick, is it?" I asked.

"Matter of fact, it is."

"Not a chance I'm going to get naked with you under these blankets," I argued.

"Oh, get over yourself, Lucy. I mean you're a fine-looking woman—and I ought to know since I've seen pretty much all of you already, but I'm about froze to death and if it will keep us warmer what's the problem? We can at least give it a try."

I don't think I'd ever been so cold and wet and miserable and so I relented because being naked with a man like Red Dog was preferable to shivering to death.

We shucked out of our clothes and wrapped ourselves together and in a matter of minutes we started benefitting from each other's body heat and I no longer cared what we were, naked or dressed, friends or enemies, at least we were warmer than we had been by a damn sight. I lay on my side spooned in behind him.

"Now ain't that better?" he said.

"I have to admit it is," I said.

"Least we can get us some sleep now," he said.

But I was already dozing off by the time the words left his lips.

I woke with the first gray light and found that sometime in the middle of the night we'd switched positions and he was spooned into my back. His hand also happened to be cupped around my breast. I did not move at first for feeling mortified but why exactly I couldn't say, for it seemed as natural as anything on one hand and as wrong as anything on the other.

I lay thinking about it as the sky overhead lightened to a still grayness while the wind yet whispered cold and I feared a threat of rain. And to tell the truth, lying there like that, pressed together and feeling so warm, I didn't even want to ever be cold again, even if I had to stay like that the rest of my days.

Still, I gently removed his hand and scooted away and dressed quickly in dry clothes as he came awake and watched me with the hungry eyes of a normal man and not one shot and living with a slug of lead still in him.

He sat up and moaned and said, "Damn I'm stiff and sore."

I helped find him some dry clothes as well and helped him dress into them. Then I pulled from the gunnysack a couple of corn cakes and some deer jerky and we ate a hasty breakfast after heading off into the bushes for our morning constitution.

Then rode on.

"How will we know when we get to Texas?" I asked. "Will there be some big sign stating such? For to me the land looks all the same no matter."

"There will be a trading post at the border run by a one-eyed Frenchman named LaRue if he's still there. I've dealt with him before."

"How do you know this man?"

"He married one of my wives."

"One of your wives?"

"I had two or three. He married one—Janice Two Birds. Her people were Muscogee Creek. It didn't last long between us. I heard she was fooling around with the Frenchman LaRue when he ran a store over in Muscogee. It took me a while to figure out how she was able to afford so many pretty things."

"You didn't go and kill them over it?"

He laughed.

"Hell no, I was glad he took her off my hands."

"And this other wife of yours, what about her?"

"Oh, we're still married, I think. She was also Muscogee Creek—Janice's cousin, Mary Little Horse. I started fooling around with her after I learned Janice was fooling around with

LaRue. Figured why not, fair's fair, eh? But then I learned she was one of those two-spirits women so I didn't fool with her after that."

"Two-spirits women?"

He looked at me slyly. He'd taken over the driving, for something to do, he said.

"You know, women who . . . it don't make a difference who they share their bed with—men or other women."

"Oh," I said. "Other women? Really?"

"That shock you?"

"Nothing shocks me. Well, maybe a little."

"Good," he said.

"But you didn't divorce her, you're still married to her?"

"Ah, I figured someday I'd get around to it but then that trouble came up with the policeman's wife and I had to leave out of there."

"It's some life you've lived, mister."

"And I ain't done yet, I hope."

Two more long days and nights of travel, each night eating a meager supper of creek water, jerky and corn cakes, then wrapping up together, naked as jaybirds and telling each other things about ourselves to while away the time till we fell asleep.

I told him about Mama, all the places we'd lived, the lovers she'd had. Told him about Frank James too, about how I believed he was my real father.

He seemed duly impressed.

"Now those were some wild boys," he said. "I heard about them when I was still a kid. My father would read to me from the *Police Gazette* of their exploits. Said they invented bank robbing. I always thought it would take a lot of nerve to do what they did."

"I reckon," I said as Red Dog spooned against me, his arm around my waist this time, thinking I wouldn't protest if his hand moved up and cupped my breast again, for I was feeling a bit antsy lying there naked with a naked man. In spite of all that had transpired these last several days I was still a young woman with a young woman's wants and needs, I'll be honest about it.

I never was one shy about making sex. I always liked it from the first, even though the first wasn't that great and mostly clumsy. It left me with an itchy feeling for more. I reckon Mama and me were much the same sort of women.

I remembered as still a girl looking forward to the day when I would marry and have all the sex I wanted without recrimination or guilt for enjoying it. But my dream had not lasted long enough and now I was a widow far too soon and not yet grown out of my womanly desires.

"It must have been something for the Jameses and Youngers to get shot all to hell up there in Minnesota trying to rob that bank," Red Dog said, his breath warm against the back of my neck. "But Frank and Jesse got clean away. It was the Youngers paid the price."

"And Clell Miller, too," I said, remembering Clell and how he wasn't your typical bad man.

"You know him too, Clell Miller?"

"Yes, he and Mama were friends of a sort," I said without going into detail.

Red Dog rambled on about the James boys, and I was half sorry I ever brought it up, for my mood was for something other than swapping stories, something real and in the moment. But I also knew I wasn't going to make the first move, either. And then I did.

I reached my hand back and touched his hip and he stopped talking, as if that simple touch had poleaxed him.

Neither of us said anything. It was just the sound of our breathing and the night wind that seemed to scrub the blackness and finger its way along.

His hand crept up from my waist, his fingers trailing light as feathers along my ribs. I remained still as a rabbit hiding from a hunter.

Then his hand cupped under my right breast and caused a sharp intake of my breath.

He held it there and my own hand did not move from his hip. It was as if we were doing this slow dance, like two blind people trying to feel our way to some sort of discovery that would tell us everything.

"Lucy," he whispered.

"Yes," I said.

"Do you like that?"

"I don't hate it."

"But do you like it?"

I hesitated as if the rest of my life depended on what my answer was.

"Yes," I said. "I like it."

"Good," he said.

His forefinger and thumb gently massaged my nipple and goose bumps prickled my skin all over.

"Do you like that too?"

"Yes, I like that too."

He kissed the nape of my neck.

"And that?"

I nodded.

The wind played through the chaparral and shifted the scent of sage. The night was black as a chalkboard and the sky salted with stars.

I felt his erection throb against my backside and turned over so that we lay face-to-face.

"I don't want you to think . . ."

He pressed his mouth to mine cutting me off. I kissed him back.

"I don't think nothing, Lucy," he whispered huskily. "We're just here and who we are and this is what this is and nothing more unless you want it to be. But for right now this is just what it is."

"Yes," I said and reached down between us and took hold of him and raised my leg over his hip and guided him into me and in doing so let the rest of the world be what it was just as we were what we were: two insignificant souls on a windswept tract of nowhere land under midnight sky and stars waiting for dark to turn into day. And our passion kept us warm and safe and distant from all trouble.

And later as he slept pressed up against me, or I him, I thought of our act as simple and sweet—as simple and sweet as the taste of cold plums.

It was all I could think or wanted to think.

I didn't want to think about grievous things, about murder and bloodletting and sorrow and loss. There was plenty of time yet to think of those things.

But for that moment, that peaceful moment, I just wanted to think about the sweetness of life and that moment.

And then I closed my eyes and slept, mercifully warm and feeling loved, even if it wasn't love.

Morning came too soon, too early and neither of us wanted to rise and dress in the cold dawn nor eat the scant breakfast of jerky and corn cakes or drink old water. But eat and drink it we did and most miserable we felt because our moments of pleasure had long since passed. We started off down the road for the border hoping upon hope we'd find the trading post this day, before nightfall at least and get something decent to eat and maybe a real bed to sleep in.

We did not speak about last night I think because each of us wanted to hold onto that memory for as long as possible. A good memory is one that will carry you through the hard cold reality of life that stares at you like a daft person.

"If I remember correctly, Lucy," Red Dog said. "LaRue used to have a small room he'd let to weary travelers. It might be we could sleep in a regular bed tonight if you're interested?"

"Is that a proposal?" I asked.

"I reckon it is, in a way. Just thought you'd like sleeping in a real bed. I don't have to sleep in it with you. I'm fine sleeping in the wagon."

"I'll keep it in mind," I said.

"Well, I wish you would."

It was all we said that even came close to discussing what had happened.

I was already beginning to lose some of that sweet feeling. How could I not? Like life its very self, pleasure, once it is born, begins to die, to become a memory that loses shape with time.

Chapter 24

When we reached the borderline there stood the trading post as Red Dog predicted and not a day too soon. We were both tired and half starved for decent food and it was a welcome oasis in a land that otherwise didn't have much to recommend it. It stood at the crossroads—empty though they were, that ran east and west, north and south, to where and from where I knew not which.

When we crossed to that store, Red Dog said, we were then in Texas.

"How the hell can you tell?" I asked.

He shrugged.

"Can't exactly, just is."

Red Dog had told me during our journey that many men had lost their way in that empty country and became forever disappeared. Said it was part of what some called the Llano Estacado, or Staked Plains. We'd hardly seen so much as a tree in three days and hadn't come across a single soul on the roads.

"I don't care where we're at," I said. "I am about hungry enough to eat one of these horses," and he said, "I am too, Lucy."

We got down from the wagon stiff and sore-bottomed. Nothing harder than a wagon seat to make you feel like you've been spanked by a cruel schoolmaster.

"I got to pee real bad," I said.

"Yonder is a privy," he said nodding toward one that sat off to the side and just slightly behind the east wall of the log structure. It had a moon cut in the door which meant it was for women. Well, at least that is what moons cut in privy doors used to mean. Stars were cut for the men. But anymore those old symbols had more or less gone out of style and you used what you found. I just hoped I'd not run into anybody already in there, and if I did, well they might just get wet. I hurried to it as Red Dog said he'd meet me inside the trader's.

I finished up right quick especially on account of a big spiderweb up in the corner. Down in El Paso some of the better hotels had indoor plumbing. And what a luxury it was. I wished I was there right now still enjoying my honeymoon, or at least that part of it when it came to eating in nice restaurants, shopping and soaking in a bathtub and going about feeling newly made—before all this sad and terrible death business.

I met up with Red Dog inside the store standing at a wood counter talking to a man behind it.

"I ordered us dinner," he said. "This here is LaRue."

"My wife, she cooks," LaRue said with a French accent wheezed through his long bony nose.

He was a wiry, hatchet-faced fellow with heavy black mustache and eyes that trapped the flames guttering in the glass chimneys of the several oil lamps. It was dim inside the store, like being in a cave. I noted a woman farther back rattling pots and a big potbelly stove. The scent of food mixed with that of leather goods, sage, and wood must.

The store was jammed cheek to jowl with dry goods: shelves of canned foods, blankets and bullets. From the rafters hung several saddles, coiled ropes and bundles of sage. There were jars of candy, boxes of cigars, barrels of flour and sugar and beans.

LaRue was well braced with a pair of matched pistols hooked to a bullet belt fastened round his narrow waist. I figured living way out here alone he needed to be pretty well armed against pillagers and miscreants.

"Sit, sit," he said, pointing with his hand to a small table just inside the door with two chairs. "Marie will have your food in a moment, eh?"

"You remember me?" Red Dog asked.

"Oh, yes," LaRue said. "Last time I see you, you ride a big white horse, eh? Had three or four friends with you."

"That's right," Red Dog said.

"Was men after you, eh?" LaRue grinned. "You run like the devil."

"No, other way around," Red Dog said, casting a worried glance at me. "We were chasing some fellows is what it was."

"Oh, yes, sure, I remember now. Marie, hurry up with the food, eh?"

"Coming!" she called and quickly came carrying two plates.

"Special of the day," LaRue said. "Zee hare. I shoot them just this morning. So fresh he is almost still breathing." LaRue laughed at his own humor.

The rabbit was fixed in a stew with carrots and wild onions and quartered potatoes and a thick brown sauce. It was so delicious, I nearly fainted. LaRue stood by watching us eat, seemingly enjoying himself as much as we were.

"Is good, yes?"

All I could manage was "Mmmm" and smacked my lips.

Red Dog ate like they were going to hang him in ten minutes.

"Could we get another plate each?" he said.

"Marie!"

The woman came. She was quite pretty, dark and small and dressed in a faded cotton dress. Her straw-colored hair was twisted into a long braid that hung nearly to her waist but with sprigs of it loose and plastered to her thin face. She had high cheekbones and pale lips to match her pale eyes. She was terribly thin like a half-starved child. There was a sadness about her, it seemed to me. I wondered if she was LaRue's daughter.

We ate our second plate and ordered a piece of gooseberry pie.

"Marie, she cook everything good, no?"

"Yes," we said almost simultaneously.

"So this your wife, eh?" LaRue asked.

Red Dog and I shared a glance.

"No," he said. "She's a friend. We're just traveling together."

"Ah, yes, I remember now, you have a wife who is like you, Indian no?"

"Yes, that's right," Red Dog said. "You have a good memory."

LaRue tapped the side of his head with his finger.

"LaRue, he don't forget, no."

We had coffee with our pie and while it was strong enough to take the varnish off a board, it still set good with the pie.

"How about a little of the wine, good for the belly," he said rubbing his stomach. "I make myself two years ago now. Just right, eh."

"Sure," Red Dog said. "What the hell."

I was less inclined, but partook anyway. The three of us, Red Dog, me and LaRue. He hadn't invited the woman to join us. She was still in the back clanging pots and pans.

The wine was sweet and strong and it made me a little light-headed.

"You still rent a room for travelers?" Red Dog asked.

"Oui, sure, sure. Can let you have room and meals altogether, five dollars, okay?" He held up five fingers. Thinking I guess, we couldn't count.

"What do you think?" Red Dog asked me.

"Is it a good bed?"

"Oui, very good bed. Big enough for you both, and maybe one more." Again with the laughter.

"We'll take it," Red Dog said.

"Good, good. Marie!" he summoned with a flick of his fingers.

The woman came forth wiping her bone-thin hands on a flour-sack apron that wasn't much better than the dress she wore.

"Show these peoples the room, eh?"

She nodded.

"You go with Marie, she show you," LaRue said.

As we walked out he called, "Marie!" She stopped but didn't look back.

"When you finish, come fix my supper, eh?"

She nodded and we followed her around to the side where a room had been cobbled onto the trading post. She flipped the latch to the door and pushed it open.

Still she hadn't spoken.

The interior was small and dimly lit from the later afternoon sun coming in through a small square four-paned window of watery glass. There was just enough room for a bed. It had a patched quilt and two feather pillows.

"It looks like it used to be a woodshed," Red Dog said after Marie left. "I can sleep in the wagon and you can sleep in here."

"Yes, it might be best," I said.

He gave me a questioning look then said, "Yes, if that's what you want."

"I mean last night was . . ."

"You don't have to say anything about last night," he said. "I wasn't expecting anything then and I ain't now. It was just something happened. I don't regret it and I hope you don't."

"I appreciate that," I said.

"Well, all right, then."

"All right, then."

We both stood there a moment judging whether we should

change our minds, but that moment had passed and so he went out.

I found a box of matches by the oil lamp and set the wick aflame then adjusted it to give the room a nice warm glow. It wasn't yet dark but I felt like I could sleep for a week.

I lay on the bed and quickly dozed off. When I opened my eyes and looked out the window it was dark but I saw something extraordinary: the woman was walking alone in the moonlight as if a wandering wraith seeking some long-lost home.

I grabbed the quilt and threw it over my shoulders and went out. Red Dog had pulled the wagon around to the far side of the trading post and was no doubt asleep in the wagon's bed. There wasn't any light on inside the store. All was quiet.

I walked out to where the woman was now standing looking off toward the north as if waiting for something.

"Are you all right?" I asked.

It startled her and I quickly apologized.

"Didn't mean to frighten you," I said.

The look she gave me made it appear as if she was about to cry.

I touched her shoulder lightly.

"Is everything all right?" I said again.

"Yes," she said so softly I could barely hear.

"I saw you from the window. I couldn't sleep either," I said.

"What is it like?" she asked.

"What is what like?"

"Out there, where you came from?"

"Well, I mean . . . it's like anyplace else," is all I could think to tell her.

She wore a shawl around her shoulders and I realized for once the night wind wasn't blowing. It was still and almost lovely with the moon full overhead bright and round as a silver dollar. She was hugging herself as carefully as if her arms were the arms of a lover.

"Where did you and LaRue hail from?"

She shrugged.

"Saint Louis," she said. "But it's been ever so long ago I can't recall much of what it even looked like."

"It must get lonely out here. Are there neighbors close by?"

She shook her head.

"It's only travelers who come now and then. Sometimes it's weeks between times when they come and they usually only stay long enough to buy something or eat and then they are gone again. Nobody wants to be around here any longer than they have to be."

"Well, I suppose they bring news from other places," I suggested.

Again she shook her head.

"He don't let me talk to them. I'm all the time working, cooking, straightening, cleaning, taking care of him, butchering the meat he brings in."

"Doesn't your father know a girl needs friends?" I asked.

She looked at me then.

"He's not my pa," she said. "He's my husband."

"How'd you end up with a man old as him, pretty and young as you are?"

She touched the side of her face, as if overly conscious of who she was.

"He bought me," she said.

"Bought you?"

"From a family in Saint Louis."

"Forgive my ignorance, but I don't understand. Lincoln freed all the slaves some time ago. People can't be bought and sold no more."

"I was an orphan. Me and my brother, Willy. We was sent out here on a orphan train and they was our assigned family. But all they really wanted was hands to work for them. Slave is more what it was than anything. My brother took sick and died. I reckon he was the lucky one. They worked me hard, then one night the man started visiting me in my room."

"He did something to you," I said.

She nodded.

"His wife found out and blamed me for corrupting her husband. Beat me bad and sold me to LaRue for fifty dollars. LaRue brought me here. That was ten, twelve years ago. I was but fourteen years old, still a girl, but they seen to it I wasn't to be a girl for long."

"And there is no way you can escape him?"

She looked at me with the saddest eyes I'd ever seen on anybody.

"Where would I escape to? What would I do?"

Then LaRue was calling her.

"Marie! Marie!"

"I have to go," she said.

I stood there while she hurried back to the house then went to the wagon and shook the foot of Red Dog.

"Wake up," I said.

He came alert.

"What is it?"

"Come on in the room, I don't want to be alone."

He cast aside his blanket and eased out of the wagon and followed me to the room.

"No point in you sleeping in that hard old wagon," I said.

"What made you change your mind?" he asked.

"I just did."

We lay down together in silence as if both of us were afraid of what the other might do or say.

"LaRue's wife," I said.

"What about her?"

"Hers is a very sad story."

"You want to tell me about it?"

"No."

"Why not?"

"Because it will just make me sadder than I already am."

"Is there anything I can do?"

"You can kill LaRue and take her with us," I said.

"If that's what you really want, I'll do it," he said.

"No. I only wish it."

Then we fell silent. I fell silent.

"If I wasn't so sad, I would make sex with you," I said after several minutes.

"You mean love," he said.

"No, I mean sex," I said. "Love is something entirely different."

"Best we get some sleep, then," he said.

"Best we do."

Chapter 25

We were eating down a breakfast of fried eggs, hash and diced potatoes when the riders came in. Two of them.

They strode in, their spurs jingling like loose change. They both wore long dusters that hung to the tops of their boots and creased crown Stetson hats banded by sweat stains and brims hand rolled. You could see the bulge of their pistols under their dusters easily enough.

I looked at Red Dog and he at me.

They didn't see us at first, those two men. They went straight to the counter where Marie stood. LaRue was out back splitting firewood. You could hear the crack of his ax blade into the wood.

"How do, Marie," one of them said touching the brim of his hat.

She offered a weak smile to the man.

"Where's LaRue?" he asked.

"Chopping wood round back," she said.

" 'Bout time that damn Frenchie did somethin' round here," the other man said in a jovial way.

"Got any grub fixed to eat?" the first man said.

"Yes," she said.

Then the one man turned, the one with the heavy dark beard, and he looked at Red Dog and me as if he'd known all along we were there. He didn't speak, just looked at the two of us then turned back to the counter.

"Business is good today, eh?" he said to Marie.

"A little, yes."

Then the other man turned halfway and glanced at us and held his stare for a lot longer than I was comfortable with. Felt like he was undressing me with his eyes and maybe he was, but it wasn't anything that hadn't happened before so I held his stare until he turned back again.

"What you got on the stove?" the first one asked.

"Chili," she said.

"Give us two bowls and a couple of bottles of beer."

"Sure," she said and disappeared toward the kitchen area.

One of the men asked the other: "You want a cigar too, for after we eat?"

"Sure. Nothing like a good smoke afterwards."

Then the fellow reached into a humidor and took out two cigars and put them in his shirt pocket and then turned slightly again and looked at Red Dog and me.

"I seen you somewhere before?" the man said to Red Dog.

I couldn't see his hands, but I wondered if maybe Red Dog had slipped his revolver out and was holding it cocked under the table.

"You don't look like anyone I know," Red Dog said coolly.

"Gyp," the man said to the other one. "Don't that look like Ed Hardy?" The one he called Gyp turned halfway round and looked.

"He does."

"Your name Ed Hardy?" the man with the beard asked Red Dog.

"No, it ain't."

"You sure do favor him. Had red hair like you. Maybe not as dark skinned though."

"Say, Gyp, wasn't Ed Hardy killed over in Waco some months back?"

Gyp rubbed his chin.

"Trying to think if he was or was it Ed Pierce was killed in Waco?"

"It could have been Ed Pierce. Maybe I got him and Ed Hardy mixed up."

"Well, if it was Ed Hardy," Gyp said, "then that fellow there surely couldn't be him."

"What about you?" the one with the beard said to me directly. "Who might you be?"

"Rose Dunn," I lied. I knew the name from stories Mama told me about her. Mama said Rose used to be the teenage sweetheart of an outlaw named Bittercreek Newcomb and that her brothers gunned him down for the reward. According to Mama's account, some say that Rose set her lover up and shared in the reward money. I figured if all that was true, then Rose was quite a woman.

"Rose Dunn? We heard that name, ain't we, Gyp?"

Gyp thought a moment then said, No, he did not believe he had.

Marie came then with their bowls of chili and bottles of beer on a wood tray and set it down before them and they paid her for it and the two cigars saying they'd take and eat outside since there wasn't any place in to sit.

She pocketed the money and watched them leave.

"We best move on," Red Dog said.

"Who are those men?" I asked Marie.

"That's Gyp Jones and the other is Lee Colt. They are Texas Rangers. They come around every now and then just to check on us—LaRue and me."

"Yeah, we best get going," Red Dog said a little more anxious now. "Why don't you buy whatever we might need for the rest of the trip and I'll hitch the team."

I nodded and Red Dog left and I went to shopping.

I bought myself a new shirt and a pair of trousers and a Stetson like men wore. I wanted to look like a man just in case word had gotten spread I might have been kidnapped and the law was looking for me, a woman. I got canned peaches and some of potted meat.

"Did you sleep good last night?" Marie asked.

"Yes. You?"

She shrugged and looked sorrowful.

"You know how it is," she said.

"Yes, I think I do."

Her face went friendly and soft—one woman to another, a secret shared without speaking, just knowing. I asked if there was a place I could change into my new duds and get out of my old and she took me back to a small storeroom behind a curtain and I changed and left the old things in the corner.

When I came out I heard LaRue outside talking to the rangers, asking them how they were and them asking him about the folks inside, the woman and that fellow who came out and was hitching the team.

"You know them people?" one of the rangers asked.

"Just people stopped by for the night," LaRue said. But, in fact, he had claimed to have known Red Dog and must be covering for him.

I breathed relief.

"Can I get you anything else?" Marie asked having packed a small box with the foodstuffs.

"You want to go with us?" I whispered as LaRue's voice got louder as he came in.

"Can't," she said.

"Why can't you?"

LaRue stepped back out when one of the men called, "LaRue, come here."

"He would track me down and just bring me back and I'd pay for leaving him."

"What if we didn't let that happen?" I asked.

"Oh, I wish it would be so," she said shaking her head. "But like I said, I was to run away where would I go and what would I do?"

"We could maybe help you. You could always worry about that later, once you escaped from here."

Then LaRue came in again and went straight over to the counter.

"Don't worry," he said. "About them," indicating with a toss of his head the rangers outside.

"I'm not worried," I said. "Why should I be?"

He offered me a quizzical look.

"No reason," he said.

I started to pick up the box and carry it out, but he took hold of it instead and carried it out to the wagon for me. I could feel the rangers' eyes following me. They had squatted just outside eating their bowls of chili with large spoons, their bottled beer set down in the dust.

"You all take care, Rose," one of them said. I kept walking without comment.

LaRue set the box in the wagon bed.

Red Dog was just finishing stringing the last trace on the off horse and running the reins back to the wagon.

"Don't worry," LaRue said to Red Dog like a coconspirator. "I didn't tell them nothing. Maybe they are looking for you?"

"They ain't looking for me for nothing," Red Dog said.

"Well, who knows what anyone is looking for, eh?" LaRue said. "Sometimes a few extra dollars helps a man loose his tongue when other men are trying to get him to say certain things."

"You threatening me?" Red Dog asked.

"Oh, no, I'd never do that, mon dieu!"

"Like hell you wouldn't," Red Dog said.

"I swear it," LaRue said raising his hands in supplication.

I'd climbed up into the wagon and sat and saw Red Dog glance past LaRue toward the two rangers, one of them sipping from his beer and watching the three of us carefully now.

Red Dog leaned in close to LaRue.

"You sic those lawdogs on me, I will come back here and cut your throat after I kill 'em. We clear?"

LaRue's face grew rosy of a sudden.

"Oh, LaRue never say anything about you. Not to worry, eh?"

"I'm not worried. Just make sure you don't slip up."

Then Red Dog climbed up and sat beside me, took up the reins and without a further word or glance snapped and hawed the horses into getting up and off we went in no real hurry, Red Dog playing it cool.

"You wanted in Texas?" I asked calmly.

"Might be," he said.

"Might or do you know and just aren't saying?"

He shrugged.

"We'll be all right, Lucy, just as long as I can get to my friend's place."

I looked back after we'd gone a mile or so but didn't see anyone following.

"I don't think we have to worry," I said.

Red Dog smiled in that way of his that made me want to do nice things for him.

"I just said that, didn't I, Lucy?"

"Yes, I guess you did."

He patted my knee and said, "I like your hat."

Chapter 26

We camped that evening by a willow-lined creek thin as a hair ribbon and not deep enough to wet your ankles, but at least it was water, which was scarce enough that if Noah had lived in north Texas he'd never have had to worry about getting flooded out, I remember Mama as having said.

Mama favored cities and wasn't much given to the hinterlands of any place. That is why it was so surprising to me she'd agreed to be moved to outside of Hadley's Jump with Daddy Sam.

She'd told me a long time ago that when her own daddy and mama had come to Texas from Indiana they'd come down through the panhandle and said it was the most godforsaken-looking country she'd ever laid eyes on. Said the cows outnumbered the people a thousand to one. Her daddy being a barber by trade kept on heading for Dallas where she quoted him as saying to her mama Ethylene, I don't believe there is enough heads of hair to cut in this upland country to keep me and you and baby Belle in beans for a day much less a week.

Mama always smiled so prettily when she talked about her folks. I never got to meet either of them. They were both dead and gone by the time I came into the world. All she had was a copper-framed tintype of them. They could have been anybody.

I set out to make the evening meal while Red Dog gathered what he could for a fire, which was dried cow flop. The green willows were the only form of tree wood in sight and he said they wouldn't burn.

But for the smell, the cow flop made an admirable fire and we ate heated beans in a can and potted meat and washed it down with a pot of Arbuckle coffee.

"Damn Lucy, if you could cook I'd marry you," Red Dog teased.

"Well you can set your hand to the breakfast if you think you can do better," I said.

He laughed.

"Shit, you ought to learn to take it easy, Lucy. I was just foolin' with you. You're always so damn serious."

"Maybe it's because I don't see nothing humorous about our situation," I said.

"Well, neither do I, but least we can do is not be so grim about it. Least we ain't dead."

"No but there is plenty of others who are," I reminded him.

He grew quiet then. The light of the fire shone against his face making it look like bronze and I felt kindly bad for being harsh with him.

"I'm sorry," I said. "I just got so many things on my mind is all."

He looked up, the flame light now leaped into his black eyes.

"It's okay, I understand," he said. "It won't be but a few more days and we'll get to Buck's place and won't have to worry about being caught by the law."

I wanted to tell him right then that as soon as we got to his friend's place, I was heading back to Hadley's Jump. Alone. I aimed to tell the truth of what happened and take the blame for Deputy Book's death and face whatever I had to face because of it. But more importantly I still wanted to find out who killed Mama and Jim and I couldn't do that hiding out in Texas.

Way off to the west we saw the flash of lightning.

"You think it will rain?" I asked.

"No, it's too far off," he said.

"Well, reckon we ought to turn in and get an early start on tomorrow."

"Reckon so," he said.

He went and hobbled the horses while I scrubbed the tin plates in the creek using handfuls of sand and grit and water.

"How is it you want us to sleep tonight?" he asked as the fire burned down to just a small flame.

"Apart," I said.

He nodded.

I got up in the wagon bed and fixed my pallet and he got down under the wagon and fixed his.

"Good night, Lucy," he said.

"Good night," I said.

I wondered what it was my heart wanted or didn't want when it came to Red Dog. I just couldn't figure it. For one thing, even though I hadn't ever had the chance to learn to love Jim like I should have, his death was still too soon for me to consider taking on another lover. On the other hand, Jim was gone forever and good men, in my experience, was hard to come by. Every man I'd ever become intimately acquainted with had their good points but just as many bad ones, too. Jim included. And certainly Red Dog had already proved himself to be no prince of purity and possibly a killer of the first order.

Mama had told me once, "Lucy, you can get mighty taken with lots of men for lots of reasons, but just know that most have a dark place they'll take you too if you ain't careful and that is a place you do not want to go, trust me."

Then she told me by way of example how once when she was just a teenage girl of being taken to a tent revival meeting run by a firebrand preacher. How she'd become mesmerized by him and how later her folks had invited him home to their place for a chicken dinner and offered him to stay the night.

"Well, he snuck into my room, Lucy, that mean skunk.

Clamped his hand over my mouth and whispered the worst obscenities into my ear. Told me if I didn't let him do what he wanted he'd kill us all then set the house on fire with us in it, said that he'd done it before. I was so scared I peed myself."

I asked her what happened then.

She had tears in her eyes telling it and by the time she finished, I had tears in my eyes too.

"Lord, Mama, he might have killed you all anyway," I remember saying.

"I know it," she confessed. "But he didn't. He just went off like nothing had happened."

"Why didn't you tell Granddaddy after he left so maybe he could have tracked him down or called the high sheriff?"

"You don't understand, Lucy," she said. "I was so scared, and the deed was already done and I felt I was the blame for it. You see, earlier before dinner, he asked if I'd show him about our farm and I agreed, eager to get his attention of me. Well, he openly complimented me on my comeliness and how he met many lovely girls in his travels and preaching, how many of them came to him for counsel and advice and how some of them even offered themselves to him and so forth. Why I'd never heard any man talk such to me. He asked that I keep what he told me between just us. That as a man of God he so seldom had anyone to confide these things in but especially a wise young lady such as myself. Said he thought I was special and that God had wanted me to come into his life. 'God sends us special angels, Belle.' Well, I fell for it hook, line and sinker.

"I remember we were out in the barn looking at Daddy's prize racer and he asked if he might kiss me. I didn't know what to think, this great man fawning all over me, trusting me to listen to his personal burdens and such. I allowed he could kiss me and he did, in the most tender way. I nearly swooned from it all. Again, he made me promise not to say anything to my folks, how they wouldn't understand. I promised I wouldn't.

"So you see, Lucy, it was my fault he come into my room and did what he did. I led him on and I let him take me to his dark place. And I learned then and there that every man has a dark place and they will take you to it if you let them."

I thought Red Dog must have such a dark place in him, too, even though he had saved me from being raped.

I lay a long time staring up at the stars and the moon still so bright and far away, like a dream you want to be part of but know you can't ever because it's out of reach.

Then, as sleep does, it snuck up on me and the next thing I know I was gone.

But something bestirred me and I opened my eyes quick and felt the presence of Red Dog beside me, there beneath the blankets.

"I thought we weren't going to do this," I whispered.

He didn't say anything.

I reached to touch him, to get him to say something. But when I did, what I felt wasn't Red Dog at all and I screamed and jumped up and clean out of the wagon.

"What the hell's wrong, Lucy," Red Dog yelped scrambling from beneath the wagon and banging his head in the process and yelping because of that too.

"Goddamn!" he swore.

She peered over the wagon's sides.

"Sorry," she said, "I didn't mean to scare you."

It was Marie.

"What the heck are you doing here?" I asked.

"You said I should leave him," she said in a quivering voice.

"But I . . ."

Red Dog looked at her then at me then back at her.

"Something I should know about?" he said.

Lord, I thought, what have I done?

"How'd you get away from LaRue?" I asked.

"I just ran off after he was asleep."

A saddle horse stood at the edge of the creek cropping the wet grass that grew along its borders.

"You said he'd come after you and you'd pay a price for leaving," I reminded her.

She began to blubber.

"Well, now, don't start that," Red Dog said. "Anything I hate worse than banging my head is hearing a woman crying. 'Sides, I'm confused. You tell her to leave LaRue, Lucy?"

"I sort of did," I said.

"Well, now, I reckon you just asked for a peck of trouble, more'n what we already got," he said.

"He's been cruel to her," I replied. "How come you to climb in with me, Marie?"

"I was lonely and tired and cold," she said still in that slobbering quivering voice like a child that's been whipped with a switch.

"Oh, hell," I said. "Stop crying. Everything will be okay. Won't it, Red?"

"Why you asking me?" he said, still rubbing the top of his head. "I'm just a fool way out here in the middle of no damn where with two women running from men."

"We'll take her with us to your friend's place then figure something out," I said weakly.

"Well, hell, Lucy, why didn't you say that in the first place," he said sarcastically. "Why, sure. That's a damn great idea. I'm sure LaRue or them rangers won't be looking for us, and her. While they'll just sit around on their haunches and shrug their shoulders and let bygones be bygones and not think nothing of it."

"Oh, don't be such a shit," I said. "What is this world coming to if one person can't find it in their hearts to help another in need? You helped me, remember? Now I want to help her."

Red Dog cursed some more under his breath and walked around rubbing his skull.

Marie just seemed so meek and sorrowful that Red Dog never thought to ask if she'd stolen that horse from LaRue, or maybe if she'd killed him so he wouldn't follow her.

I never thought to ask either.

Chapter 27

We rattled along the whole of the following day looking more like a family of Mormons than desperados and made camp that evening in an old abandoned stone building that had half a roof on it made of rotting timbers that hadn't yet fallen in but looked as though they could any minute. It lay off the road about one hundred yards but in a shallow ravine so that it could not easily be seen. Red Dog had the best eyes for spotting things of any man I ever knew.

"Somebody sure went to a lot of trouble to haul these timbers all the way out here," Red Dog said, for there wasn't a tree anywhere in sight and hadn't been for the last many days.

"Wonder why they go to all the trouble and then abandoned the place?" I said.

"Look around," he said. "You see any reason for anybody to stay?"

Marie was quiet, almost pitifully so.

"We can burn some of this old timber wood for a fire," Red Dog said, tugging a piece of busted wood from the end of the house where the roof had fallen in.

Marie and me set to making a meager supper. I did not fail to notice how Red Dog took her in as we sat around the fire eating our impoverished meal. It sort of ruffled my feathers the way he kept looking over at her. I asked myself was it jealousy on my part, then quickly answered that it was not. But maybe it was. A little.

I told myself, Let it go, Lucy, it ain't none of your affair if he finds her comely, and if that is what he wants then so be it. He is obviously a faithless so-and-so and you should not be surprised. Besides you don't even care for him all that much.

Still, it bothered me.

I felt like a fool for having lain with him realizing he'd probably run off with the first wench who'd have him—like some old hound chasing whatever rabbit he sniffed.

Well, if that's what he wanted, he could have her.

We ate as evening closed in around us, the three of us like a coven of witches gathered around the fire, its crackling wood sounding like bones breaking, the flames licking at the darkness and throwing our shadows up against the stone walls.

"I bet this was some old sheepherder's place," Red Dog said at last and standing up and going to one of the walls and running his hands over the stones.

"I bet if he was a sheep man, the cattle bosses ran him off is what it was," he added.

"This could have been a caveman's dwelling," Marie said. "I read about them in school when I was a girl. How they had to eat dinosaurs and we all are descended from apes."

"Apes?" Red Dog said. "Why my folks and their folks was pure Irish and Cherokees. Wasn't no apes in our families. Yours maybe but not mine."

"You are both a pair of fools," I said. "Dinosaurs lived about a billion years ago and humans didn't come along till about two thousand years ago, in Jesus's time," I said.

"My grandmama told me Jesus lived once in the belly of a whale," Marie said.

I just shook my head.

"It was Jonah lived in the whale," I said. "Jesus just caught fish and fed the multitudes." I wasn't sure if I even knew what I was talking about, truly, but it sounded a lot smarter than what those two were talking about.

"You white people sure tell some tall tales," Red Dog said. "Apes and whales with men in them."

"And what about the Irish thinking about little people finding pots of gold at the end of rainbow?" I countered.

"It's true. You find you a rainbow's end, you'll find gold."

I shook my head, the conversation was ridiculous, and so changed the subject.

"What makes you think some sheepherder lived here?" I asked.

"It looks like a place a man herding sheep would live," Red Dog said. "Them is some lonely people. If he wasn't run off by cowboys, he probably got sick of living alone way out here with nothing but sheep baaing the whole night long and just up and left one day. A man can't hardly do without the company of a woman for too very long and he probably didn't have nothing but them sheep."

His white-tooth grin radiated even as he stood by the walls, as if I didn't know what he was implying.

"You are right," Marie said. "No woman with a brain in her head wants to live way out here on this godforsaken land. I ought to know." And surely she did know, I thought.

He looked at Marie and me, his eyes moist with desire now that the subject of living with or without women had arisen.

"Well, it just goes to show the weakness of men and the strength of women if you want my opinion," I said. "For a woman can make do being alone. She can cook and clean and do the things necessary to sustain life, whereas a man would live all his life on beans and potted meat and wear the same clothes till they rotted off his body. A man is useless without a woman to guide him, whereas a woman can make due quite well. You heard of grass widows, but you never heard of no grass widowers, have you?"

He patted the stone as though testing its strength or gauging its age.

"No," he said, "I ain't. But I don't believe humans are meant to be alone, man nor woman. It ain't natural for a fellow to go without getting his needs met. Women neither, I reckon, at least in my experience. What do you say to that, Marie?"

"I don't know," she said softly. "I ain't got no thoughts on such things. I've been kept locked away in this godforsaken frontier too long to have any notions."

He came to a window opening that looked toward the road and stuck his head out like a damn fool and said, "Boy howdy, this could use some window glass, couldn't it?"

"What do you see out there in the dark?" I said sarcastically.

Marie seemed confused about Red Dog looking into the dark.

"Why, I see the whole world," he said. "I see mountains covered in snow and big blue lakes. I see ladies dancing on a stage lit by candles. And ponies doing tricks. I can see the oceans and San Francisco. Come and look and see for yourself."

"No thanks."

Marie got up.

"Do you really see San Francisco?" she said naively. Or maybe not as naive as she'd have you believe, and went and stood next to Red Dog. He let her squeeze in next to him so she could look out a window with no glass into darkness. The pair of them the two biggest fools I ever saw.

"I'm going to bed," I said and stood and walked to the wagon and climbed into my pallet of blankets and tried to shut my eyes and my ears, determined to let the pair of them have at whatever it was they were seeking to have at.

I could hear them talking, Marie's tittering questions and it put a knot in my stomach. I thought if he fornicates with her I'm going to take one of the horses and ride out of here and he can do whatever the hell he wants, and her too.

But then in a few minutes she stood at the edge of the wagon.

"Can I sleep with you tonight, Lucy?"

"No," I said and tossed her a blanket. "Sleep on the ground." She began to cry and mew like a lost kitten.

"Come on," I said and she crawled up into the wagon's bed and lay down next to me.

"Is there something wrong, Lucy?"

"I'm just tired is all. Go to sleep."

"You ladies sleep tight," Red Dog called from the darkness of the old skeleton of a house.

Marie scooted close to me and it made me feel uncomfortable to be so pressed up against another woman, especially her. But soon enough she was snoring lightly and I was too.

But then Red Dog was shaking me by the foot.

"Get up," he said in a low harsh whisper. "Someone's coming."

I sat bolt upright, my heart thumping like the hind foot of a snared rabbit.

"Who?" I whispered.

"Don't know, but I heard their horses."

I started to wake Marie but Red Dog said, "Leave her be." And so I hopped out of the wagon and followed him into the ruined stone house that stood between the wagon and the road. Red Dog was carrying his rifle. I followed him to the open window from where he'd seen San Francisco and dancing women and all manner of crazy things, and he levered a shell into the rifle's chamber.

"Hesh, now," he said. "Maybe they will pass by in the dark."

I hardly breathed.

Then we heard the snort and soft thud of horse hooves on the hardpan and the voices of men.

"They might have turned off somewhere back yonder," one of the voices said. "Where we run out of daylight. What do you want to do, Lee?"

"I think we've lost them, but seems they'd have stayed on this road."

"They could be anywhere in this country. We'll never find them in the dark anyway. They could be laying out there right now listening to us and we not even know it."

"Yeah, they damn well could be."

"Hesh, listen?"

After a time of silence: "Don't hear nothing, Lee, you?"

"Nope."

I'd leaned against Red Dog so I could see too. Suddenly a light flared on the roadway not fifty yards distance: the flame of a match, then the glow of a cigarette when the light went out. I thought Red Dog might shoot at the cigarette glow, kill whoever was holding it. I placed my hand on his wrist and squeezed it to let him know if that was what he was thinking he should hold off.

"I'm for going on to the Double J and lay over the night and get a fresh start at daylight, see if we can't pick up their tracks again."

"Yeah, I guess we oughter. I'm as beat as a rug."

"Plus," said the other. "We'll get another look at the old man's daughter. That's worth the trip alone."

The other one laughed.

The glow of the cigarette moved up and down like a firefly as the man smoked.

"Shit, you ever think she'd stab ol' LaRue to death, that little slip of a thing?"

"Maybe it wasn't her. Maybe it was them two we saw eating. Maybe they came back and did it and kidnapped Marie."

"It's a possibility. They both looked sort of heinous, didn't you think?"

"That big Indian especially."

"Wonder what that white gal was doing with him. Maybe that's all he does, go around stealing white women."

"You mean like they was horses or something?"

"Why not? He could trade 'em off for horses or sell them as slaves down in Mexico couldn't he? He'd probably get more for 'em as slaves than if they was horses."

"That's true."

"Shit, some of these white women even go for them bucks."

"She wasn't a bad looker, either."

"Neither was Marie it come down to it."

"No, she wasn't."

"I bet he's already done things to 'em."

"I bet you're right."

"Well, nothing we can do about it now. Let's go on to Hemp's place at the Double J if we're going and get some supper and a look at his daughter."

"I sure do pity them gals that Indun stole."

"I do too."

"Don't worry, we'll catch 'em. Traveling with a wagon they can't be going fast."

"We'll run 'em down tomorrow or the day after."

"Let's go, then."

"Hell, I'm already gone."

We heard the thud of their horses fade off into the darkness.

"Well now we're in the jackpot for sure," Red Dog said.

"What are we going to do? They think we have kidnapped Marie."

"We have to get rid of her."

"Get rid of her? How do you mean?"

He didn't say anything. I could hear his breath passing through his nostrils.

"They catch us and she tells them a story to save her own skin about knifing LaRue, they'll hang me and maybe you if she blames you too."

"She wouldn't do that."

"How can you be sure? People will say all sorts of things to save themselves."

"I just know that she wouldn't, is all."

"Just like you knew when you saw her that first time, she wouldn't kill LaRue. Hell, I bet she stole that horse of his too, another hanging offense."

I didn't know what to think. It seemed like every mile brought new danger and more trouble.

"We'll leave her with your friend," I said at last afraid of what Red Dog was contemplating. Still he did not speak. I imagine his mood was as dark as the night.

Directly overhead I counted three stars that fell one right after another and thought: that's us.

The fallen ones.

CHAPTER 28

Somehow we managed to avoid running into the rangers and made it to Red Dog's friend's place. Red Dog said his name was Buck Harrow but did not say how he knew this man or anything about him.

When we pulled within sight of the place, what you saw was a windmill churning its rusted metal blades for all they were worth and a shack of a place constructed of weathered and unpainted clapboards under a further rust-streaked metal roof. A cottonwood corral with a few mangy horses lazing in the sun, their eyes troubled by about a million flies feasting on them and the droppings. There was a canted outhouse and naught else but wind troubling sagebrush.

It looked like someplace a bad man would go to die, but certainly not one where any sort of body would go to live.

"Y'all don't come no closer," a voice called from within the shadow of the door frame. "Who ye be and what ye wantin'?"

Then we saw the blue barrel of a rifle poked out and aimed our direction.

"Hold off, Buck, it's me, Red Dog," Red Dog shouted.

"Red Dog who?"

"Goddamn, how many fellas named Red Dog do you know, damn it?"

There was a pause in the palaver and all a body could hear was those rusty windmill blades clacking this way and that as the wind shifted to and fro and causing water to spit out of a spigot over a large watering tank.

"The onliest Red Dog I know got hisself shot dead somewhere in Indian Territory and I don't doubt it a bit, mean sumbitch as he was."

Red Dog laughed.

"Well, hell, living way out here I imagine you don't hear too very much about what takes place in civilized country that would be true or otherwise," Red Dog said.

"Ha. You call the Nations civilized? Now I know you're brain addled."

"Step out here and take a look at me."

"All right then, but if ye'd be thinkin' to pullin' one over on me, I'll blast ye to hell and gone."

The man stepped out.

He was thick-bearded and nearly bald and dressed in ragged calico shirt and wrinkled trousers and wore mule-ear boots rough and run-down at the heels. He waggled the Winchester about like trying to decide which of us he was aiming to shoot first. But he sure did let his gaze rest on Marie and myself like a dog staring at a fresh ham.

"Step on down and come closer so I can have a look at ye," the man said.

"Just don't shoot me while I'm doing so," Red Dog said.

"I won't shoot ye, though I might just to take them wimmen off'n ye hands."

His laughter was similar to that of a hen cackling.

Red Dog climbed down and walked toward the fellow with his palms upraised and paused before him.

"Well, shit, it is ye," he said.

"I told you it was me."

"My eyes ain't so good no more."

"Why ain't they?"

"Oh, hell, ye know." Then he lowered his voice and said

something I couldn't hear and Red Dog laughed and the fellow said it wasn't funny—whatever it was he told him.

"We come a long way," Red Dog said. "We're all tired as hell and there could be a couple of curious Texas Rangers back there somewhere." Red Dog waved his arm toward the big empty we'd just come in from.

"Well, come on in and get out of the sun."

We climbed out of the wagon, Marie and me, and followed them inside.

I thought the inside couldn't be much worse than the outside, but I was wrong. It was just one big room with cobbled-together handmade furniture and a single cot shoved up against one wall with an old cast-iron stove in the center of the room and a stovepipe running up through the ceiling. The walls were lined with old newspapers, yellowed and curling and peeling loose and there was a wood box by the stove with no wood in it. There was a shelf of canned goods, mostly peaches and beans and some potted meats and a box of Blue Diamond matches.

Above the cot was a gun rack holding a shotgun and on the table a deck of playing cards with pictures of naked women printed on the backs and some of the cards were laid out like a game of solitaire interrupted. The stove held a blackened metal coffeepot and the only extravagance I saw was three chipped china cups hooked on pegs alongside the stove.

Buck Harrow invited us to set down as he put it. Not sit, but set. And we did. Me and Marie on the two available chairs and Buck pulled up an empty apple crate and offered it to Red Dog for a seat and tugged the bed over from the wall and sat on it.

"Where ye hailin' from?" he asked once we got situated.

"Hadley's Jump over in the Nations," Red said.

"Never heard of it."

"It doesn't matter. We're in a bit of a tight," Red said, "is the reason why we come."

"What sort of tight?"

"Let's just say there was some serious bloodletting and a deputy marshal was killed."

I thought maybe this Buck person might express astonishment or fret, but all he said was, "Well, one more for our side, then."

"It's not like that," Red said.

"Well, hell how is it I can help ye?"

"We just need a place to lay over for a time till things cool a bit and plan our next move."

Buck shifted his gaze back to Marie and me.

"Hell, if ye brought a case of spirits, along with these pretty gals ye can stay till we're all dead of old age and go to Jesus."

It was more a hoot than a comment and I felt a shiver down my spine and I imagine Marie did too.

"Didn't bring no whiskey," Red said. "And the women aren't the partying type."

Buck scratched his scalp while offering a look of disappointment.

"Ye always did come the bearer of bad news," Buck said. But then he relaxed and said, "Ye'all want some Arbuckle and beans?"

We ate the meager meal in silence, Marie and myself, while the two men talked among themselves about the old days, the last time they'd met and about old acquaintances who were now dead. Then Buck Harrow got out a bottle of rotgut whiskey and splashed it into the coffee cups but both Marie and I declined the offer to which Buck, unfazed, merely laughed and said more for him and Red, then went on to tell of old pards of theirs.

Rainy Roberts got shot through the neck and lay paralyzed for two weeks in jail before he died. Karl, the big German, drowned in the Nueces trying to outrun a posse. Ye remember how damn afraid of rivers he was. Well, seems he had a reason to be. Should have at least bought hisself a hoss that could swim. That one didn't.

Buck Harrow's talk was punctuated by hardy laughter as if everything, every tragedy was humorous.

Kirby Kitlow was killed taking a bubble bath with a banker's wife over in Silver City he was wooing, or trying to. I bet Kirby never figured he'd get shot to death by some damn banker after all the banks he'd robbed—leastways not in a bathtub. Said his bean floated to the top and it is to this day displayed in a pickle jar in one of them Silver City saloons.

I touched Marie's elbow under the table and rolled my eyes toward the door.

"Marie and me are going out for some air," I said.

Buck Harrow looked disappointed at our stepping away from the table.

Once outside and out of earshot I asked Marie the important question.

"Why'd you kill LaRue?"

Her face was a storm of trouble.

"How do you know?"

I explained to her about hearing the rangers on the road that night.

"They said you stabbed him to death."

"He came at me and I happened to be holding a knife at the time," she said with shifty eyes.

"You sure that's what happened?"

"Yes," she said.

"I thought you were afraid of him? I thought you said you didn't have nowhere to go when I offered you to go with us."

"I changed my mind. I thought about what you said."

"Well, did you have to kill him to run away?"

She shrugged.

"What choice did I have? I knew I could catch up with you if I went when I did."

"Damn it, Marie."

She offered me a pouty hurt child look.

"Are we going to stay here with that man? He looks dangerous to me. He's been peeling my clothes off with his eyes since we got here," she said.

In that, Marie was telling the truth.

"You're not the only one," I said.

"Oh, Lucy, are we women always to be so abused?"

"Obviously not," I said. "You took care of yours. Don't let that dog in yonder bark at you."

"They're in there getting drunk and you know what that means," she said.

"Don't worry," I said. "Red won't let anything happen to you. I won't either."

She hugged me and wept. Weepingest woman I ever met.

We remained outside until dusk descended on the place and the night covering up its ugliness, but for the clattering windmill that never stopped because the wind never stopped. I had intended to leave out and leave Red Dog behind, but now there was a new concern about leaving Marie with this Buck. I knew if I left her, she was doomed, one way or the other. Either Red Dog would get rid of her or he'd leave her with Buck Harrow and he would get her and she'd be no better off than she had been.

A light came on inside the house and I could see the shadow of one of them passing back and forth behind the lone window. I couldn't tell if it was Red Dog or his friend.

Marie and I got into the wagon's bed and lay there silent.

"What if that old scamp comes for me?" she whispered.

"He won't."

"How can you be sure?"

"I know Red won't let him."

She trembled with fright. I stroked her hair and hushed her like I would a child frightened by a nightmare.

The distant rumble of a thunderstorm sounded and only added to Marie's terror.

"Be still now and try and sleep," I said.

Eventually she lay still, the rhythm of her breathing brushing warm air against my arm. I couldn't imagine her killing LaRue with a knife. It's such mean work, stabbing a body is. I was shaken by having shot off part of Deputy Book's head. What must it be like to plunge a knife into someone and feel them wiggling at the end of it? I hoped I never had to find out.

From inside the shack I heard loud singing, the kind of loud singing that drunken men do and it did not ease my mind any that Red Dog was one of the two doing it. The longer it went the angrier I got. He was supposed to be helping to watch over us, to keep us from harm's way even though he never made any vow to do such. I had just assumed he would and now he was betraying our safety by drinking with that damn blackguard Buck Harrow.

I closed my eyes and tried to sleep hoping it would help pass the night and that daylight would bring about some sort of relief.

How long I'd been like that, eyes closed, a protective arm around Marie, I couldn't say but then Red Dog shook me awake.

He was good and drunk and slurring his words.

"Hey," he said. Said it twice in fact.

"What?" I said.

"Was thinking maybe Marie could spend the night inside with Buck. Buck's awful lonely and Marie, well, she ain't married no more . . ." He giggled like a damn fool.

"Are you crazy?" I said.

"Probably," he said.

"Crazy and drunk. Get away and sleep it off."

"Now, why you got to talk to me like that, Lucy. Damn it, what'd I ever do wrong to you?"

"Why'd you bring us here?"

Either he failed to understand the question or the whiskey had completely stolen his brains.

"Why?" he said. "Why?"

"That man is nothing but pure trouble," I said.

"Why, he ain't," Red Dog said then fell down and said "Ouch," then laughed again.

"Jesus, you stink," I said. "Go on get off with yourself, don't be an ass."

"Oh, hell," he said still lying on the ground. "Oh hell . . ."

In a matter of minutes he was snoring loudly and I was sorely disappointed in him for the first real time. Mama had always warned me about men who drank excessively. "Lucy," she said. "A drunkard shames himself and the woman who loves him."

Well, I sure didn't love Red Dog but lying there in the dirt and snoring like a bulldog sure was a shameful thing.

I was ready to ignore him when I heard shouting coming from inside the cabin then suddenly saw the door fly open and Buck Harrow standing in the lighted doorway in his altogether.

"Hey! Hey!" he shouted. "Where's that gal, Red, ye promised me."

Oh God, I thought.

"Hey! Hey!" he shouted again. "Goddamn, where's she at?"

Marie stirred beside me.

"Lucy," she muttered.

"Go to sleep," I whispered.

But that damn fool kept on shouting and she sat up.

"What is it?" she said.

"Don't worry yourself," I said. "He's drunk is all," I said trying to calm her.

"Why is he without any clothes?"

"He's drunk," I repeated. "Men do stupid things when they're drunk. Don't look."

"He's going to hurt me," she whispered, clutching at me.

"No he's not," I said.

He came forth from the cabin and toward the wagon. I took Deputy Book's pistol from where I'd hid it under the blankets.

"Don't you come any closer," I called.

He stopped there in the yard halfway between shack and wagon, his arms held wide.

"Red promised me to lay with one of ye," he cawed. "It don't matter which. Ye both fine-looking wimmen."

"Well, Red is a damn fool and so are you if you think any woman in her right mind would lie down with a dirty dog such as you, Mr. Harrow. Now, go on back in the cabin and sleep it off. Good night."

He seemed befuddled for a moment, muttering to himself. Even with it being a dark night, his body was as white as lard, a terrible sight for anybody to have to look upon. I held the revolver cocked in my hand. I surely did not want to have to shoot another man and run my total to two, but I'd do what I had to, to protect myself and poor Marie.

"Why goddamn," he said at last and turned around in a complete circle as if confused as to what he should do about this turn of events.

"No sir!" he shouted. "I aim to get what I was promised."

I fired a shot into the air hoping I'd aimed high enough not to shatter his skull like a melon, for I'd seen the results of such already and did not want to ever again see another man's brains blown out.

He jumped and scatted like a frightened rabbit back to the cabin and slammed the door.

From inside I heard him shouting: "Ye lying sumbitch, Red.

Why ye can just git off my damn propty."

I waited until the light went out and the cabin grew dark, making sure that Harrow would not put in another appearance.

"My ears are ringing, Lucy," Marie said.

"Hesh now," I said. "It's okay. I don't think that fellow will trouble us further."

After a time I lay back and she next to me and I was so tired of it all: the running, the death, missing my mama and Jim too, a little. I just wanted to close my eyes and sleep a thousand years.

I was nearly asleep when Marie kissed me on the mouth.

It was as if I'd suddenly felt a snake crawling over me.

"Why'd you do that?" I said harshly. "You shouldn't have done that."

"I love you, Lucy."

She said it so sadly and needful it was again as if she'd become a child and I couldn't stay angry at her even though I wanted to.

"It's okay," I said. "Just get some sleep."

"Yes," she said. "I'm sorry."

As I lay there trying to settle my nerves down again, it struck me that her kiss was in a way the most decent and tender thing that had happened to me since my honeymoon—a gesture full of tender need, a wanting to be healed. I put my arm about her as we lay back to front and fell asleep with my face in the tendrils of her hair. I just wanted some peace and quiet.

Chapter 29

The morning found Red Dog acting quite contrite.

"I guess maybe I drank a little too much of Buck's bug juice," he said.

"I guess you did," I replied.

"I hope I didn't say or do anything to insult you," he said.

"Well, that is a hope that is gone wanting," I said. "You told that damn piece of trash he could have Marie for the night."

Marie had gone off to the privy.

"I did?"

"I nearly had to shoot him last night."

"You did?"

"I've made up my mind that we're not staying here," I said.

"Well where are you aiming to go?"

"Nearest town that's got more than a saloon and whorehouse. A town town."

He rubbed his jaw.

"A town town?"

"You keep repeating everything I say. It's annoying."

"I do?"

I glared at him.

"I think that would be a big mistake, Lucy. Least here we don't have to worry about the law every time we turn around."

"No, we just have to worry about your boozehound pal and his lascivious nature," I replied. "That, and the fact if the law does come around the two of you are likely to kill them. I'm sick to death of killing."

"Lascivious," he repeated, chewing on the word as if the rest of what I'd said about killing hadn't even registered.

"So you can either come with us or stay here and you and your partner can drink up all the whiskey in Texas and act like damn louts."

"Well, shit."

Marie returned from the outhouse just as I was asking where the nearest town town was.

"Amarillo would be the closest," he said.

"Then that's where we will go."

Still rubbing his jaw, he brightened.

"You know, maybe that's a good idea. The two of you traveling by yourselves. Nobody would suspect two women of being dangerous killers of men. I could lay over here for a time and join you later."

I nodded not sure what the hell he was thinking.

"Good, we'll take the wagon and you can have Book's saddle horse."

Red Dog gave us directions on how to find the road to Amarillo. We shook hands like business partners even though the only business we'd been joined in was murder, at least murder the way the law was sure to look at it.

My thinking all along was to get somewhere I could catch a train back east and get Marie settled in someplace where she'd be safe.

"I'll see you all in a few weeks, then," Red Dog said and I snapped the reins and off we went, Marie and me and if anyone saw us from a distance, at least, me dressed in shirt and trousers and my hair pinned up under my Stetson hat and her in a dress they'd think we were just a man and woman riding along somewhere like men and women often do.

Red Dog said we should make Amarillo in a day or two if the

weather held and the roads didn't turn muddy. He said there were a couple of decent hotels there that had indoor plumbing and some good restaurants and whatever else a body needed, that it was a real going town, the biggest in the panhandle. He also said that maybe there was some sort of Christian organization that might take Marie in and help her to a new life.

It suited me right down to my toes.

Marie and I rode along in silence but every once in a while she would spot a herd of white rumped antelope or some sort of colorful bird and would shout and point and say, "Lookit, Lucy." And I would look, every time, even though I wasn't much interested in the flora and fauna.

The landscape looked flat but it wasn't. It would dip and rise and was cut here and there by canyons and arroyos you couldn't see until you came upon them. It was a fooling sort of land without much to recommend it, but in a way, its plainness was its own sort of beauty too.

Sometimes we'd spot a windmill way off in the distance that indicated a ranch house but we were intent on making Amarillo as soon as possible. We stopped only enough to stretch our legs and arch our backs and give the horses a blow.

Marie would talk to the horses like they were human beings. She named them Jasper and Ike.

"Why name them?" I asked.

"Just because they need names," she said. "All living creatures should have names, don't you think so, Lucy?"

"You mean like even turtles and fishes and birds?" I said trying to make light of her silliness.

"Why not?" she said. "We got names."

"Seems to me just calling a horse a horse or a bird a bird is name enough," I said.

"Oh, Lucy. Don't you think life should be romantic and not so plain and uninteresting?"

"I'd say it's been real interesting so far without giving names to horses."

She laughed, her little teeth showing. The more I took stock of her, the more like a child she seemed to me. A child in a woman's body who probably would never grow up no matter what.

"Does it trouble you greatly what you did to LaRue?" I asked during one of our stops while she twined wildflowers in the horses' manes.

"Well, I think he deserved it," she said simply. "For what he did to me."

A simple truth, no doubt.

"I wish I had some sugar cubes or carrots for them," she said happily.

It did not seem to me that it bothered her, stabbing a fellow to death.

We rode until the evening caught us and I pulled off the road into a little dry wash and we unhitched the team and hobbled them up the draw where there was some fodder for them then ate jerky and wrapped up in our blankets.

She hugged me.

"No kissing," I said.

"Oh, why not, Lucy?"

"Because," I said. "I ain't that way."

"What way?"

"You know, one of those women who like other women, what Red Dog calls two-spirits women. I like men, pure and simple."

She lay quiet for a time.

"Men have always treated me mean, Lucy. I never knew any man who was nice to me."

"I take it somewhere along the line there was a woman who was nice to you, then?"

She gave a little sigh.

"Yes," she said.

"Well then, I guess that accounts for your feelings."

"LaRue was awful rough with me, and before him so were the others. I never liked to learn it—doing it with men."

"Okay," I said. "I get the picture, Marie. We don't need to be jabbering all night and miss out on our sleep."

"Okay," she said.

She turned her back to me and lay there for several minutes.

"Could you just put your arms around me, Lucy, and hold me a little, like you did last night. I like being held gentle."

I did without saying anything and it seemed to calm her greatly, and I guess it did me too.

It rained all the next day. A soft gentle rain and we rode under it with the blankets pulled up over our shoulders and I told Marie about Mama and how terrific she was and how I'd just gotten married and was on my honeymoon when the news came that she'd been killed and then I told her about Jim and about his being murdered too.

"Life just kicks you when you're not looking," I concluded.

"Seems as if we both have known trouble and heartache," Marie said.

"Seems so," I said.

A wagon came along toward us and I eased ours over as much as I could to let the other pass. It was an old man and a woman, both of them dressed in black, like mourners, the woman's bonnet covering most of her face. The man eased his team to a halt alongside ours.

"How do?" he said, touching the brim of his broad black hat.

"Good day if you're a duck," I said.

"You all heading for Amarillo?" he asked.

"We are."

"Just come from there day before yesterday, me and my woman."

The woman seemed to want to hide her face within the folds of her bonnet.

"How far is it still?" I asked.

"Oh, it's a good day's ride farther on yet," he said. "Maybe a bit more if the road continues to worsen under this rain."

Then he looked skyward and blinked his eyes at the falling rain.

"I do believe it will be an all-day rain," he said, "the way my ankle bones are aching."

"Ankle bones?" Marie said.

He looked downward at his feet then up at Marie.

"That's right, child. Broke 'em when I was a young rascal running from a band of Comanche. They got us in an ambush and I had to jump off a cliff into a river to save my sorry hide. It must have been a hunnert foot drop at least. You wouldn't think of water as being hard, but jumping that high up into it was like hitting rock. Snapped 'em like twigs and nearly drowned."

"Gracious," Marie said with real wonderment.

"Well, now, I know at least when it's going to be a hard rain a coming," he said. "Say, you ladies need a dry place to lay over, ours is not too far from here. I imagine you passed by a lane not too far back?"

"We did."

"Well it leads to our little place if'n you two would like to lay over till the rain quits. Zelda here is a mighty fine cook."

He patted the woman on the knee but she had yet to speak.

"What do you think, Marie?"

"It would be nice to get shed of these wet clothes," she said.

"Turn your team around and foller us," the old man said.

It was a delay. But the prospect of not riding all the rest of the day in the rain—and maybe even getting a hot home-cooked meal—was a temptation too great to refuse.

Our detour was only a matter of a couple of miles. You'd never have known their homestead was even there without going down that lane for half a mile or so. It was invisible from the road. I imagined there must be other homesteads in that country as well, you just couldn't see from the road.

Once inside, the woman removed her bonnet and I was surprised at how much younger she was than the man. She had lovely light-brown hair woven and pinned up and a thin pale face with clear gray eyes.

While her man was outside caring for his team she had us follow her to a room where she opened a wood trunk with leather straps.

"I have some dry clothes you can change into," she said. "Nothing fancy, and if you don't mind that they're just shirts and pants and not dresses."

No, we didn't mind at all.

She left us to change and went out into the main room.

Marie and I shucked out of our wet duds, and Marie's gaze livened at the sight of me stripped down.

"You have nice ones," she said.

"You stop looking," I said.

She averted her eyes and seemed wounded by my rebuke until I said she had nice ones too.

"Oh, they're small," she said.

"I don't imagine such makes a difference to a man," I said quickly shucking on the plaid wool shirt I was given.

"At least it never has been my experience," I added.

She half smiled.

"No, mine, either, far as I can tell."

I turned my back for the rest of the getting dressed. I felt uncomfortable being naked in a room with her, maybe even more so than if she had been a man.

We finished dressing and came out into the big room.

It was a nice clean cabin with handwoven rugs on the plank floor and fine furniture of table and chairs and a divan even covered in red damask with curved wooden arms. There was a shelf of leather-bound books and the mounted head of a mule deer on the wall. There were two stoves, one to cook on and another to heat the rooms with. There was even a pantry in the kitchen and a sink with a hand pump and sideboard.

"I'll have us supper in an hour," she said over her shoulder as she busied herself in the kitchen.

She asked our names and we told her and she said, "Oh, those are real pretty names, Marie and Lucy. Are you two sisters?"

"No, just friends," I said, even though that wasn't exactly true.

"How nice. Are you going to Amarillo to go shopping?"

"Our husbands are waiting there for us," I lied.

"Oh."

I quickly added that we'd been visiting my sick auntie a day's ride north to make the lie sound more true. Mama always claimed that whenever she told the truth it sounded like a lie and whenever she lied it sounded like the truth.

"I don't know why I was so afflicted, Lucy," Mama told me. "Telling the truth has gotten me into more trouble than I ever got in telling a lie. You might say I've been cursed in that way." Then she would laugh and tell me a story and had me guess whether or not I thought it was true or not. I rarely got it right.

"North of here?" Zelda said as if trying to figure in her head what was north of here. "You all aren't related to the Sweets are you?"

"No," I said. "My auntie's name is Rose McGee. You ever hear of the McGees?"

She thought and thought whilst stirring whatever was in the pot on the burner plate.

"No, I can't say that I have," she said. I sighed with relief.

"Well, it's way out of the way," I said. "Up near the border."

"Oh. Well, how is she faring?"

"She's coming along just fine," I said.

"What was it that ailed her?"

Damn this curious young woman. Why'd she have to ask so many questions?

"Something I can't even pronounce," I said. "One of those funny medical conditions the doctors have names for but no ordinary person's ever heard of. Something to do with her blood," I lied.

"Oh. Well, I'm glad she's doing better."

Mister came in just then, taking his hat off and slapping it against his leg.

"It's still coming down cats and dogs," he said. "Wouldn't you know." He went over to where his missus was and kissed her on the cheek.

"Zee, I see you got these young ladies some dry clothes."

"Yes, Hank. We've plenty to spare."

"Ain't it the truth," he said. "Now I must go and change my own self."

There was also a Regulator clock that filled the void of conversation with a steady ticktock much like a metallic heart beating.

We later sat down at the kitchen table and held hands while the man, Hank, said grace followed by "Dig in."

It was a pot of tasty stew and she'd baked a pan of clabber biscuits on which we smeared apple butter.

Hank ate lustily like a man twice his size. He was small and wiry and had a dark spade beard and keen brown eyes.

"I've not seen the likes of you two before," he said.

His missus told him what we'd told her about visiting the sick aunt and going to Amarillo to meet our husbands.

"So, you're traveling alone," he said, not as a question but as a confirmation.

"That's right," I said.

"Well I hope you are armed," he said. "Lord knows there are road agents out there and you must beware."

"Oh, we can take care of ourselves," I said, patting the butt of the revolver I'd shoved into my belt.

"Yes, I see that," he said. "But it's one thing to carry a gun and another to shoot someone with it."

"I know," I said without way of explanation.

He appraised me then, arching one eyebrow as his gaze went from the gun handle to me.

Nodding, he said, "Well, somehow I don't doubt that a bit. You'll stay the evening with Zee and me will you not? Looks like your horses could use a rest. I took the liberty of turning them out with my own, grained and watered."

"That was kind of you," Marie interjected.

Hank cast her an appraising look.

"Least a neighbor can do for a weary traveler," he said. "We often take in folks for the night. Ain't that right, Zee?"

Reaching across the table he patted her hand and she offered him an approving look.

"We have a extra cabin out back for folks such as yourself, travelers needing a place to stay. It's far out country from here to Amarillo and north to nowhere. Why, I know of no other place north of here until you cross over into the Pistol Barrel and even there I'm not at all sure of too many accommodations."

"That's right," Hank enjoined. "It's lonely country this around here is. Now south of here you've got Amarillo of course and all manner of other little towns with accommodations, but it's still a good day's ride even to there. A traveler can use some good rest and a warm meal, we've learned."

I likened as to how he was right about that.

"Might I ask how much you charge for the accommodations?" I asked aware of the limited funds I carried.

"Well," he said rubbing his chin. "You know, normally we'd charge five dollars for supper and a bed overnight and care of your horses, but you two sprites, well, I reckon Zee and I could do you both a good turn and just let it go at a dollar apiece. How does that sound?"

"Sounds like a bargain," I said. But there was something about all this friendliness I couldn't quite put my finger on. I told myself I was just too jaded anymore to trust anyone and I was reading into something that wasn't there. That indeed there were good people on this earth—that they weren't all bad, killers and cutthroats and rapists.

Marie piped right up and said, "That would be great."

"Then it's settled. Zee, why don't you show these two ladies to the guest cabin and I'll clean up the table."

She lighted a lamp and we followed her out the back door and across the yard and past a nice-sized barn to a small cabin.

"It provides you with nice privacy. Hank snores like a horse," she said.

We entered and there were two cot beds with a small night table between them and a small window cut into each wall. The room smelled of cedar and the lamp lit it nicely. There was also a trunk at the foot of one of the beds.

"The privy is next to the barn," she said. "It's the one we use for guests. Hank and I have our own so you won't be troubled any."

"It's quite commodious," I said.

She smiled and said, "Yes, isn't it?"

I looked at Marie and she was smiling at our good fortune.

"Sleep well," the woman said. "Breakfast will be at eight in the morning. But don't worry if you don't get up in time. I always have something ready. Good night."

"Good night," we said.

She went out and closed the door behind her.

"This is really a piece of good luck," Marie said.

I agreed that it was.

Marie sat on one of the cot beds and bounced a little. The wire springs creaked.

"It's comfortable," she said.

I sat down on the other across from her.

"What's wrong, Lucy?"

"Something," I said.

"Something?"

I nodded.

"I can't quite square it," I said.

"I sure am tired, ain't you?" Marie said starting to undress.

"Yes."

"Don't worry, Lucy. We'll be in Amarillo tomorrow hopefully."

"You're most likely right," I said.

"But?"

"You notice anything strange about those folks?"

"Well, she's a lot younger than him, but then so was I when I was with LaRue. But that's all. Other'n they're nice."

"Too nice," I said.

"Oh, Lucy, I think you're just wore out. I think once you get a real good night's sleep you'll feel more sunny in the morning."

"Yeah, I reckon," I said and pulled off my boots and hung my hat on the knob of the bedpost. I turned out the lamp and the room went full on dark, dusk having come early because of the weather.

I lay there a long time thinking.

"Marie?"

"What is it, Lucy?"

"If something were to happen . . ."

"Yes, like what?"

"Like anything."

"You mean if you was to die or something?"

"I mean anything. Do you think you could do as I tell you and not ask a bunch of damn questions but just do it?"

For a moment there was just silence.

"Yes," she said. "But what would happen?"

"There you go asking those damn questions. Nothing is going to happen. I'm just saying if something did, could you do what I told you?"

"Yes, I already said I could."

"All right, then. Go to sleep."

"You want me to come over and get in bed with you?"

"No."

"All right, then. Good night, Lucy."

"Good night."

CHAPTER 30

Try as I might, I could not sleep. Mama used to say that a full moon brings out the haints and you best beware, daughter. Mama would sometimes stay up thc whole night when there was a full moon just pacing the floor and looking out the windows—for haints, I suppose.

I got out of bed and threw on my clothes feeling the need to use the privy and went out. The night world looked vaporous and spirit made; and the moon so big and close it looked like you could just reach out and touch it. It was so bright it even cast shadows. No wonder you can't sleep, Lucy, I told myself as I walked to the outhouse feeling as alone as the last soul on earth. Hell, I felt like some old haint myself walking a graveyard. It put prickles on my arms.

I noted that there was a lamp yet lit inside the main house and could see them moving around in there. Figured maybe they couldn't sleep, either. Then as I got closer to the jakes, I noticed what looked like a garden patch off to the right—a large square of ground but with nothing growing in it. That struck me as odd. Why'd you have a garden with nothing growing in it? Some of the dirt looked freshly turned too, over in the right-hand corner. Maybe they was just then fitting it for planting, but then considering how late in the season it was, it seemed like they'd get nothing to grow before the snows fell.

I entered the jakes and sat down. I missed the indoor plumbing in the hotels down in El Paso, a world of difference from these country places. I wasn't sure I actually had to go as much as just not try and sleep when I thought about El Paso and going back there someday, probably to live once everything got resolved with the killings. I was like Mama in wanting to be in a lively town with plenty to keep me busy and happy. I sat there thinking on it all and then I heard voices.

Low whispering voices I'd probably not heard but for it being so still and quiet out. I quick stood up and pulled up my trousers and looked out through the cut moon in the door thinking maybe they were coming to use the jakes too and I'd get out of the way so they could.

But no, I saw them skulking toward the little house where Marie was still sleeping. The pair of them, him and her almost the same as if it were day. My heart jumped up into my throat.

What the hell?

He held something in his hand and she did too. I reckoned it was a rifle but then I saw it was a mattock he was carrying and her an ax.

Jesus Christ I almost screamed. What the hell were those two aiming to do but kill us in our sleep!

I had nothing to defend myself or Marie with. I'd left the revolver back in the house by the bed.

I pushed open the privy door and screamed.

"Hey you sons a bitches! What do you think you're doing!"

They stopped dead stride not three feet from the door of the house and turned my direction. I could see their startled ghostly faces and dread spilled through me like cold water.

"Go get her!" the woman yelped. "I'll take care of the one inside."

I was already running as he turned to come after me. I had to try and direct them away from Marie. Poor defenseless Marie asleep inside that soon to be death house if she didn't wake up and fight for her life.

I heard the man's heavy footfall on the caliche as he came charging after me yelling, "Stop, stop, it ain't nothing. We ain't gone hurt you all."

I ran toward the corral and flung myself in between the rails landing in a pile of dung, jumped up and ran between snorting and stamping horses that had been sleeping standing up but surprised to have a wild thing in among them suddenly. The man scrabbled after me. I had no plan, no time to think, I just let fearful instinct take over and it ran me into the barn and as soon as I was inside, in the darkness of it with its sweet scent of hay, I realized I'd just run right into a trap.

It was just enough moonlight coming in the door, I could see a ladder leading up to the hayloft and quick started to climb up, figuring worse came to worse I could maybe jump out the loading window if I had to. It would probably break my legs or maybe worse, but at the last moment changed my mind and slunk back into the farthest horse stall hoping I'd trick him into believing I'd climbed up top and he'd have me trapped and then I'd scramble for the door and outside again.

I hunkered down and peered around the stall post in time to see him outlined in the doorway of the barn. His dark shape framed against the moon's light made him seem bigger than he was. He was a terrifying thing, holding that mattock in his hand.

He whistled low like he was calling a dog.

"You come on out now and don't make me come in and get you, else it will go a lot worse."

Worse! I thought. How the hell was it supposed to get worse? My heart was tripping over itself so hard I figured he could hear it knocking. Suddenly I heard Marie screaming and my heart nearly jumped clean out of my chest. I had to clamp down from screaming too because of it. I didn't even let myself imagine what might be happening to her, prayed she was putting up a fight; told myself she killed LaRue, maybe she'd do the same to the woman.

Dear God in heaven, I prayed. If you've any compassion at all you won't let them hurt that poor child, or me.

But apparently God was tending other matters because that mean son of a bitch came inside the barn and I heard every footfall of his and could damn near smell him.

He paused midway and looked about, listening and maybe sniffing for my fear as well. I was sure he knew where I was and was any moment going to swing that mattock down and that would be the end of me. Then he got to the ladder and put a hand to one of its rungs.

"You're up there in that loft, ain't you?" he said. "I guess I got to come up and get you down. Don't know why you're making this so hard."

I debated whether I could run past him or not, like a rabbit he'd spooked from the bush and catch him by surprise. But then he was holding that mattock and all he'd have to do was swing it and cut me down. God, God, God, I prayed.

He stood there what seemed the longest time with that one hand on the ladder's rung and I thought if he goes on up there I'm going straight for the house and my pistol and save Marie. Even without the pistol I figured I could beat hell out of that damn skinny little wife of his, or die trying. I kept hoping Marie would scream again just so I knew she was alive, but there wasn't another sound from outside.

"Come on down now," he said, like he was coaxing a child. "I promise nothing's going to happen to you or your friend. It ain't like what you're thinking."

I wanted to scream, What in the hell do you think I'd be thinking, you and your crazy wife walking around with tools of destruction in the middle of the night? But I pressed my lips together.

I eased myself to a standing position getting ready to bolt if he went even halfway up that ladder. It was so dark in the barn I could only make him out by skylighting him against the light of the front door. I told myself if I ever got out of this mess, I'd never again go into a barn after dark. I promised God if he'd let me escape with my life, and that of Marie's, I'd turn Catholic and go to church every day and never commit another sin, that I'd marry a good Christian man and have lots of babies and raise them Christian and do charity work.

I'll do whatever you want of me Lord, I prayed. I mean anything!

The man rested the mattock against the side of the ladder and began to climb. Then as I eased to full standing my hand felt something as it slid up the stall post I was using for support, I was so shaking: a hand sickle impaled in the wood. I almost peed my pants.

I take back those mean thoughts I had about you, Lord, being all busy in my hour of need. Thank you kindly for this instrument of death, I silently prayed as I took hold of the handle and worked it free. Once free I ran my thumb along its edge to the point. Yes, it would do the trick if I used it right. The handle was wood and smooth as bone and it felt exactly made for what a girl needed to defend herself with against a madman.

But then, with one foot on the bottom rung, he paused and turned his head my direction even at the slight sound of my having freed the sickle from the post and stepped back down again and was reaching for the mattock just as I scurried from my hidey-hole and swung with all my might in a wide looping swing burying the sickle's point into the side of his neck.

He cried out and stumbled backwards clutching at the terrible thing hooked into him and as he did he dropped the mattock. It was all I needed. I grabbed hold of it and swung it with striking force, slamming the pointed end into his chest knowing as it struck that it tore through shirt and muscle and bone. He let out a loud gasp then groaned and slid down to a sitting position his hands weakly flailing as if unsure of which thing to grab—that which was hooked into his neck or that which was buried into his chest.

"Damn . . . damn . . . ," he uttered.

"Let me help you," I said and worked the mattock free and not in a gentle way either. It was heavy and I ran carrying it in two hands toward the house.

The small house was now lit from inside by lamplight, the soft yellow glow filling the window. Tears streamed down my face as I ran; tears that came from unreleased anger and smothering fright.

I crashed into the room calling Marie's name.

But it was too late.

Marie lay slumped over on the floor. The ax buried in her skull had cleaved it partly open. A wash of blood covered her face and ran down her front. Her arms were flung out and her hands open. The woman stood over her and when she turned, her face was a face unlike any I'd ever seen: a mask of pure madness, eyes glazed and nostrils flared. As evil as anything you could imagine. Eyes bulged and mouth open, she'd streaked blood, Marie's I guessed, across her cheeks and forehead.

"Why?" I screamed. "Why did you do this?"

"Oh, deary," she said. "For your wagon and horses and whatever else you have, of course."

I could hardly believe my ears. And then she said, "Why for the sheer pleasure, you stupid girls!"

She was pure madhouse crazy. I was stunned at the sight of her and Marie, a nightmarish vision worse than any nightmare.

I heard a bone-rattling scream and realized only later that it was my own.

I swung the mattock, striking her in the face. The force of the blow knocked her back against the wall and knocked over the lamp which spilled its oil and fire on the empty cot and its blankets. The simple flame of a single wick leaped into a hungry fire that seemed to complete the mad scene. She did not move, the blow of the mattock had done its work.

I dragged Marie outside. It was such terrible ghastly work carrying my dead friend that I wretched into the weeds. I could not bear to look upon her as I freed the ax and cast it aside.

"Oh God, oh God," I swore over and over at the insanity of it all. It surely has to be a dream I told myself, one that I will awaken from. The flames of the small house licked upwards, the heat burst the window glass and in short order caved in the roof and walls.

I lay down next to Marie and closed my eyes. I could take no more that night. No more.

When I opened my eyes again, the gray light of morning had replaced the silver light of night. I glanced over at Marie thinking that perhaps it had all been a nightmare of the worst kind and that she'd be sleeping and I'd wake her and we'd go to the house for breakfast and then continue on our way to Amarillo.

But, of course, that was not to be.

The house and the madwoman in it were but smoldering ashes now and I could have cared less about her. I looked off toward the barn, its door open. But since I wasn't dead, I figured that son of a bitch inside still was and I hoped his dying took a time and allowed him to think about his evil before he died.

I stood and went back in and sure enough there he lay, sitting up against the loft ladder, legs spread and blood everywhere.

To hell with you, I might have said, then found a shovel and went to the garden spot where the dirt looked soft and began digging a grave for Marie. As far as the man inside the barn, well, he could rot on earth and then could rot in hell.

I punched the shovel's blade into the dirt and began to dig. It was easy going but after several shovelfuls the blade struck something like a thick root, something that gave but didn't allow the blade to go through it. I scraped away the dirt and then I saw what it was: a hand, the fingers curled and bluish gray and I leapt back.

Holy mother of God!

It didn't take me long to figure the truth about these people. Marie and I were not their first victims. I wretched again until there was nothing in me to come up anymore and I vowed I would not bury poor Marie in such a corrupt piece of ground.

I went to the main house and took the fine quilt from their bed and wrapped Marie's body in it then carried her into the wagon and hitched the team. I could not wait to get away from that hellish place. But before I left I searched the house for traveling money since whatever I had, had been lost in the fire. I found a tin box with more than enough money for a real nice funeral for Marie and a one-way train ticket back home to Hadley's Jump and on to Daddy Sam's.

I think I wept all the way to Amarillo.

Once I got to Amarillo the first thing I did was make funeral arrangements for Marie with an undertaker there. I ordered her the best casket they had and said I wanted her buried in a pretty place. The undertaker charged seventy-five dollars including flowers and mourners and showed me the nice glass-sided hearse she'd be carried in to the cemetery. I went to a shop and bought her a pretty peach dress to be buried in and told the lady to take it over to the funeral parlor. Then realizing I was in need of some new clothes myself, bought myself a blue organdy dress, bone button shoes, and underclothing. Had her wrap everything and watched as she tied it with a string.

Then I located the law and told them the story and they said they had long suspected something like it because other travelers over the last few years had been reported as missing along that stretch of road. It made me angry and I cursed them for not doing anything about it before.

"Lady, do you know how damn vast this country is?"

"Yeah, damn right I do," I said. "But that don't mean you shouldn't have been looking."

I'm sorry about your loss was as good as the marshal could offer, that and he'd send some men out to collect the bodies.

"Well, I am sure they'll be grateful for being collected," I said sarcastically.

There wasn't a train out until the next morning so I rented a room at the hotel and discovered much to my surprise they had indoor plumbing. I had the boy who worked there bring me supper and a bottle of champagne from the restaurant down below. It was a real swell place and I damn well deserved to treat myself to a real swell place after all that had happened.

I was soaking in the bathwater so lovely and warm and pleasant when there came a knock at the door.

"Come in," I called.

It was the boy with my supper and champagne. He called from the front room, "Miss, I have your supper and bottle of champagne. Where would you like me to put them?"

"Leave the food out there but bring the champagne in here," I called.

He came in carrying the bottle and saw me there in the tub, water up to my breasts and blushed bright red.

"Can you pop the cork on the bottle?" I asked.

I watched as he wrestled with it but finally got it to pop and some of the bubbly spilling down the sides. I reached for it and when I did I guess some of me exposed myself to his youthful eyes. He blushed even more.

"How old are you?" I said.

"I'm nineteen, miss."

"Then you're old enough not to be embarrassed."

"Yes, ma'am."

He was a right handsome young man and had the world turned a different way and this was a different time and place and not all the people I loved and cared about were dead and and and . . .

But all I wanted was peace and quiet.

"What's your name?" I asked.

"Wayne, miss."

"Wayne, would you take those old clothes of mine out in the other room and get rid of them."

"Yes'm."

"Oh, and there is money on the bed, take five dollars for yourself."

He beamed.

"Yes ma'am."

"Oh, and Wayne?"

"Yes?"

"Stop calling women under thirty ma'am, they don't like it."

"Yes, ma—miss."

"Thanks and close the door on your way out."

He left. I drank the rest of the champagne and while it wasn't as strong as hard liquor, it left me feeling sleepy and light. I climbed out of the cooling water and toweled off and looked at myself in the mirror nicely placed on the wall with its striped wallpaper of dancing cherubs and I saw a face I nearly did not recognize staring back at me.

Lucy, I might have muttered. Is that you?

The woman's face didn't look so much like me as it did my mama's, but she had Marie's eyes and I wept.

And then I found the bed and lay down in it and drew the nice bedding up over me and slipped down into a much needed and wanted sleep giving thanks to the Lord or angels or whatever for my salvation and that I was still alive and not dead, dead, dead.

Chapter 31

It took three days and several changes of railroads to get back to the Pistol Barrel and then to Daddy Sam's over near Hadley's Jump. I'd only been gone but a short time but already everything seemed somehow different.

Daddy Sam was sitting alone on the front porch, a pint bottle rested down between his feet.

He looked startled to see me. His eyes were bloodshot and his hair a muss.

"Lucy," he said in a croaking voice. "My God, child where have you been? I thought surely you were slaughtered what with all the blood in the house."

"I left you a note, Daddy Sam."

"I know, but still . . ."

I explained it to him, everything and he sat there staring as if in a fog.

"They's been two or three deputies has come out here from Fort Smith searching around looking for Deputy Book," he said. "You say you flung him down a well?"

"He was dead already," I said. "It don't excuse it but you have to understand it was Red Dog who saved my life and I only did what he'd asked me to do so he wouldn't be falsely accused even though I was willing to admit I'd killed Book. Red Dog was worried with his past and him being an Indian he'd be accused anyway, and that the courts would just see it as me lying to protect him. That's why I done it. I'm not proud of the fact."

He reached for the bottle. I could smell the liquor on him already and I noticed the bottle was nearly empty. His face was flushed and it seemed to me he must have been drinking all day.

We sat for a time saying nothing then, him thinking, me thinking.

"Any news about Mama or Jim?" I asked.

"I'm afraid to have to tell you this," he said. "But it was your brother, J. R., what killed them."

I wasn't completely surprised by the news but still it came as a shock.

"How'd you find out?" I asked.

He shrugged.

"J. R. confessed it to me."

"He did?"

Daddy Sam shook his head like some old dog waking from a drowse and placed his sad gaze on me.

"J. R. killed your mama because she favored you more than him. That boy was insane, you know that."

I felt myself fill with righteous anger and thought that if Daddy Sam hadn't killed J. R., I would have.

"But why Jim?" I asked.

Daddy Sam spat a gob between his boots. "He killed Jim, he said, because he hated that you were happy. I reckon he wanted to make you as miserable as he has always been. I figure it was just plain ass meanness on his part. That boy had the devil in him is what it was. Some is just born bad, Lucy."

Such news hit like a hammer blow. I knew then why I'd always found J. R.'s presence a tremble in my blood.

Daddy Sam watched me close to see my reaction. But I didn't show him any. It was a private matter with me. Then he went on to tell the rest of it:

"It wasn't easy. We got into it when he came back around. Fought about it and he pulled his gun and I pulled mine. It was a Mexican standoff for a minute and that's when he confessed it and said he aimed to kill me too. We both shot at the same time. He missed but I didn't, not completely, anyway. I didn't kill him outright. He ran off trailing blood. I don't know how bad it was I shot him but I figured he'd just crawl off and die somewhere."

He hit off the bottle again as if swallowing away the memory of it.

"My god, Daddy Sam, you're lucky he didn't kill you."

"I know it. But at least it's over with now."

I felt like the world had tipped over and it wasn't ever going to be right again. Nearly my whole family wiped out, just me and Daddy Sam left. It seemed impossible.

"Well, at least it's finished, Lucy. We can get on past this thing now that we know."

Daddy Sam drained the last of his bottle then flung it out into the yard.

"You think Red Dog will show up round here again?" he asked, wiping his mouth with the back of his wrist.

"No," I said. "I think he's scared off this place forever."

"I am sorry you had to go through such a terrifying ordeal as you had."

He reached over and patted my hand.

"I'm sorry too, Daddy Sam," I said.

He placed his hands on his knees and pushed himself upright.

"I reckon I will go on in and get me a little bit of a nap. I hit this busthead a little too hard today."

"Why is it you were drinking so bad, Daddy Sam?"

He looked at me like some sad old dog.

"I don't rightly know," he said. "I reckon I just felt like doin' it, is all. I've been waitin' around to see what happened to you, Lucy. Seeing if I'd hear you was yourself dead, and now I see that you are not, and I guess, well, I guess, I'm surprised, is all."

Then he held out his arms and I rose and stepped in close and he hugged and held me tight.

"It's just me and you now, Lucy. We're all the family we got left."

This he said with such anguish in his voice that I nearly wept.

"Yes," I said. "Go on and get you some rest."

He started into the house.

"Are the deputies looking for J. R., then?" I asked.

"I don't reckon so," he said. "I never did mention it to anyone but you just now. Me and the law ain't exactly on a friendly basis no how and they might not accept my story, the same as you say Red Dog is worried about 'em. Best to let sleeping dogs lie."

It seemed awfully cruel of him to shoot J. R. and let him run off and maybe bleed to death.

"When'd this happen, that you and him got into it?" I asked.

Daddy Sam blinked as if having trouble remembering.

"Two days ago," he said.

"I should send word to Judge Parker as to what happened with me and Red Dog and the deputy," I said.

"It can wait, Lucy. One more day won't make no difference. You ought to get you some rest as well."

I allowed as he was probably right. Another day wouldn't change anything. I looked off toward the woods.

"Did he run off on his horse?" I asked.

"What?"

"When you shot J. R., did he run off on his horse?"

He stood a moment looking about. "No, his horse is out in the corral yonder. He run off on foot, his blood trail leading off into those woods yonder."

"Maybe we should go see if we can find him," I suggested.

He looked at me sternly then, sternly or with disappointment.

"He's most likely dead by now, he surely is. And if he ain't and we go in there and he's just wounded, he's liable to kill us both, Lucy. No, let it be. Come a few days more I'll go in search of him, that or look for the buzzards circling overhead. He's just a waste of a human being, worse than a coyote as far as I'm concerned."

I felt torn between hatred and sympathy for my half brother.

I climbed the stairs to my room. The window was open and the breeze lifted and dropped the curtains as if they were dancers of cloth. I stripped down to my underthings, bloomers and camisole, and sat forlorn on the side of the bed, a thousand thoughts running through my mind. It still all felt like some disturbing dream I was having I couldn't awaken from, and yet I knew that it was not.

J. R. had a sickness that could not be discerned. And to think what would have happened to old Wilson had he not fled the country. Surely we would have killed him for Mama's murder and it would have been one more crime added to the annals of crimes thus far starting with Mama.

I stared at my hands and swore I saw them smeared with the blood of Deputy Book and the man and woman back in Texas, and rubbed and rubbed them trying to get the blood off when there wasn't any blood there.

I remembered Mama's diary then and pulled it out from under the mattress. How I wished she was alive and there with me now, someone to talk to and explain to me why I was going through the turmoil of grief and loss, why all this was happening, one thing right after the other. I felt like Job's wife.

I lay back and read and read the entries at random. I read of lovers and hard times and bad, of my birth and that of J. R.'s, of Mama's desires and dreams, of a horse and a dog she once owned. There were days and weeks with no entry at all. I turned to the last pages and what I learned, what she'd written in her own hand, surprised me greatly:

Sam and I have grown apart. His drinking has become for me a problem. I told myself a long time ago I would not tolerate a drunkard and made him swear off, and for a time he'd given it up. But lately he's turned back to the bottle, to drown his regrets, I suppose, for he tells me more and more about the misdeeds of his days before we met. But more so I think he grieves for his lost youth, that he is a man pinned down by everything. By us.

What he claims bothers him most is some murders committed not by him, he says, but by the men he rode with: the murders of a family that included a child. He says the memory of it has come to haunt him and put wild thoughts into his head. I asked him what kind of wild thoughts, but he refuses to tell me. I asked him again to stop drinking, threatened to leave him if he did not. It seems as though it makes no difference. He loves the liquor more than me these days. I seem to make no difference in his life.

I've nagged him, perhaps overly much, to move us to a city, Saint Louis or Denver or the like. Told him how so lonely way out here it is for me never seeing anybody, hardly ever getting a chance to go shopping, none of the normal things people do. I don't know why I should have to pay for his misdeeds and now his drinking. And worse, I suspect he keeps a woman in town, a harlot he's been seeing. I'm ready to pack my bags and leave and have told him as much. Hopefully he will get right with me, but if not . . .

I noted that the entry was dated two weeks before her death. I felt sad that she was in such turmoil in her last days, that she couldn't have lived in a city, that Daddy Sam was drinking and maybe chasing some harlot. Oh Mama, I cried, the tears streaming down my cheeks. I should have stayed closer to you and not fallen in love and ran off and got married and not been here for you.

I felt so dismal sitting alone in that room.

"Lucy you are not yet thirty years old," I heard Mama saying. "You're too young to be old and too old to be a child. You must take care of your business while you can. Don't let any man keep you from living the life you want . . ."

Whether I dreamed or actually heard her voice I couldn't say for I'd fallen asleep in that warm room with the gentle breezes touching my wet stained cheeks.

I had a dream of Red Dog and Marie. They were sitting beneath a crab-apple tree together holding each other, Red Dog stroking her hair and before them ran a wide river—as wide as any I'd ever seen with the far shore so distant it was just a blurred gray line and the water was churning and all a rage moving swift with bobbing trees and dead cattle floating past in stark contrast to the peacefulness of the two lovers there on the grassy bank.

Marie was saying, "Look, there goes another one," but Red Dog was so taken with her he did not even notice what the river was carrying away and he had one hand on her stockinged knee and the other on her bosom.

The sky itself was a strange and disturbing color: dark blue and orange with swift running clouds whose shadows floated over the boiling river with its churn of floating trees and dead animals, and worst of all, the river was creeping over its banks getting ready to carry the two of them away as well.

Then that pair of folks who tried to kill Marie and me arrived on horses and threw ropes over the limbs of the crabapple tree, ropes with nooses and shouted it was time and Red Dog said, "Time for what?" And Marie answered: "Time for us to go." And the crazed man and his wife took hold of them and put the nooses around their necks and started hoisting them up till their feet were just barely off the ground and kicking at the air.

I woke gasping, sitting bolt upright, as if I was strangling. It took me several seconds to draw in enough breath to feel safe again.

Then I saw him, sitting in a chair in the corner, there, by the window: Daddy Sam.

"What is it?" I asked, startled.

"Nothing," he said.

"I was having a bad dream," I said still trying to get my heart to slow down.

His gaze was leveled at me, no humor in it at all, no nothing.

"Are you okay?" I asked.

"Yes," he said. "I am okay."

I was confused. His eyes watched me intently and I thought it was from the liquor had him a bit strange.

"Well, did you need something?"

"No," he said. "I don't need nothing."

I felt almost naked before him, naked and uncomfortable in a way I never had before.

"Then why are you here?" I asked feeling more and more upset. He was sitting there in the room with me only partially clothed.

"There is something I need to take care of," he said, eyeing the open diary on the bed, the last pages Mama had wrote about her and him.

I noticed he held a piece of unfolded paper in his right hand.

"There is this," he said looking down at the paper. "The reason I was going to go to Tahlequah but drank too much and lost track of the days. That, and I was waiting to see what news might arrive of your fate. Figured sure you was dead."

"Well, what is it, the paper?"

He rose slowly and came over and stood at the side of my bed and it seemed to me he had grown in size, bigger and more looming as he stood there. He held it forth.

"It's your mama's last will and testament," he said.

I took it from his fingers and read it.

"It needs to get documented by a court before it can be executed legally," he said.

His voice was flat, officious, without any kind of the warmth I'd always heard in it. "She left you and J. R. everything," he said as I was still reading it over. "About twenty-five thousand dollars in all between her life-insurance policies and a saving account in Dallas. Woman sure knew how to save her money and mine. She held out on me. I always wondered why it seemed we never had enough to go around even though I'd quite a little nest egg from my past business."

Then he grunted a short hard laugh that wasn't a laugh at all.

"Robbing wasn't a bad business, neither. I guess she figured I'd robbed Peter to pay her instead of ol' Paul the way it went down. Took my money and hers and socked it away in life-insurance policies and some in a hidden savings account. And now you get every damn dime of it."

I felt anger filling my chest. What the hell was wrong with him but greed?

"She left me nothing," he said, "when it should have been me she left it to instead."

His face was full of red rage, his fists knotted.

"I don't know what you're getting at," I said. "But you need to leave out of my room right now."

He stood huffing his liquor stink breath, like some old bear.

"No, this will not stand," he shouted and filled me with sudden cold fear.

"You see, gal, you get it all, unless you're not alive to collect it, that is. And as far as your half-witted brother, well I made goddamn sure he wasn't alive to collect it neither. I shot him and would have done a principal job of it too if I'd been completely sober and he'd been less quick. But as it stands, he's out there dead somewhere and you're here and I ain't drunk enough this time to miss."

And suddenly he was upon me, his hands around my throat, his full weight pressed down on me, his knees against my arms, his hands grasping my throat.

"I'm sorry it's come to this, child, but I can't just begin again with nothing, not at my age . . ."

His hands were like a noose of muscle and finger bone around my neck and I realized then why I had that hanging dream: it was a portent Mama had passed onto me. She was trying to warn me in the dream.

I did my best to squirm out from under him, and got one arm free and clawed at his wrist but it was a hard knob and he pulled it free and pinned it again beneath his knee, his weight bearing down on me even more and all I could see was red fear, like blood flooding behind my eyes.

As he bore down on me, choking the life out, his face was a fury above mine. I reckon now that the cat was out of the bag and the truth be spoken he decided to tell it all.

"J. R. didn't kill your mama—I did!" His spittle flecked my face. "I aimed to blame him for the killing but it went sideways and we shot it out, only he lost. Now I just need to take care of you."

He squeezed harder, his face blood red.

Was this how it was all going to end, me like the others, death by murder's sake?

"Please," I managed to croak.

But there was no mercy in him and I could feel my strength rapidly being sapped even as my fear ravaged me. There had been a neighbor boy when I was just a child who drowned in the river by our house and I remembered thinking then how horrible it must be to drown, to smother to death. And now it was happening to me.

Daddy Sam's face began to blur and fade as the life went out of me. The only thing that even helped was that the mattress was soft and yielded some beneath us and I sunk in, and though he had a good grip on my throat I probably wasn't dying as fast as he'd wished for it.

I made one last effort at bucking my knees into his back and to plead with my eyes but to no avail. Daddy Sam was gone way off in his head somewhere, flat gone and I knew I was to die at his hands. Greed. The love of money was a sin. It sure was. Even a man like Daddy Sam would sin because of it.

I felt myself sliding down into darkness, my limbs gone limp and useless now. I had no fight left in me.

Then a crashing sound and suddenly Daddy Sam released my throat and I heard him swear as though he was far away.

"Goddamn, it's you! I thought I killed you! Put that gun away, you son of a bitch!"

Daddy Sam came off me and there was a thrashing in the room as I sucked in lungs full of air and life started easing back into me like water filling a bucket. There was a crashing I couldn't quite grasp even as I sat up gasping for all the air I could get. Then I saw it: Daddy Sam and J. R. entangled in a struggle, J. R.'s shirt and right sleeve a bloodstained mess as he gripped a gun in his left hand and Daddy Sam fighting him for it, the two of them dancing like mad lovers to their music of grunts and groans and curses, each trying to take the lead and each refusing to give it.

I wanted to run from the room, flee to a safe freedom I didn't know even existed anymore in a world so washed by blood.

But I was frozen by the sight of the two of them fighting, each trying to kill the other and wishing that they would both somehow win.

Daddy Sam had a grip on J. R.'s gun hand and it looked as though he might lever it loose. I knew I couldn't let that happen. If he killed J. R. he would kill me too.

Then I remembered the gun I'd taken from that hell house of a place where they'd killed Marie. A small silver pistol heavier than it looked. The kind of gun a body could hide easily and come out with it when he wanted to. An assassin's gun, and it was right there under my pillow and I grabbed for it.

I damn sure did not want to shoot yet another man even though at least one of them deserved it.

I thumbed the hammer back and pointed it at them both, trying to draw a bead on Daddy Sam, but they were struggling so much, moving back and forth and twisting about, I dared not pull the trigger lest I shoot the wrong one.

They came close together, J. R.'s gun between them, pressed up against the wall and then the gun went off and one of them made a sound like he'd been punched in the stomach and I watched as J. R. slowly slipped to the floor.

Daddy Sam had the gun now and stood looking down at J. R., the whole front of his shirt blossoming in a fresh bloody flower. A cloud of blue smoke filled the air above them.

Daddy Sam stood a moment too long studying his handy work and when he turned, I shot him, high up, the bullet knocking him backwards like an unseen blow from a fist. And then I shot him again as he sank to the floor. And then again as he sat there, eyes looking for something that no longer existed.

He'd slumped down next to J. R. and together they were there on the floor like a couple of tired men in from a long day in the fields but for the blood soaked across the front of their shirts. Damn it, I thought. Damn it all to hell.

CHAPTER 32

The circle of death was complete.

I attended the funerals and burials of Daddy Sam and J. R. in the boot-hill cemetery in Hadley's Jump, preferring that neither of them grace the same ground that Mama and Jim was buried in.

The same women, including my two fake aunties, attended, as did almost everyone in Hadley's Jump because a double funeral, caused by a double murdering, was quite an interesting event. The saloons were giving a free beer with every shot purchased and candy suckers for the kids. Two photographers came, one from Tahlequah and the other from Ardmore. Stringers from several newspapers wanted to interview me but I refused all their requests and so they wrote whatever they wanted.

I was hauled into Fort Smith by the roving deputies and stood before Judge Parker where I explained once more the details of what had transpired, including the part about my having to shoot and kill Deputy Leviticus Book as he tried to rape me. I was sure the old boy would send me to prison regardless of the circumstances.

I explained that I wanted to come clean and start fresh regardless of what punishment might be leveled against me and the time for lying and betrayals was over. I wanted clean hands. No more blood.

He listened intently as did the courtroom full of spectators, for never before had they heard of such doings performed by the sweet and comely daughter of the well-known Belle Moon, a woman of note in her own right, as the *Southwest Times Record* had described me. An artist had even sketched me and Mama's pictures over the article and made us look attractive if a bit severe.

"And where now is Red Dog to be found, Miss Moon?" Judge Parker inquired.

"I don't know, sir. We parted ways over in Texas and I've not seen or heard from him since and don't really care to."

"I see. And are you remorseful for your role in the killings as described before this court here today?"

"Yes, sir. I am greatly so. I wish a thousand times none of it ever did happen."

He pondered a bit, asked me a few more questions and then found me not guilty of the crime of murder by way of self-defense, slammed down his gavel and said, "You are free to go Miss Moon, and I hope to never have to see you in my court again."

Then as I turned to thank my attorney, the judge called me to his bench and in a low voice said, "I am deeply sorry for your loss, Miss Moon. I knew your mother well and she was a very fine woman, may God rest her soul."

I couldn't be sure, but I thought I detected the merest hint of something in his look, something veiled but intimate when he mentioned Mama. I'll just say this: It wouldn't surprise me that theirs was more than a casual acquaintance.

I never again heard nor saw Red Dog. Never read a thing about him in any newspaper.

He simply disappeared.

Or was he a pure figment of my imagination?

ABOUT THE AUTHOR

Bill Brooks is the author of more than thirty historical novels, including the John Henry Cole series by Five Star. His novel *The Stone Garden: The Epic Life of Billy the Kid* was named by *Booklist* as one of the ten best Westerns of the past decade.